Praise for Grayton Beach Affair

"Present day Grayton Beach, a quaint village on the sugary sands of the Florida Gulf Coast, is taken back to the WWII era in this action packed novel. Harvey convincingly weaves together a thrilling tale of espionage and Southern romance, bringing the reader's imagination to life with lucid historical detail."

— Lindsey Kafonek, *Panama City News Herald*

"A war story for the men and a love story for the ladies, *Grayton Beach Affair* combines the action and suspense of war with the passion and romance of a beautiful love story in one compelling novel. Harvey does an exceptional job of painting a vivid picture of the Southeast U.S. in the 1940's. From the sleepy seaside town of Grayton Beach to locales throughout Atlanta, it is easy to visualize the setting for this unexpected story of action and romance during WWII."

— Tracy Louthain, Beaches of South Walton Tourist Development Council.

"It is refreshing to see a beloved place like Grayton Beach portrayed in a work of fiction. It provides both a historical and cultural context of the area as well as giving the reader a sense of time and place in parallel to one of the most significant World Wars in history."

— *The Thirty-A-Review* Magazine

"Captures the romance of Grayton Beach in a pulse-racing action adventure story of a war-torn love affair."

— Glenda Beasley, former Grayton Beach homeowner.

Grayton Beach Affair

James Harvey

To Lindsey,
Thank you so much for
your support! you can
see that it has been very
important to me.
I hope we can meet soon

Jim Harvey

Published by T.D. Bailey & Associates Publishing

Copyright © 2011, James Harvey

Printed in the United States of America

ISBN: 978-0-9845564-0-3

Library of Congress Control Number: 2010905113

Cover Design by TLC Graphics, www.TLCGraphics.com

Photo Credits
Man: © iStockphoto.com/sandoclr; Woman: © iStockphoto.com/rgbspace

This is a work of fiction. Names, characters, places, and incidents either are the product of the author's imagination or are used fictitiously, and any resemblance to actual persons, living or dead, business establishments, events, or locales is entirely coincidental.

This book is dedicated to my wife, Marie Elise, who not only did a superb job of helping write and polish the story but was also instrumental in the development of the characters, and as result of her effort, took the book to a higher level. Thanks for your help.

"Love is the flower of life, and blossoms unexpectedly and without law, and must be plucked where it is found and enjoyed for the brief hour of its duration."

—D. H. Lawrence

Chapter One

CHRISTIAN WOLFE COULD NOT SLEEP. THE STEADY, IRRITATING sound of the clock ticking on the table by his bed throbbed in his head, and his constant tossing and turning had turned his bedcovers into a hopeless, twisted jungle. The clock showed 2:00 A.M.

He climbed out of the warm bed—his pajamas damp from the heat of the covers—and was assaulted by the chill of the room. Lighting a cigarette, he wiped the condensation from the windowpane and stared at the dark silhouette of the city. He was fitful, but the acrid fumes from the sulfur match and the taste of tobacco calmed his nerves. *I've grown too dependent on these,* he reflected for the thousandth time.

He leaned against the window frame and inhaled deeply, then exhaled a stream of cigarette smoke into the chilled air. Wiping the condensation from the window, his thoughts drifted aimlessly while his eyes searched the street for any sign of the Germany he had known in his youth.

A quarter moon was still rising, although it was hard for him to see it through the layer of spotty clouds hovering over Berlin. The city was cloaked in darkness and deadly silent. The only movement was tree branches swaying rhythmically in the wind, creating a graceful but erratic dance. Spring was arriving late this year, and the freshness of the budding flowers and trees that might have given the citizens a sense of hope and renewal was dragging its feet. The cold wind made contact with the warmer windowpane, creating a curtain of condensation in lacey patterns that soon turned into rivulets of water pooling on the windowsill.

Since the war began, the military enforced a complete blackout of the city to minimize potential Allied bombing damage. To date, there had been almost no retaliation bombing on German soil by Allied forces; still, the city maintained a depressing and foreboding atmosphere, mirroring his mood.

His small apartment was located down a narrow cobblestone street and a block off a once-tidy square. A Lutheran church sat on one side. On the other side was an assortment of produce markets, bookstores, cafés, and a few small shops, now shuttered. Trash and debris had accumulated in the dry pool of what used to be a splendid stone fountain in the center of the square.

Also gone was a wonderful bakery on the square where he frequently bought coffee and strudel for breakfast. The memory of the smell of warm strudels and hot coffee made his mouth water and his soul ache. He remembered leisurely Sunday mornings when he sat at a café overlooking the square, watching happy families walk by. That had been the Germany of his youth.

He had overheard that the owners of the café, as well as some of the other shop owners, had been taken away to some unknown location because Jews were no longer allowed to have businesses or even homes and possessions. Christian was troubled over the stories, not only because he liked the bakery owner and his family, but also because he had a hard time believing his home country could do such a thing to its citizens who were simply trying to survive like everyone else in Germany. As the months went by, he had heard more and more stories like this, beginning to give the rumors credence. He finished his cigarette, resolved once again to quit smoking, and returned to bed to try to get a few hours sleep.

Christian had been told the previous afternoon he would be summoned to a meeting with a high-ranking German officer for a special assignment. Apprehensive, he wondered why they would want to meet with him. He had spent the past few years keeping his head down, trying to maintain the lowest profile he could. Obviously, he had not been successful.

Two incidents had brought Christian into the spotlight of the military. A year earlier in the spring of 1941, a gas explosion in the building next to his apartment started a tremendous fire. Several people were trapped on the third floor. Hearing the cries from an open window, Christian ran through the crowd of onlookers and into the building. He climbed the stairs through the thick smoke and found two small children and their mother inside an apartment. Grabbing a child under each arm, he instructed the mother to hold on to his belt, leading them outside to safety just as the roof collapsed. He was surrounded by the crowd and hailed as a hero in a newspaper the next day.

The second event happened just 2 months earlier while he traveled in France. French Resistance fighters had wired a bridge with explosives, which was blown up just as a group of soldiers ahead of Christian started to cross. Several trucks were destroyed, killing or seriously injuring more than two-dozen men. Christian jumped from his vehicle and ran to give first aid. His quick actions saved several lives, including the nephew of a high-ranking officer. As he ministered to the soldiers' wounds, he defended himself with his pistol against the Resistance fighters who shot at him from the trees on the riverbank. He used one of the soldier's radios to communicate with medics a few kilometers away who were able to provide further assistance. Unfortunately for Christian, his name was again brought to the attention of the German army.

At 9:00 the next morning as Christian arrived at his desk, he was summoned to his supervisor's office. His supervisor, Hans Ulrich, was a nervous and unkempt man who reeked of garlic and constantly rubbed his hands together. He introduced Christian to a German officer who stood in a leisurely stance at the side of his desk. The officer approached Christian, raised his arm, and spoke the words to which Christian had become very familiar: "Heil Hitler!"

Christian's first impression of the man standing before him was one of astonishment. He stood over 6½ feet tall with snow-white hair and cold piercing eyes that peered through round, steel-framed eyeglasses. Those eyes expressed intelligence and confidence. His uniform was freshly pressed, and his sidearm was snapped into a highly polished leather holster and belt. He wore tall boots, polished even more than his belt and holster. Christian would need to look up if he were to speak directly to the man standing in front of him.

The officer appeared courteous but seemed inclined to skip any polite conversation. He motioned Christian to a chair and, as soon as both men were seated, he began.

"Herr Wolfe, I am Colonel Rolf Schmidt, head of engineering for the Reich's effort to develop a new long-distance bomb. We have a serious problem and need your help. It seems that one of our lead scientists overseeing a test in France was taken prisoner by Allied forces 2 months ago when they overran a facility in which he was working. The scientist, Dieter Braun, was smart enough to leave his laboratory before being taken prisoner and commingled with the other German prisoners so as not to give the Allies any sense of his knowledge and unique skills.

"He was transported to England, and now we have learned from our spies that he and several hundred other POWs have been relocated to America where they are being held in camps. Our sources in the area have informed us that he is being held in a camp in the southeastern U.S. near the Gulf of Mexico. The camp is in Florida, near the small town of DeFuniak Springs, close to an American Air Corps training base called Eglin Field. The Allies have established these work camps in rural areas where the prisoners are assigned to build roads and labor in the fields.

"It seems the Allies believe the German prisoners would have very little success escaping and making their way out of the country because very few speak English and there is nowhere for them to go. As a result, the camps are minimally guarded and, in some cases, the guards have nothing in the way of weapons except for a few pistols and wooden clubs. They are surrounded by a high, barbed-wire fence with tent barracks for the men. Because of your early life in America and your ability to speak English perfectly, we want you to help us get Dieter out of the camp and back home."

Stunned, Christian looked the colonel directly in the eye to make sure he was not making some kind of joke.

"I'm an engineer with no military experience. All I want is to survive this war so that I can get on with my life. How the hell—excuse my language, sir—would I know how to break someone out of a POW camp, even if I do speak English? And how do I know I would not get caught and shot as a spy? I will take my chances on surviving the bombing and stay here in Berlin. That is dangerous enough for me. Find someone else, Colonel." Christian stood up to leave.

Colonel Schmidt stepped in front of him and placed both hands on Christian's shoulders.

"Since you have no military experience, I will instruct you that you are not to leave this office until I dismiss you. Please be so good as to take your seat. You seem to misunderstand. This is an order, Herr Wolfe, not a request."

Christian reluctantly resumed his seat realizing he had made a huge blunder.

"I will make this very clear, Herr Wolfe," continued the officer. "We need Dieter Braun back in Germany to help us with the war effort. You are the best person to help get him off American soil. You have a choice, and you have to make that choice now. You will help us get him out, or I will personally see you are transferred to active duty and sent immediately to the Russian front. As you know, your life there will be like nothing you can imagine, and, based on the current situation, that life will probably not be long."

Christian felt sick to his stomach. *Son of a bitch,* he thought to himself. *I can't get a friggin' break. I get treated like a second-class citizen in America, and when I come home to help my native country, all control of my destiny is taken out of my hands. I should have just stayed in Havana working on ships. I could have opened a small bar near the harbor and lived a simple life of cheap rum, good cigars, and hot-blooded Cuban girls. Why am I subjected to a life of misery over and over again?*

"If I'm going to do this, how am I going to learn how to keep my ass from being shot off or end up on the wrong side of the barbed-wire fence knowing that I put myself there?"

Colonel Schmidt looked at him and smiled. "I thought you might see the brighter side of your options. Tomorrow, come to my office. My specialists and I will begin to teach you what you need to know and explain more details about your task."

With a gleam in his eye, Schmidt added, "By the way, I hope you are not prone to seasickness or claustrophobia because you are going to spend a lot of time underwater."

What the hell does that mean? Christian thought, but at that moment he was so overwhelmed with the whole conversation all he could do was go back to his desk, light a cigarette, and stare at the wall across the room. Agitated and still in disbelief, his only thought was, *What the hell have I gotten myself into?*

Chapter Two

CHRISTIAN RETURNED TO BERLIN IN 1936 WHEN HIS PARENTS, WHO moved to the United States after World War I to pursue what they thought would be a better life, had died. Christian's father, Maximilian, was an engineer in a steel mill in Berlin prior to World War I but could only find a job on the assembly line of a factory in Atlanta when they arrived in the United States in 1920.

Postwar sentiment against the local German population was prevalent. Christian's parents suffered from the prejudices of his coworkers and neighbors, who could not overcome the pain that they had suffered during World War I. People made frequent comments to his parents about their heritage, and after being repeatedly passed over for promotions and raises, Christian's father became increasingly skeptical about ever achieving the "American Dream." He would talk about returning to his homeland where he and Christian's mother, Katrina, would be given the respect they deserved.

As the head of the family, Maximilian conceded that perhaps he made a mistake moving his family to America. He loved both his wife and son above everything else and often caught himself looking at Katrina and chuckling as she gently tried in a hundred small ways to convince him to move back to Germany. Being the dutiful and submissive wife, they never openly fought about it, but Katrina never missed an opportunity to expound on her birthplace by recollecting fond memories painted even more rose-colored by nostalgia.

Katrina was born the daughter of a successful merchant who owned several dress shops in Berlin. She grew up in a warm and generous home with a cook and house servant attending to her family's needs. She wanted that life again. She missed her homeland and combined with the anti-German sentiments, the seeds of depression and anger took root. Although Katrina and Maximilian tried to keep their feelings to themselves, Christian also began to develop a doubt that he would ever fit into his adopted homeland.

He had been an outstanding athlete and a model student but had also suffered from schoolyard taunts from his fellow students who had overheard their parents referring to "those Krauts." He tried tirelessly to fit in and worked hard to be a typical American. He practiced his English until he had no trace of his native accent. He learned to play American baseball and football, although he never understood why Americans did not prefer soccer, which he thought was a superior sport. As a result of his high-school grades, he was given a scholarship to the Georgia Institute of Technology in Atlanta, where he excelled in engineering and graduated with honors.

At a school dance during his senior year in college, Christian met Rose Abbot, the daughter of a wealthy doctor. Soon, they were in love and discussed marriage. One weekend he was invited to her parents' home for dinner and after a pleasant time, Christian decided to speak to Rose's father. He was nervous, but looked Dr. Abbot squarely in the eye and asked for permission to marry his daughter. Christian was floored by the response.

"Christian," Dr. Abbot began, "you seem to be a fine young man, and I'm sure that you will be successful in whatever endeavor you follow; however, you should know right now that Rose's mother and I will never allow her to marry someone of a German heritage. Rose will marry a young man who comes from an established Southern American family with a professional background, not from an immigrant family—not Italian, not Russian, not Polish, and certainly not German."

Shocked and reeling from such an unexpected insult, Christian asked that Rose join them. He was confident she would tell her father that she would marry Christian with or without his blessing. However, Rose did not respond. Her eyes issued the unspoken acceptance of her father's statement. On shaky legs and with as much dignity as he was able to summon, Christian nodded his head, turned, and walked out of the house without another word. On his way home, he vowed that from that moment until he died, he would prove to the world that his family and his German heritage would be a source of pride and a guiding force in his life.

He graduated from college in the height of the Depression with a degree in civil engineering. Unable to find a job utilizing his new skill, he went to sea working on a freighter for 4 years, travelling the globe as an engineer and then navigator. This lifestyle suited the needs of a rejected suitor perfectly.

While Christian was at sea, his father died of cancer. Soon thereafter, his mother succumbed to a heart attack, probably brought on by a lack of will to continue living a loveless and lonely life in a country that had not accepted her or her family.

After burying the last of his family in America, Christian left the sea and returned to Berlin with the thought that he would help rebuild Germany after the war and reestablish his life in his native home where he felt he would be welcome and where he could offer his skills to improve both himself and his new home.

He secured a position with a civil engineering company that was building roads and bridges throughout the country. For the most part, he was satisfied with his new life. He applied himself to his new occupation, choosing to ignore the political and economic changes that were taking place throughout his homeland. Even so, he was aware of the poverty and economic depression that engulfed Germany and saw the effects of the massive unemployment and inflation. The country seemed to be looking for someone to take it out of its misery, and that person was a volatile orator by the name of Adolf Hitler.

Hitler appeared to have the ability to bring order and direction out of chaos. He preached of creating a superior civilization with a clean and superior German bloodline. Christian was not interested in politics at all, but the idea of having Germany rise out of its severe economic straits did appeal to him. Other than that, he did not give Hitler or any other politician any thought. Occasionally, he would reflect on his life in America, but those thoughts were clouded with bitterness and with no desire to return.

Over the next few years, it became increasingly difficult to ignore the serious and dangerous activities taking place throughout the country by the new ruling Nazi Party. Their disregard of the Versailles Treaty and their expansion of their military forces that were forbidden after World War I became more and more popular. Conscription into the military began, and the Luftwaffe, Germany's air force, was created in direct opposition to the terms of the Versailles Treaty.

Then Hitler spoke of annexing Austria and Czechoslovakia, reclaiming land lost in the war. Speaking up against the rising Nazi Party invited swift and severe repercussions. Initially, Christian was able to survive these turbulent times without personal involvement, but as the months went by, the situation grew worse. It became clear that war was imminent as the world stood by and allowed Hitler to invade Austria and Czechoslovakia.

On September 1, 1939, Germany invaded Poland. This time, the world rose up. One by one, countries declared war on Germany. The company Christian worked for was taken over by the government, and Christian was assigned to work on military projects. During this time, he was not drafted and was allowed to keep his apartment in the city. Although he was no longer insulated from the war as he had been while working as a civil engineer, he was assigned to a department to help design the transport systems the troops would need to take them into battle.

For the next 2 years, he traveled frequently throughout Germany and the newly occupied countries, most recently,

Poland and France, which had given Christian a new perspective. He witnessed violent and dramatic scenes of destruction caused by his own military, as well as the result of constant bombings by the Allies. He saw imprisoned French and Polish citizens and heard in graphic details stories of Jews, gypsies, homosexuals, and other minorities sent away to "work camps" for the duration of the war. No one seemed to know where they went—only that they never returned.

On December 11, 1941, Germany, in a show of support of their military alliance with Italy and Japan, declared war on the United States. Christian was so involved with his work and had such negative feelings about America that this news had little effect on him. He was through with that part of his life. Although he could never visit his parents' grave again, he had come to terms with it. His life was in Germany now.

Chapter Three

MAGGIE GAZED INTO CHARLES'S EYES AND WISHED THE MOMENT could last forever. They were dancing together at the country club. She loved the feeling of his arm encircling her waist, moving ever so slightly upward to caress the side of her breast as they moved slowly to the beat of the music. Then he pulled her close so that their bodies were touching in the most intimate places. A breeze from the ceiling paddle fans cooled her flushed cheeks, and with the lights dimly lit and a glow from the cocktails they had enjoyed at dinner, she was ready to take the next step.

"I adore you, Maggie," Charles whispered softly into her ear.

"And I love you, Charles," she replied as she gently kissed his warm neck above his collar.

Then she awoke. *Oh, God.* She had the same dream again. He was there with her; then he was gone. Maggie's reaction never varied. Physically, her heart pounded, and her stomach was queasy. Emotionally, she reeled as she went from euphoria to the depths of despair in seconds. She could still feel his kisses and smell his masculine scent. Her body had already begun to respond and longed for fulfillment. She doubled over in pain, tears drenching her cheeks. She felt unable to deal with the grief and loss any longer. If she could only have him back, if she could just hold him one more time, she would never let him go. Instead, here she was alone in a place called Grayton Beach. She lay in the dark thinking how she would do things so differently if she had another chance.

Maggie had graduated from the University of Alabama with a degree in teaching. While in her second year, she met Charles Watson II, a young lawyer from a well-established family at a party one weekend. Soon, they were a couple.

Although Maggie came from a modest family whose father worked in the steel mills, Charles introduced her to the Birmingham social scene. His parents had immediately taken to her. Margaret Watson loved the thought of having a daughter and often bought Maggie jewelry and outfits for her birthday and special occasions, mostly because she wanted to spoil her. Maggie's life was centered around teaching elementary school during the week and attending parties and country club events with Charles on weekends.

Maggie was 5 feet 9 inches tall, thin, and attractive. Her lean body allowed her to look good in any clothing, although she preferred casual slacks and shorts. She carried herself with confidence and grace. Her friends referred to her as the Katherine Hepburn of Birmingham. She had warm hazel eyes, blond hair bleached from the sun, and a slightly off center nose with a small bump, the result of a collision on the softball field in school. Her cheekbones were high, a small dimple graced her chin, and her teeth were straight and very white.

Although athletic, she loved to be feminine when she deemed it necessary, and was quite striking when she dressed for the parties and cotillions at the country club. For the most part, however, she preferred not to wear makeup and allow her hair to flow freely.

Charles had gone to work at his family's law firm, and life was good. Then the war changed everything.

CHARLES ENLISTED IN the navy in January 1941 because he felt a patriotic need to help America win the war against the evil German Axis. America was not yet at war with Germany, but there was sympathy with the British and French. Many of his friends were enlisting as officers to go off and help free Europe from Germany's aggression. Much to his frustration, he was assigned to the Pacific where he would be part of the Judge Advocate Corps in Honolulu. He had never heard of a place called Pearl Harbor, and it seemed too far away from the war action that he was seeking. He said good-bye to Maggie in July 1941, and promised that he would return as soon as he could get leave.

Maggie received the dreaded news from her fiancé's family on December 8th. The man she was to marry had been killed in the attack on Pearl Harbor. Charles and Margaret were devastated. They had lost their son, and now their dear Maggie would no longer become a part of their family. Aware of her need to go away for a while to grieve, they gave her the money that they had set aside for the wedding.

Maggie quit her job as a schoolteacher during the Christmas break and told her concerned but understanding parents that she was going away for a while. Although they trusted their daughter, they were uncomfortable knowing she would be wandering around the country alone. After her constant reassurances that she would be safe, she left home and drove south from Birmingham in her 1939 Chevrolet to the Gulf Coast.

She arrived at a small seaside motel that sat on the sand dunes of the fishing village of Destin, where she stayed for a few days. Although the ocean was a tonic to her bruised soul, her room depressed her. It was small and musty and lacked any feelings of home. She had also quickly tired of the local cafés. Bad coffee, fried fish, and greasy food were all they seemed to offer on their limited menus. Since she had nothing else to do, she filled her days driving up and down the coastal roads. Then she found Grayton Beach one day as she was driving aimlessly along the narrow two-lane road east of Destin which continued on to Panama City. When she turned down the sandy trail that led her to the beach, she immediately felt that she had found a refuge where she could be alone and determine her next steps in life.

Maggie drove through the community, parked in the middle of the sandy street, and walked through the sand dunes down the wide, white beach to the edge of the water. There were no waves. The emerald water stretched to the horizon where it met the sky. The clear water and warm sand on her bare feet were like a heavenly balm to her wounded soul. *I think this is where I want to live for a while*, she thought to herself.

Grayton Beach, Florida, could best be described as an outpost for those looking for solitude. It was a small beachfront settlement consisting of a dozen wooden single-story cottages and a small store that sat on the beach. The paved road leading into the community terminated at the sand dunes. Sandy trails led to all the cottages and the one store.

Driving a car in the soft sand was difficult, so many residents used horses to travel short distances. The cottages were owned by families from southern towns who came to escape the heat and humidity of summer inland. Each cottage had a large screened porch extending across the front of the house to catch the Gulf breezes. These porches were the center of hospitality. Families would sit with a glass of iced tea or lemonade and anyone passing by could stop to visit and enjoy a cool drink.

The store was the gathering place on summer weekends where locals would come to socialize, buy beer, or perhaps bring their own liquor and mix it with Coca-Cola or 7 Up. The store offered basic staples, including bread, milk, and canned goods on one side, with a pool table and a simple wooden counter that served as a bar on the other side. During the rest of the year, Grayton Beach was as quiet as a cemetery, and that suited Maggie perfectly.

A SIGN ON a weathered picket fence in front of a simple cottage indicated that the house was for rent. Like the rest of the cottages in the tiny settlement, the house sat 2 feet above the ground on concrete blocks to allow for air circulation and to reduce the risk of flooding in the event of hurricanes.

The outside was constructed of wood siding with a tin roof. Peering through the hazy windows, Maggie could see that the interior contained two small bedrooms with pine floors and walls, plus a single bathroom with a claw-foot tub and shower. The kitchen had a counter with cabinets above a porcelain sink and a small refrigerator. A small, white enamel table that served as a worktable to prepare food was set in the middle.

The screened porch stretched across the front. A wooden swing hung from the ceiling on one side. On the other side was a grouping of rattan chairs with cushions covered in a bright fabric containing a red and yellow hibiscus flower pattern. Inside the house was a square wooden table for dining. Casual, overstuffed chairs sat in the small living room.

On both the porch and the interior of the house, paddle fans hung from the ceiling to help move the sultry, coastal air. Sitting on a side table under a window was a shortwave radio that would allow the residents to listen to the news around the world.

The cottage was located a block from the beach on the sandy road that led from the main highway. Other than a good cleaning and some light yard work, it was perfect. There were other homes around this cottage, but Maggie could tell from the weeds and debris in the yards that no one had been living in them for months.

The store where she would be purchasing her basic provisions was only a short walk down the street. Maggie drove to the store and after pulling a chilled bottle of Coca-Cola from the ice chest on the front porch, she used the pay phone to call the number listed on the sign.

A couple of days after she moved into the house, someone knocked on her screen door. A young, attractive Negro girl stood there wearing a crisply ironed but faded plaid cotton dress. The hint of laundry soap filled the air. Her hair was curled in the latest fashion, and her poise gave the impression of a strong work ethic.

"Good mornin', ma'am. I'm looking for work. Is there anything you need help with? I'm good at cookin' and cleanin' and babysittin'. I would certainly appreciate an opportunity to help you with anything you need doin'."

Maggie did not need help but there was something in the girl's eyes that expressed desperation. Noticing the beads of sweat on the young girl's forehead, Maggie guessed she had been out in the heat all day looking for work. She invited her in and asked her name.

"My name is Theresa. I'm a hard and honest worker and would appreciate any job that you might have for me to do."

Theresa explained that she and her husband had left Alabama when her husband was laid off from his job as a groundskeeper for a large landowner, so they were now both looking for work. She told Maggie she had experience looking after children as well as cooking and cleaning houses.

Maggie felt sorry for Theresa and decided on the spot to hire her. Other than initially helping Maggie get the cottage into a more livable condition, she wasn't even sure what Theresa would do, but they would work it out.

"Why don't you help me with a little cleaning and cooking. We can see how it goes for a little while. Come back in the morning and we'll get started."

Theresa's eyes lit up at the news, and a smile broke across her face. "You won't be sorry, ma'am. I'm a good worker. You'll be pleased you hired me." She turned and walked back to where her husband was waiting in an old, beat-up pickup truck that looked like it was on its last legs.

Over the next few days, Maggie and Theresa got to know each other a little better. When Theresa couldn't understand how a person with Maggie's education and background would choose to live in such a remote area, Maggie explained her reasons. A bond soon formed between the two women, and they became as much companion and friend, as employer and domestic.

For the next few weeks, Maggie spent her days walking on the beach, catching small fish and blue crabs in the coastal lake that lay adjacent to the settlement. She thought of Charles often, wishing he could be with her to share this wonderful place she had stumbled upon. In the evenings after Theresa had gone home to the shantytown several miles north, Maggie would read and listen to the news on the shortwave radio.

Occasionally, she would walk to the store to catch up on the local gossip, avoiding the weekends when some of the local men would come in to the bar, have a few drinks, and try to engage her in conversation or offer to buy her a drink. She had no interest in fending off unwanted advances. Maggie hoped that eventually her heart would heal, but she was in no hurry. She felt adrift and lonely. Thinking of Charles made her feel connected to him. Right now, she was in limbo, attempting to hold on to the past while looking to the future. She knew she had to move on, although she thought her life would never be what it had been with Charles before the war. The war! How she hated that word.

Chapter Four

CHRISTIAN ARRIVED AT COLONEL SCHMIDT'S OFFICE THE NEXT morning and was ushered into a conference room containing a large table surrounded by chairs where he was directed to sit. On one wall hung a map of Europe showing the positions of the German and Allied troops. On another wall were two maps of the United States. The larger map showed the contiguous 48 states. The other, slightly smaller map showed the southeastern part of the country. An aide asked him if he would like coffee and when it had been brought to him, Colonel Schmidt began to speak.

"Over the next few days, we are going to spend a lot of time together. I would like to keep our meetings informal. If it is acceptable, please allow me to call you Christian. I ask that you refer to me as Colonel only because we are in a military office and my staff, as well as my superiors would think it more appropriate.

"As I indicated to you yesterday, we need your help in getting Dieter Braun out of an American POW camp. You were selected for this task for several reasons. First and most important, you speak English like an American and with the appropriate clothes, can easily pass as an American. This is critical because you are going to have to interact with and talk to American citizens. You may even need to engage their assistance with problems that may arise. Also, having lived in the States, you know the customs and habits of the American people. In addition, your education and athletic strengths are proof that you have the intellectual and physical skills to pull off this important assignment.

"We are aware you have shown bravery on at least two occasions within the past year, so it is obvious that you can think and act quickly. These are skills that are needed for this assignment. You have also made it clear that you hate America for how you and your family were treated. I am confident that you are the right person for the job.

"In 10 days, one of our U-boats will sail from the port of Lorient, France, to the Gulf of Mexico. This submarine, the U-67, is under the command of Kapitänleutnant Günter Müller-Stöckheim. His assignment is to seek out and sink Allied vessels in the northern Gulf near New Orleans, Louisiana, and Mobile, Alabama. The Americans have large ports in these cities. Ships carrying fuel and supplies are being transported throughout the Gulf and along the Atlantic Coast to New England. The kapitän has been given orders to sail east to an undeveloped beachfront area called Santa Rosa Island and drop you off. He will return when the two of you determine a date.

"Our navy has recently been able to increase the distance that the submarines can travel by having larger vessels, or 'mother ships,' that carry fuel and supplies to resupply our U-boats in the Atlantic before they enter the Gulf in the Florida Straits near Key West, allowing our sailors to remain in their target areas much longer than before. This information is not currently known to the American intelligence. We expect the voyage from France to the northern Gulf of Mexico will take approximately 21 days, putting you at your destination in early June.

"Kapitänleutnant Müller-Stöckheim will take you as close to shore as possible under the cover of darkness and give you an inflatable raft. The Americans are beginning to impose blackouts along the coast because they have realized their ships are visible in the lights in from the shorefront communities. You are to find your way to a deserted area of beach. Once you have reached land, you will deflate and hide your raft.

"Then you will then make your way inland to find the camp where Dieter Braun is being held and help him escape. You will then both return to the beach and signal the U-boat, which will pick you up a couple of kilometers offshore where the water is deep enough for U-67 to wait. The submarine will surface, take you onboard, then return to France. While you are ashore, Kapitänleutnant Müller-Stöckheim will continue with his orders to seek out and sink enemy ships coming and going in and out of the ports along the northern Gulf between the port cities of Mobile and Tampa.

"From what we can determine, Dieter Braun is working as an agricultural laborer to help cut timber or plant and harvest crops for the local farmers. He is frequently transported several miles back to the military base to help with maintenance and warehousing duties. The camp is located in a rural area several kilometers from the town.

"You are going to have to make your way inland to the camp, then find a way to get a message to him. This may not be as difficult as it seems because the local newspapers tell of how the locals communicate with the prisoners while they work in the fields, particularly the girls who are attracted to the 'strong, handsome, blond men.' Once you have scouted the area, it will be up to you to determine the best plan for the escape. Do you have any questions so far?"

Christian sat silently for more than a minute. "Quite frankly, I am so overwhelmed that I don't know how to respond. First of all, why is Braun so important that I have to risk my life to save him?"

Schmidt replied, "Dieter Braun is an engineer with a specialty in designing airborne bombing electronics. He was working on a new long-range bomb that can be released, then directed by remote control from a plane to its intended target. We believe that this technology is vital to win the war. He is also a member of the Nazi Party. As you probably know, some soldiers support the Nazi Party, while others joined the military with a sense of patriotism or were drafted. Orders from the führer are to bring Braun back so that he can continue with his work.

"Even the other prisoners do not know who he is or what he does. There are both pro- and anti-Nazi Party supporters among the prisoners in the camps, and there has been strife between the two groups, much to the amusement of the American guards. The sooner that we can get Braun out of the camp, the safer it will be for him."

Colonel Schmidt produced an envelope containing papers and maps and $1,000 in American money.

"Please study these maps and information carefully. Included are directions on how you can find your way inland to the camp. Because this area has minimal development, we believe that this area of the coast is best for our U-boats to get closest to land safely. It is the closest landing in proximity to the POW camp. Here is a photograph of Dieter Braun so that you will know how to identify him. Do you have any questions, Christian?"

"No sir," responded Christian as his head whirled.

"You will be transported to the submarine base at Lorient on May 16. I suggest you attend to your personal affairs. Do not under any circumstances tell anyone of your mission. Good luck, Christian. I look forward to seeing you upon your return with Dieter Braun. If your mission is successful—and your country is counting on it being so—the führer will award you with a Medal of Valor at a special dinner in your honor."

Colonel Schmidt rose from his chair, bowed, saluted "Heil Hitler," and walked out of the room.

Chapter Five

JOHN LOGAN LOVED WOMEN. HE LOVED THE SMELL OF A WOMAN AND the touch of a woman. He loved the whole game of chase and seduction, and he was very good at it. The fact that he had a wife and two small children back home in Alabama did not bother him at all. He had found early in his marriage that he missed the excitement of the chase and quickly began to come up with reasons to go away on weekend "fishing trips."

John was tall and slender with prematurely graying hair, which he wore slicked back in the current fashion. He had a small, pencil-thin mustache he thought gave him the "Clark Gable" look. He had also found he could convince women to support him financially, which was easier than having a steady job. Being a bookkeeper in a cotton mill was not only boring but restrictive.

He had grown restless with family life and weary of being responsible for anyone but himself, so one day, he went to the bank, withdrew the money that his wife had inherited, and quietly left town. He thought he might travel toward Jacksonville or Savannah and work on the docks, loading and unloading the freighters bound for war. There would be plenty of women living near the ports in order to be close to their men when they returned. John knew it would be only a matter of time until he could get into their beds.

He had escaped being drafted not only because he was 30 years old and had two children to support but also because of a bad knee, the result of being shot by a jealous husband who found Logan putting his pants on as he was running out the back door of the man's house when he came home unexpectedly early one day.

John drove into Grayton Beach on a late afternoon and decided to check out the local watering hole to see if he could find some action. He had money in his pocket and sex on his mind. As he stepped out of his car, he saw an attractive lady walking toward the store. *This might be my lucky day*, he thought. *If she is married, I hope her husband's away at war.*

Maggie had spent the morning walking on the beach and the afternoon catching blue crabs in the coastal lake that bordered Grayton Beach to the east. She was fascinated that a brackish lake could come so close to the thin strip of sand dunes that separated it from the Gulf. Theresa had taught her how to fish with a cane pole from the shore and how to catch blue crabs with a wire basket using a chicken neck for bait or by walking along the shallow water and scooping them up with a net on the end of a pole.

Theresa would boil the crabs in a large pot of water seasoned with a fragrant combination of spices; then, when they had cooled slightly, she would show Maggie how to pull off the claws and pick out the meat with her fingers. Theresa also demonstrated how the small fish could be cleaned on a simple table on the back porch and then thrown into a cast-iron skillet with a little fat to fry. An ice-cold beer and a simple coleslaw were all that were needed to accompany the meal.

Maggie thought she would walk over to the store, call her parents from the pay phone, and pick up a few items before settling down for the evening. She had become friendly with the storeowner, Mr. Bailey, and his wife, and she enjoyed talking with them when she purchased the few items that she needed. She knew Mr. Bailey was fond of her and would keep an eye out on her if there were men hanging around drinking and playing pool. More than once, he had threatened some off duty soldiers with calling the sheriff if they didn't leave her alone.

Only Maggie and Mr. Bailey knew that it would take the sheriff hours to get to Grayton Beach from Fort Walton Beach or DeFuniak Springs. Mr. Bailey loved to tease her and tell her corny jokes that only a young child would find funny, but she always felt a little better when she walked back to her cottage after listening to him.

Tonight, Maggie planned to read for a while and then turn on the shortwave radio and listen to the news of the war. She could get American news stations, though she preferred listening to the British broadcasters on BBC explain what was happening on the European front. As she was walking toward the store, she noticed a very handsome man approach her with a confident stride. *I wonder who he is and what he's doing in Grayton Beach?*

As he came closer, she detected a certain poise and sexual charm. He reminded her of a Hollywood star, a man who knew how to make a woman want something she didn't even know existed before meeting him. None of her usual warning bells rang as she gazed up into his inviting eyes. He reached out to shake her hand and in a self-assured voice said, "Hello. My name is John Logan. I wonder if I could ask a favor. Do you know where I could get a decent meal around here?"

Chapter Six

CHRISTIAN LEFT BERLIN ON MAY 16 AND WAS DRIVEN TO LORIENT, France, a small city on the Atlantic Ocean. Lorient was the home of one of the largest submarine bases in the German navy and was where they sailed out into the Atlantic to search for and destroy Allied ships. The trip took 3 days, hampered by bomb-damaged roads and bridges and convoys of soldiers and military vehicles that took hours to pass.

As they traveled through France, they stopped in villages along the road to savor the local breads and cheeses. Christian would buy bottles of the regional wines that he and the driver would share over a meal by the side of the road or in the village café. Christian noted that even under control of the German forces, the French knew how to produce good food and wine. The smell of the freshly baked baguette and the taste of a firm, garlic sausage made his mouth water. He was in no hurry to arrive at his destination.

Late in the afternoon of May 19, he arrived at the port and reluctantly left the car and driver. Carrying his seabag, which contained his American clothes, a shaving kit, his Luger pistol, and a sharp knife in a leather sheath, he was directed along the wharf to the dock where U-67 was berthed.

U-67 was a Class IX-C submarine, one of 54 that had been built to forage deep into the Atlantic. The boat was over 250 feet long, 22 feet wide, and carried a crew of about 50 men. She had a range of over 13,000 miles and could cruise at 10 knots on the surface and over 60 miles submerged at 4 knots. The submarine was powered by diesel engines that delivered over 4,000 hp for surface transit and electric engines for under the surface that delivered 1,000 hp.

This submarine could fire four torpedoes from the bow and two from the stern. In addition, she carried deck guns with the ability of firing thousands of rounds of high-caliber shells. She was capable of descending to a depth of 750 feet. None of the U-boats carried names or numbers, but each had an emblem signifying who they were. U-67 had a butting ram painted on the conning tower as its only identifying mark.

As Christian crossed the boardwalk and stepped onto the ship, he was met by a sailor who directed him to the conning tower where he was met by Kapitänleutnant Müller-Stöckheim. The kapitän, a seasoned veteran of the Atlantic campaign, was anxious to return to sea. He had been made aware of Christian's assignment by his higher command and was pleased to be part of the rescue operation. He escorted Christian below to the officers' quarters, where Christian would share living space with the senior officers.

The compartment contained four bunks separated by a corridor that ran from the bow of the boat to the stern. Christian was instructed that he would be sharing a bunk with another officer. They would take turns sleeping, as this senior officer would be assigned certain watches during the voyage.

The first sensation that hit Christian was the strong smell of diesel and machinery that permeated the entire boat. Next came the claustrophobic closeness of the space. Pipes and electric conduits covered the walls and low ceiling that stretched from bow to stern. Below the metal floor lay machinery, batteries, food, water, and fuel. Round, watertight doors separated each compartment, requiring that he stoop to pass through. It would be a long and miserable voyage for anyone who could not tolerate the smells of a submarine while confined in such close quarters without the benefit of fresh air.

Christian threw his seabag on one of the narrow bunks and followed Kapitän Müller-Stöckheim for a tour of the boat.

Beside the officers' compartment was a tiny galley containing a small stove and refrigerator. The cook had to store almost 12 tons of food. There was no room or available space that did not act as storage. From this tiny galley, he cooked every meal for the crew using fresh ingredients until they ran out, and then canned food for the rest of the voyage. Now that the mother ships, or "milk cows," had been put into service to resupply fuel and provisions, the morale of the sailors was greatly improved.

Next to the galley were the petty officers' quarters, containing a dozen bunks, the enlisted men's quarters, and the torpedo room, which also had bunks hanging from the ceiling on both sides of the corridor. As with all the sleeping quarters, each bunk was shared by sailors as their watches demanded. One of the two toilets on board the boat was located in a closet off this room.

Christian and Kapitänleutnant Müller-Stöckheim continued toward the aft of the boat, where they entered the kapitän's quarters containing a bunk, a small sink, and a table. Across the corridor but within the kapitän's compartment was the radio room. The kapitän had no more privacy than any other sailor on the boat.

Next to this was the control room, the operational center of the boat, and above that, the conning tower. The control room was where all navigation and orders for military action were given. A ladder led the way up from there to the conning tower where lookouts could stand with binoculars, seeking out enemy ships on the horizon. Behind the conning tower and exposed to the sea were the deck guns.

The kapitän continued aft and entered the diesel engine room. This long and narrow room held two immense diesel engines, each over 20 feet long and 5 feet high. These turbocharged engines produced temperatures exceeding 100 degrees and enough noise to cause permanent ear damage. There was only a small gap between the engines to allow a passageway to the electric engine room. This room held the electric motors that propelled the submarine while submerged.

Finally, they entered the aft crew and torpedo room, the rearmost compartment on the boat. Here, the crew shared bunks and space with torpedoes that were destined to be shot from the rear two torpedo chutes. The second toilet on the submarine was located in this compartment.

When Kapitänleutnant Müller-Stöckheim completed the tour, he excused himself, stating that he needed to be back on deck to assist in preparations for sailing. Christian meandered back to the officers' section, taking his time to survey the boat in more detail. He had never been on a submarine and was fascinated with the complexity and sheer amount of gauges, valves, and pipes that ran from bow to stern. The only concession to the painted metal finishes throughout the ship was varnished wood walls and cabinets in the compartments where the officers and crew slept.

He introduced himself to the other officers and crew and quickly began to realize that they had been expecting a mystery passenger but had not been told why. They were guarded with Christian, knowing that the SS would often place a Nazi agent on board to test the loyalty of the sailors. All of them were aware of instances where sailors who had criticized Hitler's strategy had been arrested and never seen again.

The submariners of both the German navy and the Allied navies were known to have the highest morale of any branch of service and truly believed they were the most elite corps in their military. These sailors of U-67 were no different. They wanted to avoid trouble of any sort from the high command. There was enough heart-stopping danger just trying to stay alive on a submarine during wartime. Christian understood the men's coolness, which did not bother him. He was confident that once at sea, his mission would be made clear and that they would accept him. What even the kapitän was unaware of, however, was that there was, in fact, an SS spy on board the U-67.

Christian left the boat and walked into the city. At a café overlooking the busy main street he ordered a bottle of chilled Sauvignon Blanc and a large bowl of steamed mussels that had been seasoned with white wine and garlic. A baguette was all that he needed to soak up the rich broth. Christian realized that this would be the last meal that he would truly enjoy for a long time, so he took his time and savored every bite of mussel and every sip of wine.

After dinner, he enjoyed a cigarette and decided, again, that this was a good time to quit smoking. Throwing the rest of the pack into the trashcan, he walked back to the boat. U-67 was scheduled to sail early the next morning, and he was as ready as he would ever be.

Chapter Seven

Dieter Braun was irritated again. Pissed was really more like it. Unlike his fellow prisoners, he refused to acknowledge that his captors were decent people and that the food they received was better than they had eaten before. It also irked him to no end that he could not proudly tell his captors of his superior standing within the German Reich. But to do so would invite severe interrogations from the Americans and threaten the freedom that he currently enjoyed within the camp. He had quickly discovered that most of the other prisoners were not active members of the Nazi Party, and although they knew that he was, they were unaware of his seniority.

Since his capture and temporary relocation to England with several hundred other prisoners, there had been only one fellow prisoner who had known of Braun's status in the Nazi Party and the technical nature of his work. Braun knew that it would only be a matter of time before word got out, and he could not allow that to happen.

On the evening before the POWs left England for America, Braun followed the soldier as he returned from the latrine. Grabbing the soldier around the head, he twisted and broke his neck, killing him instantly. Braun then dragged the soldier to a dark corner of the yard, removed the soldier's belt, slipped it around the dead man's neck, and hanged him from the post that supported the wire fence surrounding the compound. When the soldier was later discovered, it was assumed he had committed suicide. No further investigation was warranted. This took the pressure off Braun temporarily, but it did not solve the problem of how he was to protect his identity. With no hope of rescue, Braun relied on his intelligence, keen sense of observation, and cunning to survive. He would watch, listen, and plot his escape. All he had to do is take one day at a time.

When he and the other prisoners arrived at the camp, they were immediately put to work, either in the fields harvesting crops or on work details, cutting timber or laying railroad track. The northwest part of Florida, known as the Panhandle, was a part of the world that Braun had never known existed.

It was hot and humid, even in the springtime, and strange bugs and creatures inhabited this world that he had never seen before. Dive bombers zoomed in for a surprise attack on exposed bodies and departed as quickly as they arrived. Trench diggers burrowed under the skin, causing agony to the helpless victim. Mosquitoes and flying insects bit any exposed skin night or day, causing uncontrollable itching. Ticks and chiggers burrowed under the skin, causing prolonged irritation. Scratching didn't help. Doing so only caused more irritation and infection.

But the things that bothered him most were the snakes. It had become a game for the POWs when working in the fields and woods to find and kill rattlesnakes. They would skin the snakes and dry the skins on boards to make belts. The prisoners thought these belts would make great souvenirs to take home after the war. Dieter thought himself above this childish behavior and would have preferred fine European leather.

Braun shared a tent with several other German POWs. Each day they went out to work, returning in the evening to a simple but hearty dinner of vegetables and meat purchased by the prison from local farmers. It made him angry that the other prisoners seemed satisfied with their situation and did not seem to long for the homeland.

The thing that bothered Dieter Braun most was that he had to work with and even take orders from Negroes. He had never interacted with black people before because there were next to none in Germany. Here, there were black workers alongside the prisoners in the fields, and black men sometimes acted as supervisors over the prisoners when they were cutting timber and laying railroad ties. These men frequently drove the trucks to and from the fields. They were strong and tough men. Braun could tell that they had very little in material possessions and even less education. They seemed, however, to make the most of their circumstances and dealt with it in a positive manner.

These Negroes often sang spirituals as they worked and joked with each other to make the hot and dusty days pass more quickly. He saw the shacks in which they lived and could not imagine living in such poverty. He also saw the lunch pails that they brought to work that contained a cold sweet potato, a biscuit, and maybe a piece of pork. Braun could not imagine living on such a primitive diet.

It was clear that the white Americans did not treat black people equally, but he dismissed it as part of the social order. In his mind, he was part of the only pure race, and if given an opportunity, the Nazi would have all minorities eliminated. After all, he had helped plan for the mass transfer of Jews and Gypsies and other minority groups to the new concentration camps in Germany and Austria and was satisfied that he was contributing toward Germany's plan for a master race.

A Negro guard had told Dieter to move faster down the rows of beans that they were weeding in a large field outside DeFuniak Springs. They had been brought to the field early in the morning and would stay until dusk. At the end of the day, they would be trucked back to camp and allowed to shower and eat. After dinner, they would have a couple hours to play soccer in the yard or read in their tents. The American Red Cross had provided books that taught the prisoners English. Some of the soldiers studied these books, but Braun had no interest. He spoke a little English and that would see him through until he could return home.

There were also magazines that gave reports of what was happening in the war. Dieter, as well as most of the other prisoners, dismissed most of it as propaganda, but they still enjoyed reading the magazines when they arrived. The Red Cross kept a close watch on all the POW camps to make sure that the prisoners were treated according to the rules of the Geneva Convention.

The Negro man came back down the row again and spoke to Dieter. "Mistuh, I ain't gonna tell you again. If you don't get the lead out and pick up the pace with you weedin', I'm gonna tell the boss man, and he is gonna get all over your butt. We needin' to finish this here field 'fore dark, and I ain't gonna suffer the wrath of the man if'n we don't."

Dieter mumbled, "Kiss my ass," in German and reluctantly picked up his pace. He thought to himself, *God, I hope that I have the chance someday to catch that black SOB alone.*

The one glimmer of hope that Dieter saw was that there were very few guards watching while they were working in the fields. It was as though they assumed no one would try to escape because there was no place for them to go in their prison clothes and their poor English. Even speaking English without a Southern American accent would attract attention. Dieter thought that a prisoner from New York would attract just as much attention from the locals as he would with his strong German accent. As a German officer, it was his responsibility to try to escape. His only consolation was that his superiors, knowing his importance to the war effort, would make some attempt to break him out.

Chapter Eight

MAGGIE WIPED HER HANDS ON HER PANTS AND SHOOK LOGAN'S hand as she self-consciously brushed the hair out of her face. She wore no makeup, not even lipstick. She had been in the sun and fresh air all day and was afraid she looked like a local hick to this ruggedly handsome man who seemed to have drifted into her life from a world far more sophisticated than hers. It was a strange sensation to care how she looked. It had been a very long time, and her feminine senses were on overload.

"Hi, I'm Maggie Neal. It's nice to meet you." She felt like she was 14 years old. "I haven't seen you around before. Are you new to this area?" she stumbled, feeling more like a fool with every word.

He smiled. "Actually, I'm traveling through and not sure how long I'll stay. From what I see so far, however, I may be here for a few days."

Maggie could not make out whether he liked Grayton Beach or her. She hoped it was her. "There isn't a decent place to eat here, but if you go over to Destin, there are a couple of dockside restaurants that offer fresh oysters and fried grouper sandwiches. I suggest you try one of those."

"Thanks for the tip. I hate to eat alone. Would you like to join me? I could have you back before dark. I would enjoy your company, and you could tell me more about the area. What do you say?"

Maggie felt flushed with excitement and nervous. She hadn't had an intimate conversation with an eligible man since she had arrived in town and was not sure of her ability to talk with a stranger. Where were those warning bells? Why didn't she fend him off the way she had with the other men? Maybe she just missed being with a sophisticated man. Thoughts of having him pull out a chair for her, or open a car door, or gently guide her by putting his hand on her waist were intoxicating. Just this once, perhaps, she would relax and enjoy herself. It was only dinner, for heaven's sake.

"I guess that would be fine, uh, I mean, sure, I don't have any other plans, uh, I mean that would be very nice. Thank you," she stammered while wondering when it had become so hard to utter a simple sentence.

John grinned, showing his perfect white teeth while joy shone from his sexy eyes. "Why don't you tell me where you live?" he said. "I'll pick you up in, say, an hour? We can drive over, and you can show me around a little."

After giving him directions to her cottage, she waved lightly and turned to walk back to her house. She could feel his eyes boring into her backside as she walked away. A quiet tingling crept through her body, and a soft flush covered her face. She was enjoying being a woman for the first time in a very long time.

Attached to the back of Maggie's house was a metal pipe and simple showerhead surrounded by a galvanized metal enclosure with a door that closed with a spring. It was such a nice day that she thought she would shower in the fresh air. The bathroom in the house could be hot and stuffy during the day. The outside shower was more pleasant. Also, it served to wash sand off her feet from her beach walks before she entered the house.

Maggie took a long and leisurely shower, then shampooed her hair. After toweling off, she went to her bedroom and found a clean pair of shorts and white cotton blouse. She applied a small amount of Chanel No. 5 perfume behind each ear. Slipping on a pair of sandals, she was ready—anxious but excited at getting out of Grayton Beach for the evening. Other than the day-to-day small talk with Theresa, she had not had a meaningful conversation with an adult in a long time, and certainly not with an attractive man.

As she was waiting for John to pick her up, she turned on the radio to hear the news. Reports of German submarines coming up from the Straits of Florida between Key West and Cuba, sinking American ships in the upper part of the Gulf of Mexico made headlines. Further reports from New Orleans and Galveston stated that an increasing number of ships were being targeted and that the government was starting to implement a blackout along the coast to prevent the submarines using the lights to locate ships.

Maggie had heard that submarines had been spotted in the Gulf recently. It did not surprise her that action would be taken. She decided that she would go to Fort Walton Beach to purchase material for blackout shades. She and

Theresa could stitch some covers for the windows. Anything that she could do for the war effort would make her feel as if she were helping in some small way.

John pulled up in front of her house promptly at 6:00 P.M. In an effort to impress her, he jumped out of the driver's side and opened the passenger door as she approached the car. She was floating on air as they began their drive. She caught him staring at her and a little smile crept over her face at such a delicious thought.

The drive to Destin went by in a blur. They soon arrived at a small dockside restaurant and found a table overlooking the bay. When they were seated, they ordered a beer. There was an inlet from the Gulf to the bay through which fishing boats came to reach the marina, and docks jutted out from the shore for the fishing boats to unload their catch in front of the restaurants.

John had an easy way about him, and the conversation was fluid and full of laughter. He asked how she came to be living in Grayton Beach. He couldn't believe an intelligent and beautiful woman would live in such a remote place. She told him how she had lost her fiancé and needed time to grieve. She thought that honesty would be the best way to start a new relationship. Then Maggie asked him why he was traveling through the area.

"Well, my wife died last year, and I just couldn't stand to be in Atlanta anymore, so I decided to travel around. That's how I found Grayton Beach."

He was able to make his eyes water when he mentioned his dearly departed wife. It had exactly the effect he was looking for.

"I'm so sorry," she said. "Two sad souls dealing with a sad time."

John did not want to push the subject any further that evening. He knew that it would work its way into her heart. He could build on her sympathy over the next few days. Soon, they were talking about the funny things that people did during wartime rationing to cope with the many shortages and the mood was light again.

After dinner, they drove back to Grayton Beach. John walked Maggie to her door. "Maggie, I've had a wonderful evening. I hope to see you again."

"I had fun, too, John. Maybe we can do it another time."

She smiled, hesitating a moment in the hope that he would kiss her. Instead, he held her hand for a few seconds longer than necessary, said good night, and turned toward his car. She waved awkwardly to his departing back, whispered good night, and entered her house. *This has been a pleasant evening,* she thought. *I enjoyed his company. I hope we can see each other more. I really would like to get to know him better. Maybe I can offer him some solace.*

As he pulled away from her house with a Cheshire-cat smile forming on his lips, John was thinking to himself how predictable women were. It was almost too easy. *Take them out to dinner, open a door for them, and you're sliding into home plate for a score. I'm going to stay in town a while. It shouldn't be too difficult. She's more than ready.*

He drove back to Destin and found a cheap motel room near the beach. As he turned out the light and drifted off to sleep, he was thinking of good times ahead. As Maggie was drifting off to sleep several miles to the east, she was thinking that she felt like a woman again. Both wore smiles on their faces.

Chapter Nine

U-67 LEFT LORIENT IN FRANCE EARLY MORNING ON MAY 20 AND headed out to sea. It took Christian a while to find his sea legs and get used to the close quarters. Unfortunately, the smell of diesel combined with the odor of cooking kept him constantly on the verge of nausea. At least the boat cruised on the surface, which enabled him to climb to the deck for some fresh air and to think about how he was going to complete his mission.

When he was allowed on deck, he drank in deeply the fresh salt air as if to preserve it in his lungs. The cook had a pot of soup on continuously, and the odor of whatever he was adding on a daily basis sabotaged all desire to eat or drink other than a bare subsistence level. Every square inch of the boat was filled with provisions. Sausages hung from pipes throughout the boat. Even the toilet and torpedo tubes were used as storage lockers for food.

The toilets on the boat were used only when the boat was submerged, if at all possible. The men preferred to stand or squat on deck to relieve themselves rather than to use the complicated system of valves that were required to flush the toilet. It was tradition for new sailors to receive improper instructions on how to operate valves required to flush the toilet so that it back-flowed on them, much to the amusement of the veteran sailors.

Christian took it all in good humor and was soon accepted among the crew. He was quick to give up his bunk or eating space to a crewmember coming off duty and was always looking for a task, the harder or messier the better. He stayed out of the diesel room as much as possible because the noise of the twin engines was deafening. He was amazed that the sailors could work in such an environment and quickly discovered that the sailors frequently suffered from permanent hearing loss.

As the days passed, the temperature slowly began to rise. The sailors, including Christian, changed from long sleeve cotton shirts and pants to just pants without shirts, and then to simple blue or white cotton shorts. Bathing was next to impossible. When the seas were calm, those off duty could climb on deck and wash with saltwater soap, rinsing themselves with a pint or two of fresh water. Only a few sailors could be on deck at a time in case the submarine had to make a crash dive.

Occasionally, they would practice firing the deck guns or doing emergency dives. The sailors were very efficient with their maneuvers, and he was impressed with their skills. It was clear that they thought highly of Kapitänleutnant Müller-Stöckheim and wanted to perform with perfection. They also revered the commander of the entire German submarine fleet, Admiral Karl Donitz. Admiral Donitz was a natural leader and an inspiration to his sailors. He made sure that whenever possible, he was at the dock when they sailed and met them when they returned from their missions.

They took on fresh supplies and headed through the Straits of Florida between Key West and Havana, Cuba, then turned north toward New Orleans and Galveston. As they were leaving the western tip of Cuba, a tanker was sighted in the distance. The kapitän ordered the submarine to dive, then fired a torpedo from the forward tube. The ship exploded and began to sink. U-67 surfaced, and seeing that the crew of the tanker was boarding lifeboats, he shouted, "Good luck, I hope that you make it ashore safely." Then he ordered that they continue north to their next targets.

Christian was impressed with the way in which Kapitän-leutnant Müller-Stöckheim had led the crew in their first combat mission and also how the crew had responded calmly and efficiently.

A few days later, they arrived south of New Orleans in the Mississippi Delta. They waited on the bottom of the sea during the day and rose to the surface after dark to search out their prey. Their next target came in this area south of the Mississippi River, and again, a single torpedo dispatched it quickly.

The radioman approached the kapitän the next day and informed him that he had heard propeller noises nearby and thought that other U-boats might be in the area. As radio transmissions could be intercepted by the Americans, Müller-Stöckheim could not contact the other submarine but decided to move out of the area for a while. This was a good time to proceed a few hundred miles to the east toward Port St. Joe and Cape San Blas, Florida. That area had tanker traffic which had not yet been targeted by U-boats as far as he knew. It would also bring them to the place where Christian would be dropped off. The timing would work well for both him and Christian. He knew that Christian's assignment was important, but he also had his own mission and the care of his crew to look after.

The kapitän sent for Christian. Then they sat at a small table to discuss the best strategy.

"I plan to be at the location to drop you off in 2 days. During the day I will be running submerged and will only surface in the evening to recharge the batteries. When we arrive at the location for you to leave the boat, we will wait until dark to surface a kilometer or two offshore. You will take one of the small inflatable life rafts and paddle your way to shore. Hide the raft well so that it will be there when you and Braun are ready to be picked up.

"We will be waiting in the same position for a signal that you are on your way back. I will be at that position every night for a week between 12:00 p.m. and 3:00 a.m. During the day, I will cruise along the coast looking for targets. You will signal that you are ready by sending us a series of two short flashes followed by one long flash with a flashlight. Do this three times. I will respond with one quick flash only. Any more would invite detection.

"When you and Braun return to the boat, we will continue with our mission until we have to return home. If I don't see your signal after a week, I will assume that you were not successful and will continue west toward New Orleans."

Two days later, Christian was summoned again to see the kapitän.

"We are approaching the location where we are letting you off. Tonight, we are taking the boat in as close as we can go to your location. We will surface just long enough for you to take the raft and go overboard with it. As soon as you are gone, we will submerge again and continue east. Good luck with your mission. I must admit I am glad it is you and not me. I wish you well and hope to see you in a few days."

Christian was grateful to the kapitän for the information, and with some regret in leaving the security of the ship, thanked him for the ride.

Christian returned to his bunk and removed the dirty, oily shorts that he had been wearing throughout the voyage. He poured a pint of fresh water over his head and attempted to wash off as much of the diesel smell and body odor as possible. From his bag, he retrieved a shaving kit and shaved off the straggly beard that he had grown since leaving France. He then pulled on the American casual slacks and short-sleeved shirt, finishing with a pair of worn leather shoes.

Looking at his reflection in the glass cover of a large gauge, he was impressed with how much he looked like an American. When he had finished dressing, he gathered his personal items and spent a few moments collecting his thoughts. First, he would need to start thinking in English so that he would speak it without making the deadly mistake of uttering German instead.

Suddenly, a sense of doubt washed over him, quickly replaced by fear. Christian broke out in sweat, and his stomach roiled. If he screwed up, he would probably end up bunking with Dieter instead of breaking him out of the camp. He tried to console himself with the fact that at least he wasn't on the Russian front.

Chapter Ten

THE DAY AFTER MAGGIE'S DINNER WITH LOGAN, SHE ASKED THERESA to drive with her to Fort Walton Beach to purchase black cloth to make shades for the windows. She planned to buy several yards of material, then cut and sew the fabric to fit each window.

As they drove along the highway with the moist sea breeze blowing through the windows, Maggie told Theresa about her evening with John. Theresa was pleased for Maggie, while, at the same time, feeling protective of her. Maggie was still emotionally fragile. Theresa knew she could be hurt. She didn't want to lecture Maggie but decided to share a little of her own experience.

"Miss Maggie, I do truly hope that you will find someone to replace your sorrow. I was very lucky myself to find my husband Robert. You see, I got into trouble a couple of years ago. I had a boyfriend and thought I was sitting pretty. But lo and behold, I come home one day and find him in bed with another woman. I just lost my senses, grabbed a kitchen knife, and stabbed both of them right hard. Didn't want nobody messing with my man, and I damn sure didn't want my man messing around. Didn't kill either one, but they ain't gonna forget about me any time soon.

"Well, I had to go to jail for 3 months. The judge was about as understandin' as I could have expected him to be, but it was a hard time and a hard lesson. When I got out of jail, I was determined to start a new life for myself. I was able to find a job taking care of some white children for a lady, and soon, I met my Robert at church. He's a fine man and takes good care of me. We ain't got much in worldly things, but we got each other, and I guess that is about as much as we could ask for in this life.

"Robert found himself a job last week working at a pulp mill over by the bay. We have moved from that house where we lived with an old lady into a house that we rent. It ain't much, but at least we have some privacy—if you know what I mean," she giggled, looking over at Maggie with a knowing smile on her pretty brown face.

If Maggie was shocked to hear about Theresa's past, she didn't show it. She had grown fond of Theresa and discovered in her a warm, sincere woman. All one had to do was look into Theresa's eyes to know that she had a good heart. Both she and Theresa were a product of the times and were comfortable with their positions in the society in which they lived. Neither one knew of any other way of life.

Maggie was aware that Negroes were not treated the same as whites, but she was not the kind of person who was going to campaign for changes. She had been raised with servants in her home. As a child of the South, that was the way things were.

Theresa did not know of any other life either. She was used to being treated as a second-class citizen. Separate schools, churches, and restaurants were all she knew. She had heard that in cities like Detroit and New York City in the north, colored people and white people lived and worked together. However, Detroit may as well have been China, because she had never been north of Birmingham in her life.

John Logan came by unexpectedly the following day to ask if Maggie would like to drive over to Panama City and grab a bite to eat. She was delighted to see him and asked him to wait on the porch while she freshened up. The evening was perfect and passed by much too quickly. When John took her home, she thought he might try to kiss her this time, but he only walked her to her door and said good night. Again, Maggie was disappointed and wondered what she needed to do to make it clear that she would like to be kissed by him. *Longed* to be kissed by him was a more accurate statement.

But John Logan was biding his time and knew that the more slowly he played his hand, the more sure he would be of success. Maybe in a day or two he would make his first move. Perhaps waiting before seeing her again might ripen her up a little more. This always made the sex much hotter for him.

The next day, Maggie told Theresa about her evening and mentioned she was beginning to have feelings for John. Theresa smiled and said nothing.

THIRTY MILES NORTH, Dieter Braun toiled away in the hot sun. He had been in this godforsaken camp for 3 months and couldn't see how he would be able to survive much longer. The food was disgusting, and the bugs were terrible. He had almost been bitten by a rattlesnake when he went to relieve himself in the woods. Startled, he yelled at the top of his lungs, falling on his butt in the sandy soil causing laughter from the guard and prisoners.

A fighter pilot in the Luftwaffe named Federspiel who had been shot down over France quickly dispatched the snake with his hoe. He had already accumulated several skins and was earning a tidy sum from selling snakeskin belts to the local citizens. He had also constructed a crude still and concocted a barely drinkable moonshine which he bartered with the other prisoners.

Braun admired Federspiel's bravery and entrepreneurship. He would have befriended him had he not been a fervent anti-Nazi who had openly criticized Hitler. Federspiel had proven his bravery in combat many times, so Braun was careful not to push his own beliefs in the superiority of the Reich on him. He decided that they would just coexist.

Each day as he worked in the fields, he kept an eye open for any possible means of escape. He knew enough English to communicate with the guards and would innocently inquire about the area as though he were interested in learning more about America and its people.

One day, he stumbled upon an old Standard Oil road map by the side of the road that he quickly stuffed into his pants. He would study it at night in his bunk to familiarize himself with the roads and waterways in the area. If the time ever came for escape, he would be as prepared as possible. In the meantime, he continued to hoe rows of vegetables and load logs on the trucks to be taken to the mill. He could do nothing else but wait for an opportunity.

Chapter Eleven

THE NEXT DAY, MAGGIE HEARD ON THE RADIO THAT BLACKOUTS WERE to become mandatory at dusk. There had been further reports of German submarine activity in the Gulf. People along the coast were now required to turn off all outside lighting and put deflectors on their cars to hide their presence on the roads.

After listening to the announcement, she tried to find a station playing music but couldn't. During the day, reception was poor, but at night, she could pick up stations as far away as Chicago, New Orleans, and Atlanta. She listened to the news for a while, then decided to walk up to Mr. Bailey's store to pick up a few groceries.

Mr. Bailey waved her over as soon as he saw her. She could tell that he had another of those corny jokes to tell her. Sure enough, the first thing that he said was "Maggie, do you know the difference between a pilot from the Pensacola airbase and God?"

Smiling, she responded in a theatrical voice, "No, Mr. Bailey. What is the difference between a pilot from the airbase and God?"

"God doesn't think that he is a pilot," Mr. Bailey said and let out a loud laugh that could be heard across the store.

Maggie chuckled at the joke and at the obvious joy Mr. Bailey took in telling it. While she was picking up the items that she needed, she overheard a conversation between Mr. Bailey and a local man saying that the Coast Guard was planning to send a group of men to Grayton Beach to establish a lookout for submarines that might be cruising off the coast. The conversation elicited excitement because it would mean an opportunity for the citizens to rent their homes to the government for the soldiers. Any extra income would be appreciated in these hard times.

Theresa was at the house when she returned. Maggie decided they should grab a couple of cane fishing poles and walk over to the lake to catch some fish for supper. Any fish more than what Maggie could eat would go home with Theresa, along with hush puppies and anything else they cooked. She knew that Theresa and Robert were living on a shoestring, so whenever she could give them something without it appearing to be charity, she liked doing so.

The two women sat on the bank and stuck their cane poles in the sand. The fishing line had a cork float that would sink if a fish took the small piece of raw pork fatback that they used as bait. When they had caught a dozen small fish, they walked back to the house, where Theresa cleaned and fried them up with some hush puppies and fixed a simple coleslaw.

They were both surprised when two vehicles pulled up in front of the house at the same time. Robert arrived first, and John Logan pulled in behind him. Giving Maggie a quick wink that said *I know what you are going to be doing tonight,* Theresa wrapped up some of the fried fish and coleslaw and slid out the door, eager to meet her husband.

As she jumped into the truck, she caught a glimpse of the man emerging from the car. He looked familiar to her. She looked again while trying to keep her face averted from him. She couldn't believe what she saw. Theresa was horrified. Her only thought was to leave before he could recognize her. Crouching low in her seat, she hissed to Robert, "Pull out and leave right now!"

He could see the fear in her eyes. "What's wrong with you, woman?" he said as he stepped on the accelerator. "You look like you done seen a ghost."

"I have! God Almighty, Robert, that man's been courting Miss Maggie. Did you see who it was?"

"No, I didn't see who it was. Who was it?"

"That was Mr. Logan from Andalusia. I looked after his and Mrs. Logan's two boys. What is *he* doing here courting Miss Maggie? Lord, help me. What am I going to do? He's a married man with a family, and here he is acting like he is a cock of the walk and telling her all kind of lies so he can put his pecker where it don't belong. I tell you, Robert, I just don't understand men. They want to have a nice home and somebody to cook for them and raise their children, then they want to fool around like a damn tomcat."

"Well, Theresa, I ain't that away, and you know it, so don't start jumpin' all over me. Let's think what we need to do, but we gotta be awfully careful 'cause white folks ain't gonna cut us no slack. I know you like Miss Maggie a lot, and she is good to us, but we need to be careful."

Theresa looked back as John Logan met Maggie in her front yard. They both seemed happy to see each other. *Damn, what am I gonna do about this mess?* Theresa thought miserably to herself.

Maggie was, indeed, happy to see Logan. She gave him a large smile, offered him a cocktail, and asked him to help her eat some of the fish that Theresa had just prepared. Even if she only had a box of crackers, she would have thought of some way to make him stay for supper.

He smiled and said, "That would be real nice, Maggie."

She seemed to float on air as she went inside to fix two iced Tom Collins. Maggie had only known John for a few days, but it felt like a lifetime. Without John, her life was lonely, without purpose. With him, her life took on new meaning. Maggie could imagine many evenings ahead with just the two of them, enjoying life and planning a future together. She would take pleasure in helping him overcome his grief. Coming to Grayton Beach had been a good decision after all.

After they had finished their drinks, Maggie excused herself, went inside, and brought out two plates of fish with hush puppies, coleslaw, and a plate of sliced ripe tomatoes. They sat on the porch where it was cooler and listened to Glen Miller on the radio while they ate. After a leisurely supper, John suggested that since it was such a fine evening, a walk on the beach would be pleasant. They strolled down through the sand dunes and walked along the beach where the water lapped onto the shore.

After a while, Maggie suggested that they sit. The sun had long since set, and the sky was clear. With the blackout in effect, there were no lights from town to wash out the stars, and just a sliver of the moon appeared above the horizon. Combined with the sound of the waves gently lapping onto the shore, it was a perfect evening. Occasionally, a falling star would shoot across the sky and they would watch it until it disappeared.

Maggie lay back and closed her eyes. Logan reached over and tenderly kissed her on the lips, startling her. She had been waiting a long time for John Logan to kiss her. She responded by putting her arms around his neck, and he lay down beside her, and their bodies touched. Logan kissed Maggie hungrily, darting his tongue between her lips, and she responded with low murmurs of pleasure. He slowly reached up and lightly brushed her breast, causing a gasp from Maggie. It had been a long time since a man had touched her, and her entire body was responding with tingling delight. She wanted this to go on forever, but did not want to rush into making love before she was ready.

Suddenly, Maggie sat up, breathing hard, and said, "Let's go slowly. Why don't we take a swim and cool things off for a while? I want you to turn around and look in the other direction while I undress. When I'm in the water, then you can join me. Now John Logan, I expect you to behave like a gentleman. Do you understand me?" she said with such a wry smile that he wasn't sure how serious she was.

In his experience, a *no* usually meant *yes* in the end. She stood up and peeled off her blouse and shorts. She then reached back and unhooked her bra, removed it, then slid her panties down her hips and let them fall on top of her clothes. Naked, she ran through the sand and dived headfirst into the water, leaving Logan on the blanket in an uncomfortable state.

He reluctantly stood up, crouching over to hide his erect manhood, and began to undress. When he was naked, he walked more timidly into the water. Maggie giggled at his awkwardness and began to splash him to get him to relax. She was standing knee deep in the water and Logan could see only the dark form of her silhouette. He could see the long legs and the beautiful roundness of her breasts with erect nipples.

He moved closer to her and took her into his arms. Tenderly, he wrapped his arms around her and brought her closer to him, feeling the soft downy triangle between her legs. He was beside himself with desire. Without another word, he picked her up and, despite her feeble resistance, carried her to the beach, laying her down on her back.

Maggie wrapped her arms and legs around him, and they moved with each other in a furious surge of passion, each caught up in their own needs and desire. He would move quickly and then slowly, teasing her with his deftness at lovemaking. She enjoyed every changing sensation until she did not think she could take it any longer. She rolled him over onto his back and mounted him hungrily. It was only a moment before she felt herself going over the edge. She climaxed with a gasp and a soft moan.

John felt her body quiver and came immediately with a deep groan. They collapsed together, their sweat mingling as they lay panting. Soon, she rolled off and lay beside him. They stared at the stars overhead while they each caught their breath. Both of them were satiated and without being aware, drifted off to sleep as the water lapped softly on the shore.

Chapter Twelve

I_T WAS_ 10:00 O'CLOCK IN THE EVENING WHEN K_APITÄNLEUTNANT_ Müller-Stöckheim told Christian they were in position for him to leave the boat. "The sub is now at the best location to let you off. We are a little over a kilometer offshore, and this is as far as I can go submerged. Get the things that you are taking ashore and let me know when you are ready. I will surface only long enough for you to board the raft, then I will dive again. Hopefully, I will see you in a week or so. Good luck with your mission." The kapitän saluted Christian then shook his hand as a gesture of comradeship and respect.

Christian returned to his bunk and picked up his seabag containing the items that he would need. Included was another set of clothes that would allow him one change during his time ashore. He had been given $1,000 in small denominations for spending money and for whatever expenses that he might encounter, and this could purchase a used car, if necessary. He had packed the shaving kit, a toothbrush, and tooth powder. A comb would keep his hair neat.

He slipped a slender, razor-sharp knife into a sheath and strapped it to the inside of his leg. Finally, he secured the Luger pistol in a waterproof holster and strapped it behind his back. The pistol was fully loaded with cartridges. He had an additional 20 cartridges in his bag. He hoped that he would not have to fire a single shot because most likely, a single shot would result in many more in quick succession.

When he was finished, he walked back to the control room and told the kapitän he was ready to go. The order was given and without further comment, the boat began to rise, making very little noise as it broke through the surface. A sailor gave Christian the nod when the tower and deck were clear.

He walked along the wet deck until he found the raft, inflated it quickly, and without another word, slipped over the edge and began to row toward shore. There was just enough moonlight for him to see. Christian wore an American watch with a small compass on the band, which he knew he might need to find his bearings once he was on land.

After half an hour, he began to sense the outline of the shore in the darkness ahead. Listening carefully for any noise, he dragged the raft out of the water and across the beach to the sand dunes, where he quickly dug a hole and buried the deflated raft with its paddles in the sand. He found two pieces of driftwood and laid them in a rough X to give him a simple marker for his return. Next, he took a dried palm frond and swept away his tracks back to the waterline. Christian knew from studying the maps that there was a road leading inland to the west. He thought he would go that way, find a place to hide, and get some rest. Soon, he would have to find food somewhere.

Christian had only been walking for a few minutes when he heard voices. He dropped down and peered into the darkness. He could barely make out the voices of a man and woman. Slowly, he crept up on his hands and knees until he could see two figures rise from the sand, dress, and then stroll away from him along the beach, their arms wrapped around each other's waist. He could not help but smile. He had himself done the same with several young ladies at a lake near Berlin. Until the couple had made their way further down the beach, he decided to hide in the sand dunes before going into the town. As soon as they were out of sight, he quickly returned to the shoreline as there was no breeze behind the dunes and mosquitoes were attacking every bit of exposed skin.

Lost in his thoughts, he covered the distance quickly and could soon see dim lights from the houses ahead. He was sure that he was now in Grayton Beach, and he knew the road to Braun started here. Some of the houses looked inhabited, while others showed obvious signs of neglect. His best option would be to break into one of the dark houses and try to get some sleep. Maybe there would be some food in the pantry.

Keeping to one side of the road to avoid noise from crunching oyster shells, he made his way in from the beach. Soon, he saw a house that was completely dark and could see from the debris in the yard that no one had been there for a long time. Christian crept to the back of the house, where, using his knife, he breached the lock. In the dark, he found the kitchen and pantry. There were some canned vegetables and beans that would serve as food for the next day, but now he was tired and anxious for what tomorrow would bring.

Soon after he lay down on a bed, he heard voices and a car leaving the house next door. As he drifted off to sleep, he wondered if it were the couple that he had seen on the beach.

Chapter Thirteen

THERESA AND MAGGIE HAD A UNIQUE RELATIONSHIP. THERESA HAD grown to like Maggie and found she was treated by her with respect, something she was not accustomed to from most white folks. Maggie seemed to enjoy her company. It was fun to be with her and work together.

Theresa was, unwillingly, caught in a dilemma. In her head, she thought it best to not become involved with Maggie's personal life. But in her heart, she wanted to tell Maggie what she knew. All night long, she could not stop thinking or talking to Robert about what she had seen and what she should do about it. Robert could only try to be supportive.

"Honey, I know this is drivin' you crazy, but you gotta keep your wits about you. You go in there and tell Miss Maggie what you seen and all it's gonna do is cause more trouble for her and you, too."

"Don't care," Theresa replied. "She deserves to know about that lying two-timer before she gets swept up into something that gonna break her heart again. When you take me over to her house tomorrow, I'll figure out how to tell her best I know how."

Arriving early at Maggie's house the following morning, Theresa found her on the porch drinking a cup of coffee. The glow from Maggie's face just about blinded her. She didn't even need to ask what had happened. Theresa had never seen Maggie looking so content. *Damn that John Logan to hell.* She cleared her throat, adjusted the folds of her dress, and ran her fingers over her stomach before she raised her head and looked Maggie in the eye.

"Theresa," laughed Maggie, "you look mighty fidgety this morning. Is everything all right? You and Robert didn't have a fight or anything, did you?"

"No ma'am. It ain't Robert I'm worried 'bout. Miss Maggie, we got to talk about somethin' important." She sat down in one of the chairs. "I want you to know that tellin' you this is the hardest thing I've ever had to do. You can believe me or not, and if you think I'm oversteppin' myself, you can just ask me not to ever come back here again."

"Theresa, what in heaven's name are you talking about?"

"Well, yesterday when I was leavin', I saw that man you been seein'. You need to know that I know that man, and he ain't what he been tellin' you he is. Miss Maggie, that man's name is John Logan. He's married with a wife and two boys back home in Andalusia, Alabama. I know this 'cause I took care of them kids before Robert and me moved down here. I want you to know this 'cause he ain't no good for you.

"I even overheard Mrs. Logan and him arguing more than once about his seein' other women. He used to disappear for days, and when he'd come home, he acted like nothin' had happened. Mrs. Logan was gettin' mighty fed up from what I could tell. I just thought you needed to know what I seen. I don't want you to get your heart broke again."

Maggie stared through Theresa as if she were not there. She started to rise up from the swing, but suddenly, her legs began to shake. She dropped her cup on the porch floor and fell back into the swing, releasing a loud, angry howl.

"You can't be right. You have him mixed up with someone else." Theresa said nothing. Maggie continued staring at the floor and after a while, Theresa went into the kitchen to get a cloth to clean up the spilled coffee and to give Maggie some privacy.

"I sure hope that I done the right thing tellin' her," she mumbled to herself. "She needs to know the truth."

The more Maggie thought about it, the more she knew Theresa was right. Then the anguish and heartbreak began to change to a rising anger. She thought about how they had met and the stories he had told her about his past, and she realized that he had been too perfect and she had been too desperate to be held and loved again. He had taken advantage of her vulnerability. The anger rose. She stood up and yelled at the top of her voice, "You lying, two-timing son of a bitch. John Logan, I am going to cut your balls off and then let's see how you screw around."

Theresa was so startled with the outcry that she dropped a glass, sharp shards of shattered crystal spreading across the floor. Quickly, she walked out to the porch and found a

Maggie that she had not seen before. There was a look in her eyes that said, *Revenge is mine, and I am going to enjoy every minute of it.* Maggie turned to Theresa and said, "Thank you for telling me, Theresa. I know it was hard for you."

Maggie's outcry had woken Christian from his sleep. He crept to the window and saw an attractive lady on the porch next door. He looked around to see if she had been talking to someone in the yard, but there was no one. *She is one pissed-off woman,* he thought to himself. *Better stay clear of her.* Christian ran his hand over his whiskered face as he slowly stood up. He was a little stiff and very hungry, but otherwise, it hadn't been a bad night. He needed to make a plan so he decided to hitchhike north to see if he could buy a used car or a motorcycle. If necessary, he would hotwire and steal a car.

The shades in the house were pulled down, but as he still wanted to be careful not to be seen, he crouched low as he moved from room to room. He found a can of peaches in the pantry, opened it with his knife, and ate out of the can. His mind was racing in anticipation of the day. His English was good enough. He was not worried about being discovered as a German, but knew he might be mistaken for someone from the North. With the war going on, it would not be uncommon for soldiers and civilians from all parts of the country to be coming through the area. He needed a cover for his presence and decided that he would pose as an engineer assigned to check on road conditions in the area.

After he had carefully checked for activity on the street, he slipped out of the back door and casually strolled to the road. As he was walking, he held out his thumb in the hope that someone would stop and pick him up. Hitchhiking was common as soldiers frequently relied on it to get to and from their base.

It was not long before a car stopped and offered him a ride as far north as Freeport, a farming and timber town with a small port. This was perfect because it allowed him to cross the new bridge that spanned the bay separating the mainland from the island on which Grayton Beach was located. Christian thanked the driver in perfect English. He was surprised how easily the language came back after all the years he had been out of the country.

He found a café in town, and, sitting alone in a booth, ordered a lunch of meat loaf, mashed potatoes, and green beans. He had not had this kind of meal since he left America. It was delicious, and he was so full he could not bring himself to try the pecan pie for dessert.

When he finished, he noticed a used car lot down the block. He casually strolled over and eyed a 1937 Ford Sedan. It was perfect. With some haggling, Christian purchased the car and drove quickly off the car lot. Now that he had the means to take Braun and himself back to the beach, he felt a great relief. The first step of getting Braun out was accomplished. He filled the gas tank at a Sinclair station on the edge of town and drove toward DeFuniak Springs and the POW camp.

Chapter Fourteen

JOHN LOGAN DROVE UP TO MAGGIE'S HOUSE MIDAFTERNOON. HE WAS looking forward to spending the afternoon and, if all went well, the evening. Maggie had exceeded his expectations. He was ready for a repeat performance. There she was, sitting on the porch, probably waiting for his visit. It just didn't get any better than this. He stepped out of his car and with his usual swagger, a sexy smile on his face, approached the porch.

Maggie was waiting. She was waiting with a cast-iron skillet in her hand. Theresa had seen Maggie pick it up when Logan drove up. She was terrified but could only wait in the house to see what unfolded. John did not even have a chance to speak before Maggie had swung the skillet with both arms and made a direct hit to the side of his head. He dropped like a rock and lay unmoving as blood began to trickle down the side of his face. "That's not only from me, you bastard, but from all the other women you took advantage of. Not to mention your wife and kids."

Theresa looked at the prostrate figure. "God Almighty, you done killed him. Damn, Miss Maggie, look what you done."

Maggie looked down at the man and then at Theresa. "He's not dead. I just knocked him out. Go get some water and throw it on his face."

Theresa could barely hold the pot of water she was shaking so badly as she returned from the kitchen. "Throw it on him and let's see what he does," Maggie directed.

Logan grunted and slowly opened his eyes, staring off into the distance. "Get your cheating butt up and out of here right now and don't ever let me see your sorry face again."

He rose to his knees and holding on to a low table, slowly pulled himself up, swaying back and forth as he tried to regain his balance. Water and blood was dripping down his face and soaked his shirt. As his head began to clear, he was able to focus on Maggie and the other woman. The Negro girl looked familiar. Suddenly, it dawned on him who she was. *How in hell did she get from Andalusia to here?* A look of pure hatred crossed his face.

Slowly, John turned and staggered out to his car. After sitting for a few minutes to recover, he drove off. He realized now what had caused Maggie's wrath. "I will get you back, you little black bitch," he shouted as he drove erratically down the street.

Maggie fell into a chair on the porch and rocked back and forth, sobbing. *Why is this happening to me? I didn't do anything to deserve this.* Theresa sat across from her without speaking. After a few minutes, Maggie looked up at Theresa and spoke in a composed but resigned voice.

"I had a perfect life. I had everything I ever wanted. In the past 6 months, it has all been taken away, and I now realize that no matter what happens to me, I will never be the same innocent girl again. I desperately wanted John to be the person to rescue me, but he turned out to be the person who has made me sadder than I thought possible."

Chapter Fifteen

I<small>T DID NOT TAKE</small> C<small>HRISTIAN LONG TO DRIVE TO</small> D<small>E</small>F<small>UNIAK</small> S<small>PRINGS</small>, where he hoped he would be able to find the POW camp. He knew he had to be very careful not to attract attention. He parked on the main street of the small town and walked into a hardware store.

"Can I help you?" the older man behind the counter asked.

"I need a light ax, please," he responded. "Maybe a pair of wire cutters, too," he added.

"You from around here?" the man inquired. "Don't believe I have seen you before."

"No, I work for the road department. I need to cut some brush and barbed wire to get to survey markers." The explanation seemed to satisfy the merchant. As he was paying for the tools, he asked, "On the way in to town, I thought

I saw some prisoners working in some fields. Is there a prison around here?"

"Nah, just a German POW camp west of town. A couple hundred soldiers are being held as part of Eglin Base. You need anything else today?"

"No thanks, that's all." Christian had found out enough to get to the next leg of his quest, so he drove west to see if he could catch a glimpse of the camp. He would need to keep watch for a couple of days to locate Dieter Braun and to get a sense of the routine of the prisoners and guards. Soon, he would figure out a way to let Braun know that he was there and then plan to spring him when the time was right.

Shortly after driving from the town he saw a group of men working in a distant field. He slowed, parked, and after carefully slipping through a pine thicket, confirmed that they were from the camp. They wore blue pants and shirts with PW stitched on the back. He could hear German being spoken as they worked and saw two guards watching them. One carried a pistol on his belt and the other a billy club as his only weapon. *At least I have found some of the men. Now I need to find Braun and let him know I am here.* He decided to wait until they had finished for the day then follow them back to the camp.

At 5:00 o'clock that afternoon, he saw the men start to walk slowly toward some trucks and climb aboard. He waited for them to drive by the road where he was parked and then followed them at a distance, making sure not to be seen by the drivers. When they reached the compound, he saw how it was laid out.

Sitting at the edge of a pine forest, the camp covered several acres with two high wire fences surrounding the entire compound. The outer fence appeared to be about

10 feet high with strands of barbed wire on top. Separated by 30 feet of cleared ground was a inner fence also topped with barbed wire. A watchtower stood at each of the four corners standing 20 feet in the air. Only two were manned by guards. It appeared to Christian that the guards were not concerned about attempts to escape. Still, getting Braun out would be difficult and dangerous. He needed to get a message to his target to let him know he was here.

Driving back to the town, Christian stopped at a store and purchased a pencil, a small paper tablet, and a pack of Lucky Strike cigarettes. He then returned to the field where the men had been working and wrote a note in German, addressing it to Braun.

Dieter Braun, I am here to help you escape. I have wire cutters for the fences. Let me know in the same way that you received this message the best means and time to break out. It must be within the next 4 days.

Folding the paper tightly, he wrote Braun's name on the outside, discarded the cigarettes from the pack, and re-placed them with the note. He walked out into the field and carefully placed the cigarette pack at a point where it would be easily seen by a POW the next day. Christian hoped that if a prisoner found the note, it would find its way to Dieter Braun. Then he returned to his car and drove away, pleased with his ingenuity.

His mind was already racing ahead to the next phase. He knew that Braun's escape would be discovered quickly so they would need a safe place to hide until they could signal to be picked up. He drove up and down several sandy side roads looking for a place that would work. After he crossed over the bay bridge, he turned off the main road onto a road of oyster shells and sand that led him past a couple of simple houses and through a deep pine forest of palmetto palms and wild wax myrtle.

Looking through the undergrowth, he noticed an abandoned farmhouse with an old barn and outhouse behind the dilapidated structure. He made his way up the overgrown drive, palmetto leaves scratching both sides of his car. It was clear from the broken windows that no one had been here in a long time. This was a perfect place to wait to hear from Braun.

The door was not locked so he pushed it open and stepped inside. There was nothing but a rusty bed frame and a rickety wooden table. The house smelled musty and droppings from rodents dotted every room. Cobwebs stuck to his face as he explored each room.

Eventually, he found an old grammar textbook on a bedroom shelf. *A child has grown up in this house,* he thought to himself. Seeing the book reminded him of his school days in Georgia and a discomfort enveloped him as he remembered that unhappy time. To escape those depressing thoughts, he walked out to the barn. Opening the creaky doors, he found that it contained several rusty farm implements scattered haphazardly throughout. He decided to move them to make room to hide his car from anyone passing by.

An old well stood between the barn and the house. Gazing down into it, he could faintly make out a reflection of water many feet below. A wooden bucket tied to a frayed rope sat on the edge of the circular housing over the well. This place was ideal for a hideout. It was remote, and from the apparent lack of attention, not used by anyone. He had to chuckle to himself. He never would have known he possessed such a keen sense of cunning and deception had it not been for this mission. War changed men. His smile faded. Again, he focused on the tasks at hand.

Unfortunately, his seabag was back at the house in Grayton Beach, so he decided he would drive back after dark to pick it up as there was no reason to draw attention by driving down the road in daylight.

At about midnight, Christian drove back down the sandy road to Grayton Beach keeping his headlights switched off. He parked a block away from the house, slipped through the back door, and grabbed his bag, a blanket, and a can of peas from the pantry. As he left the house and walked back to his car, he noticed that the house where the attractive lady lived was dark.

Returning to the abandoned farmhouse, he opened the peas and ate a pretty miserable meal. *I'm already tired of roughing it*, he mused as he lay down to sleep on the blanket.

Early the next morning, he drove back to the field, parked off the road on a rough trail, and waited. He did not know what time the men would come to work, but he needed to be there to see if his note were picked up. He could only hope that it was not discovered by a guard.

A little after 8:00 o'clock, he saw trucks pull up and a group of men wearing the PW uniform climb down and start walking out into the field. He watched from behind a clump of palmettos as the men started to hoe in single file along each row of plants. As one of the men approached the partially buried cigarette pack, Christian noticed that he hesitated and bent down. The man looked around. Seeing that the guards were not watching him, he leaned forward as if he were tying his shoelaces.

Christian was satisfied that he had found the note and could now only hope that it would reach its intended recipient. As the man stood up, Christian could see that he was stuffing the cigarette package into his pants. He would return the following day to see if there were a response, but now, he needed to check out the routes back to the beach.

On the way to Grayton Beach, he bought some ripe tomatoes, two peaches, and a small watermelon from a truck at the side of the road and placed them on the seat beside him. Then he parked his car near Bailey's store, laid a nickel on the counter, picked a Coca-Cola from a cooler, and walked out without saying a word. He had not had a Coca-Cola since he had left America years earlier, and he enjoyed every sip.

It was a hot, sunny day so Christian decided to walk along the beach to where he had buried the raft to make sure that there was sufficient cover in the sand dunes for him and Braun to hide before signaling the U-boat. He took off his shoes and socks, rolled up his pants legs, and strolled through the squeaky white sand to the water's edge. The ocean was a brilliant emerald green that reminded him of his time in the Caribbean waters.

He walked for a while and calculated that he was about halfway between Grayton Beach and a small settlement ahead when he recognized the crude driftwood X he had left over the buried raft. He could see no one, and no footprints were in the area to indicate that people walked along this stretch of beach. Satisfied that the raft was secure and that the location to signal the U-boat was sufficiently remote, Christian turned around and headed back to where he had parked his car.

His clothes clung to him with perspiration from walking in the hot sun, so he took off his shirt. The warmth felt wonderful on his face and back. *Too bad I can't stay here for a while. The people of Berlin don't know what they are missing,* he mused. Suddenly, a loud voice broke his solitude. Christian was surprised by the closeness of the female voice.

"Ouch! Damn it all! Ouch, ouch, ouch! Shit, that hurts! What the hell did I step on? A damn piece of broken glass! Shit, I'm bleeding like a stuck pig."

Christian stooped low, peering over the sand dunes to see who was causing such an racket. On the other side, he could make out a figure sitting on the sandy bank of a large lake, holding her foot. The voice was familiar. This was the same woman whom he had heard expressing her anger the previous morning.

It was clear that she was in distress and could not walk easily. Christian was faced with a choice. He knew that his mission meant that he should leave her there. But a deep-rooted sense of morality directed him to assist her. *Oh, what the hell*, Christian thought as he approached her carefully, making sure not to frighten her.

"Hello, there. I heard you from over on the beach and came to see what the commotion was."

Maggie jumped when she heard the man's voice and then saw him. "You scared me. I stepped on a piece of glass and cut my foot. I don't think that it's too deep, but it's bleeding pretty badly. It hurts like hell to walk on."

"You're a long way from town. Did you walk out here?"

"Yeah, I was trying to catch some crabs and shouldn't have been walking barefoot. Think you could help me back to town? I would appreciate it. I don't think I can walk without it hurting like hell and dripping blood all over everything."

Christian really did not think that he had much choice at this point. He had already committed himself when he crossed the sand dune.

"Sure, be glad to help." He put his shirt on and helped Maggie stand. Placing one of her arms around his neck, he picked her up and carried her back across the dunes and toward town. She did not bother with her crab net. She could recover it later.

"Thanks for helping me. I'm Maggie. I don't believe I've seen you in town. Are you on vacation?"

"No, I work for the road department and am checking some roads in the area. I'm Christian. I thought I would take a walk on the beach, so that's why I found you. Are you vacationing here?"

"I guess you could say that," she replied.

Periodically, he would put her down for a minute to rest and then they would resume the trip back to her house. If the truth were known, Christian was enjoying himself. Maggie's body felt good to him. He liked the feel of her arm around his neck and her soft breasts rubbing his chest as they walked.

When they finally arrived, Christian was soaking wet with perspiration but was almost reluctant to end their journey. Maggie called out for Theresa. Although rather surprised by the appearance of a handsome man helping Maggie up the steps, Theresa acted as if this were nothing out of the ordinary. She helped Maggie onto the porch swing and elevated her foot. Quickly, she found some alcohol and washed the wound, then wrapped her foot with a clean cloth. The bleeding had stopped. It appeared that the worst was over.

Maggie asked Theresa to bring Christian a glass of iced tea. He had not had iced tea since he left the States years earlier, and it brought back memories. The sweet, cold drink was refreshing. In a few, quick gulps, it was gone. He could see that he was in a precarious situation and did not want to say anything that might provoke an unwanted inquiry. After the customary expression of gratitude by Maggie, Christian made his excuses, said good-bye to both the women, and left.

As he drove away, he thought how glad he was he had made the decision to help her. Meeting her had startled him. There was definitely a subconscious attraction on his part. The encounter had felt good, even if only for a short while. But now, he had to focus on his mission.

After he left, Maggie and Theresa sat on the porch and discussed the stranger who had carried her home.

"Right nice looking, if I do say so. He sure has pretty blue eyes, don't he?" Theresa said.

"Yes. He was strong also," Maggie responded. "And you are right about those blue eyes. He's a good-looker for sure. Didn't have a wedding ring on, though. Of course, that doesn't mean much after John Logan. Right now, I don't want to think about men. They all break your heart in one way or another."

Still, she continued to think of him throughout the day.

Chapter Sixteen

CHRISTIAN PARKED HIS CAR IN THE OLD BARN AND BEGAN STRIPPING off his sweat-drenched clothes before reaching the house. He walked out to the well in his undershorts, crossing his fingers that it had water and that it was clean. With the rope in his hand, he dropped the bucket until he heard a faint splash. The rotten rope strained as he heaved the bucket to the top, and he was not sure if it would make it. Finally, he was able to lift it out and rest it on the wooden shelf that surrounded the well. The water was clear, but contained a strong, sulfurous odor from the minerals in the soil. He took a small sip and found that it tasted fine, but the smell was enough to quench his desire to drink any more than necessary.

Splashing himself from head to toe, he washed off the last 2 days of sweat and grime. Christian wasn't sure which would smell better—sweat or sulfur—but at least he would feel cleaner. After allowing himself to air-dry, he changed into his one clean outfit and used the bucket to rinse out the clothes that he had been wearing, hanging them on the porch railing to dry.

Since he was biding his time, he thought it might be beneficial to try to get some sleep, so he lay down on the blanket and closed his eyes. The image of Maggie continued to resurface in his thoughts.

THE GERMAN SOLDIER who found the note in the field was named Klaus Gerber. He was a corporal in the infantry and had been captured in France along with Braun. He was part of the Wehrmacht, or regular army, as were most German soldiers. Relatively few were in Hitler's private army, the SS or Gestapo. Gerber knew that Braun was a strong supporter of the Nazi Party from conversations they had over the months.

He sought out Braun as soon as he arrived back at the camp. Gerber was not sure what he would do, but he wanted to be part of it, if possible. He had told no one of his discovery, not even his fellow prisoners. He knew that the more people who knew, the less likely that an escape would be successful.

Gerber found Dieter Braun at the mess tent having supper with the other prisoners. He sat down beside him and in a low voice whispered, "I need to see you in private. I have something that you are going to want to see. Meet me at your tent after dinner. It seems that someone has come to take you home."

Braun could not believe his eyes when he read the note. They had sent someone to get him out of this hellhole! He turned the note over and with a pencil wrote:

Will have time to escape before discovery noticed. One hundred meters west of northeast corner is best location. Forest comes close to fence. 1:00 A.M.

DB

Folding the note and placing it back into the Lucky Strike pack, he said, "Take this back tomorrow and put it where you found it. Don't tell a soul."

Gerber took the pack and put it in his pocket. "Who is here to get you out? And why you?"

Braun replied, "I have a unique skill that is needed for the war effort." He did not elaborate. In the event he was discovered, his life would be even more miserable in the hands of the Allies than it was now.

"Can I come with you?" Gerber asked.

"No, I don't know who has come or how they plan to get me out. There may not be a way to include anyone else."

This made sense to Gerber, so he made no more effort to persuade Braun. He was happy just to be participating in the escape in the role of courier. Also, he had to admit that life as a POW in America was not as bad as being on the front lines of battle.

Christian was waiting when the POWs arrived at the field early the next morning. Parking a half-mile from where the trucks would bring the workers, he walked down the road until he came within sight of the field. He then left the road, crossed a pasture, and entered into a pine and palmetto thicket that bordered the bean field. From this vantage point, he would be able to see the worker who had picked up the cigarette pack the day before. The woods were silent, but the mosquitoes buzzed around him and bit him constantly. As soon as he stopped swatting them, they reappeared and continued to attack. *God, I hope I don't have to stay here all day.*

A little after 8:00 o'clock, he heard and then saw trucks carrying the men drive up the dusty road. The prisoners climbed down, carrying a hoe or shovel, and walked out into the field to begin their day. Christian recognized the prisoner that had picked up the message the day before and watched as he made his way toward his row of beans. The man seemed to carry himself a little more sprightly than the other prisoners, which worried Christian. Anything unusual could draw attention from the guards. Fortunately, they were talking among themselves and not paying attention to the prisoners.

Gerber dropped to his knee and buried the cigarette pack in the sandy soil, leaving just enough above the surface to be seen by the person searching for it later. He then stood up and, glancing around again, raised his hoe over his head, swinging it in an arc. He then began to hoe in the same manner as he had for weeks.

When Christian saw the man's action, he crept out of the woods and walked back to his car. He could do no more until after the POWs left for the day so he decided to return to the farmhouse to rest. Tonight might be a long one.

Again, his thoughts returned to Maggie. He wondered if her foot were better. He lamented that he would never be able to see her again.

Chapter Seventeen

JOHN LOGAN WAS INTENT ON REVENGE. NO WOMAN HAD EVER treated him like Maggie had, and he meant to pay her back. He drove out to Grayton Beach and parked around the block from Maggie's house. From under the front seat he pulled out a small pistol. Although he did not have any intention of shooting her, it sure would scare the hell out of her. Maybe he would just slap her around a little. She needed to learn a little humiliation.

He stuffed the gun in his pocket and watched. He would wait to make sure she was alone, and then he would pay her a visit. He was still suffering from a bad headache from the concussion. Every few hours he took some Goody's powder to help minimize the pain. He would take care of her real good, and then he would leave the area. *If only this damn headache would go away.*

"Theresa, I'm going to drive up to the produce man on the highway and pick up some fresh vegetables. Maybe there'll be some fresh corn and tomatoes. If I pick up some fruit, would you make us a pie? You can take half of it home and share it with Robert."

"That would be real nice, Miss Maggie. It don't matter what kind of fruit you buy. I can make just about any kind of pie out of whatever you find."

"OK, I'll be back in a jiffy."

Logan watched as Maggie walked out of the house and drove away. *Damn, just my luck. Where's she going?* Logan was in no mood to wait around. His anger ticked inside him like the hands on a clock. He felt as if he were about to explode when he saw the colored girl come out to speak to Maggie before she drove away. He wasn't sure what the girl's name was, but he thought he remembered his wife referring to her as Patricia or Theresa or something like that. He recalled seeing her play with his two boys when he was home but didn't pay her much attention. Instantly Logan revised his plan and smiled.

Theresa had told Maggie who he was, ruining his conquest and causing his damned headache. He was going to get both of them through Theresa. Suffering the humiliation herself would have been more tolerable to Maggie. Knowing that Theresa had suffered it for her would be the ultimate payback.

He climbed out of the car and walked up to the front door. Without calling out or knocking, he simply walked in and found Theresa singing to herself while rolling dough out on the countertop. She looked up and gasped. Frightened to the depth of her soul, she stammered, "She ain't here. She done gone to Fort Walton Beach to do some shopping. Won't be back till late this afternoon."

Instantly, Logan grabbed Theresa by the hair and slapped her hard across the face. Then he hit her with the back of his hand and burst her lip. Blood began to trickle down her chin and onto her cotton dress. Turning her around and twisting her arms behind her, he dragged her out of the kitchen and into the bedroom, slamming her into a chest of drawers. Holding her close, they staggered together in a frantically choreographed dance, tilting pictures on the walls and causing the lamp on the bedside table to teeter.

When she realized what he intended to do, Theresa tried to cry out, but he covered her mouth with his hand and held it while he pushed her onto the bed. She tried to bite his hand, but taking his handkerchief from his pocket, he stuffed it in her mouth, pulled her dress up to her waist, grabbed her worn and frayed underwear, and roughly pulled them down below her knees.

Terrified, she pleaded, "Please, please don't do this," but her muffled voice was lost in the wadding. She was overcome with panic and could not breathe with the cloth in her mouth, but she continued to struggle as best she could.

Logan unbuckled his belt, unzipped his pants, and pulled them down far enough so that he could free his erect penis. Then he grabbed her legs and roughly spread them between his thighs, reached down, and rammed himself into her. Tears ran down her face as she prayed that it would be over quickly. He moved cruelly inside her, a demonic grin spread across his face as he held her down on the bed. Theresa closed her eyes tightly to try to make believe this was not happening.

Then Logan collapsed on her without a sound. In shock, she opened her eyes. Standing over the bed was Maggie with the rolling pin that Theresa had been using to roll out the pie crust.

"I forgot my purse. When I came back, I heard noises as I came in the house. I saw what was happening and grabbed the first thing that I could get my hands on." Maggie reached around Logan's head and gently removed the cloth from Theresa's mouth. Grabbing the back of Logan's shirt, she pulled him off the quivering girl and let him fall unceremoniously to the floor. He was unconscious.

Maggie gently helped Theresa to the bathroom where she cleaned the blood off her face with a warm wet cloth. Then she left Theresa alone so that she could tend to her personal needs. Theresa was still in a state of shock when she came out of the bathroom and could only whimper lightly as Maggie helped her fix her underwear and dress, then Maggie held her arm as she walked her to a kitchen chair.

"Do you need to go to a doctor?"

"No, I'm all right, I guess. I just hurt some down there, and my lip feels the size of a cantaloupe. Miss Maggie, I don't wants Robert to know what happened. He'd go after him for sure, and I don't want my husband locked up for the rest of his life. I'll tell him that I fell and hit my lip. You gotta promise me you'll never tell him what done happen here."

"Don't worry, it will stay between us, and before the day is over, I am going to ask the same favor from you."

Theresa had no idea what Maggie meant. It was apparent by the look on Maggie's face that whatever it was would involve John Logan.

There was anger in Maggie she had never felt before. This encounter had destroyed the innocent, trusting woman and replaced her with a hard woman in complete control.

"We're going to take care of him so that he never does *anything* like this ever again." An idea was already beginning to develop in the back of her mind. "Help me get him dressed."

As they were handling him on the floor, Maggie discovered the pistol in his pocket. She handed it to Theresa and said, "Point this at him until I get back. If he wakes up and moves at all, shoot him. I'm going to gather a few things, and then we're taking him out of here." Theresa had never handled a gun before, but she was so mad she almost hoped that he would wake up just so she could shoot him.

Maggie went to a small storage closet and found some heavy twine and other items she needed. When she returned, Logan was still unconscious. She took the handkerchief that he had used on Theresa and stuffed it into his mouth. Then she pulled his arms behind him and tied his wrists securely with the cord.

"Help me get him into the car. We need to find a place to take him." Together, they dragged him through the door and pulled him into the backseat of Maggie's car.

"Theresa, we need to find some place to take him that is out of the way. It needs to be a small wooden structure. Do you know anywhere like that?"

Theresa was finally beginning to recover from the trauma and had no problem keeping the gun pointed on Logan as they drove. "There's an old farmhouse down the road from where we live. Nobody lives there. It's the only place I can think of."

"All right, let's see if it'll work."

They drove up the sand drive, pushing the palmetto palms and myrtle branches out of the way and stopped behind the old house. The house and the barn were too large for Maggie's needs, but she saw what would be perfect.

"Theresa, help me drag him over to that outhouse. Then get a bucket of water from that well. When I tell you to, throw it on his face. I want him to be awake when I'm ready."

Maggie pulled Logan's pants down to his knees and then cut the cord that held his arms behind him. Because he was beginning to wake up, she needed to move fast. She pushed him down onto the seat just as Theresa returned with the bucket of water. "Hold that gun on him and shoot him if he moves." Maggie went back to her car and returned with the items that had been in the storage closet back at her house.

With a quick succession of movements, she poured some kerosene on the outhouse, struck a match, and threw it at the base of the structure. When she saw flames beginning to rise, she turned to Theresa. "Throw the water on him now."

As soon as Theresa did that, Logan began to regain consciousness. And then Maggie did something that neither she, nor Theresa—and certainly not John Logan—would ever forget. Calmly positioning her target, she picked up a hammer in one hand and a long nail in the other and drove the nail through his penis into the wooden seat.

The pain didn't hit Logan instantly. He just looked at her in shocked disbelief. Before she turned to walk away from the burning building, Maggie handed him a large butcher knife and said, "Your choice . . ."

Chapter Eighteen

Alerted by the sound of the car slowly driving down the sandy road toward the house, Christian took out his Luger and peered through a dirty window just long enough to take a quick glimpse. He was sure he had been discovered. With a deep sense of relief, he recognized Maggie as one of the two women getting out of the car. There also appeared to be a third person. Trying to see out of the window without revealing himself, Christian watched as an unconscious man was dragged to the outhouse by both women. *What in the hell is going on?*

Minutes later, he saw Maggie drenching the outhouse with kerosene and immediately the whole structure went up in flames. As he watched the two women drive away, he heard an ear-piercing scream coming from the outhouse and saw the man take a large knife and with a hard swing, free himself from bondage. He stumbled out of the burning structure holding on to his genitals—or what was left of them.

His pants were below his knees, and he tripped and fell to the ground with a loud groan. Blood was seeping through his hands. Christian could tell that the man was in pure agony. The screaming man stood up and with one hand, lifted his pants up. Holding his injured part in one hand and his pants in the other, Logan limped down the drive and onto the road.

Christian's legs buckled, and he slid down the wall. His breathing grew labored and sweat poured off him. He had been exceptionally lucky that they had not come into the house or barn. He would have had no choice but to kill them, and the thought sickened him. Killing Maggie would be the single-most difficult act he would ever have to commit—an act he didn't think he would ever be able to forgive himself for. But he had to wonder about her. She had seemed so different when he met her on the beach. He now saw her in a totally different light. What had happened to cause her to become so violent? He couldn't think of how to describe her, but he sure knew that she was one damn interesting woman!

He needed to put what he had just witnessed out of his mind as it was time to go back to the field. It was possible Braun would attempt the escape tonight, and he needed to be focused. Clearing his thoughts, he drove to the camp, arriving at the field after the men had already left for the day. Parking on the road near the field, Christian went to look for the cigarette pack. It was there as expected, and the directions in the note gave him a clear plan for getting Braun out.

At midnight, Christian drove to the POW camp and cautiously walked through the pine woods until he could see the camp through the foliage. He worked his way along the edge of the thicket until he found the location Braun had told him would be the best for the escape. The night was silent except for the insects. He could see the outline of the tent city where the prisoners lived and with the faint moonlight, could make out the fences that surrounded the camp.

The guardhouse closest to him was dark. It appeared that no one was manning that particular post. There were no lights, and he could not see any motion or even the glow of a cigarette from the tower.

Taking a chance that he was right, he began to crawl on his stomach to the base of the outer fence. Using his wire cutters, he cut from the ground up. Then, bending the wire back, he crawled to the inner fence and repeated the same cut. He then crept back the way he had come and slipped into the woods to wait. His body and clothes were filthy with sand and dirt, and he attempted to brush off what he could. The mosquitoes began to swarm around his head and attack every exposed piece of skin. *Damn, I sure hope he comes soon. This is torture.*

At 1:00 o'clock, Christian saw a shadow emerge from the tents and begin to walk toward the area where he had cut through the fence. Slowly, the figure walked along the edge of the fence and when he came to the cut, dropped to his stomach and immediately wiggled through the fence. Christian saw him turn and bend the wire back to hide the cut as much as possible. He then crawled on his stomach to the outer fence, slipped through it, and again bent the wire back. Cautiously, he stood up and quickly ran into the woods, stopping a few feet from Christian. The man was wearing civilian clothes.

He whispered in German, "Hello, I'm here. Where are you?"

Christian, with his pistol ready to fire, approached the figure cautiously. "How do I know who you are? I can't see you in the dark."

Braun responded, "I'm Dieter Braun, and I'm needed by the Reich to help develop a missile system. The führer has sent you to get me. Let's leave before anyone discovers that I'm gone."

They made their way back through the thicket, and when they arrived at the car, Christian directed Braun to climb into the backseat and lie on the floor. If anyone saw a car driving down the road late at night, seeing one head would be better than two.

They drove back to the farmhouse without using headlights since they had to pass by a few houses on the road. When they arrived, Christian led Braun inside and for the first time, they talked face to face.

"My name is Christian Wolfe, and I was sent here to get you out of the POW camp and onto a U-boat. We have missed our opportunity for pickup tonight because they are only waiting for us between the hours of midnight and 3 A.M. We will have to wait here until tomorrow night. I think that we are safe here, but this afternoon, some people came for a brief time and then left."

He did not think that it was important to relate what he had witnessed, and he was not sure that Braun would believe the story anyway.

"There's a blanket over there to sleep on, and you can wash in the well outside if you want. There was an outhouse, but it burned today. Go to the woods if you need to relieve yourself. Why are you wearing civilian clothes?"

"We wear the prison outfit when we leave the camp to work, but when we return, we are allowed to change into regular clothes. They will discover I am missing at early roll call. No one has tried to escape from this camp before, so all hell is going to break loose when they find I'm gone. Surely, they will bring out the dogs and start a major manhunt for me. Good thing that we were able to use a car to get away. Where are we?"

Christian explained where they were and the plan to meet the submarine.

"Why were you selected to help me escape?" Braun asked.

"I lived in America for a long time, not too far away from where we are now, in fact. I speak English without a German accent and know the culture. Plus, they threatened to send me to the Russian front if I did not help get you out."

"You made the right choice, I guess," Braun laughed.

Chapter Nineteen

Maggie drove Theresa back to the simple house where she lived with Robert. Theresa was in a state of exhaustion, and Maggie knew that she would have to treat her tenderly but firmly.

"I want you to listen to me real closely now. Today has been a horrible day for both of us. I suggest you tell Robert that you slipped on my kitchen floor and fell and burst your lip. It sounds reasonable. What that SOB did to you will stay between us. You can trust me on that. And I have to trust you not to tell anyone about what we did to John Logan. I could be convicted of murder if he died in the fire. Do we have a pact?"

"Yes, I don't know whether I wanted him to burn up or lose his pecker. I hope that he just cut it off and lived, I guess. Just so he don't bother us no more."

"I hope so too, Theresa. I would hate to think that I killed a person, even if he did rightly deserve it."

Maggie hugged Theresa and said, "I'm going to go home now and try to put this behind me. Tell Robert that I brought you home after you burst you lip. I'll see you in the morning."

Maggie left Theresa's home and had almost reached the intersection of the main road when she saw a hunched figure limping down the street. She passed him and although she did not slow down, she saw that Logan was, indeed, still alive. Breathing a sigh of relief, a smile spread across her face. *At least I didn't kill the bastard. I'm glad he lived, and I really don't think he will bother anyone again.*

She arrived home feeling dirty, both inside and outside, so she undressed and stood under the outdoor shower, scrubbing every inch of her body with soap. The water cascaded over her until the hot water had completely gone. The sun was warm. Even as the water cooled, she stood under the flow until she began to develop goose bumps, so she dried off, put on a fresh pair of shorts and blouse, and wrapping a towel around her hair, decided that what she needed was a stiff drink.

Maggie poured a glass almost full of bourbon, added a couple of ice cubes, and sat on the front porch, reflecting on the day. She hoped that Theresa would recover from the trauma. Only time would tell.

She felt as if she had aged 10 years in the past 24 hours. Maggie realized she had stepped across the line of civilized behavior and committed a serious crime. While she had no regrets over her actions, she could never discuss it with anyone other than Theresa. For the first time in her entire life, she had no one to give her support. In the past, her parents, and then Charles, were always there when she needed someone. Now she was completely alone. For a brief moment she thought of Christian. But the thought evaporated as quickly as it had come. Christian was probably long gone by now.

The bourbon relaxed her and then caused her to fall asleep on the swing. When she awoke hours later, she was stiff, chilled, and still slightly drunk.

Theresa arrived the next morning to find Maggie sitting on the front porch, sipping on a mug of hot coffee. She greeted Maggie and said, "I told Robert that I had slipped and fallen. He believes me, although I really hated to lie to him. I think I did the right thing though. He would have a hard time dealing with the rape, so it's better to just let it go. I have to say, Miss Maggie, I don't think I have ever heard of anyone doing what you did to a man before, but I'm damn sure glad you did it."

"I saw him yesterday, Theresa. He looked pretty damn miserable, but he's not dead."

"Thank the Lord. I hope he don't cause us no more trouble."

"I'm not worried about that. He certainly isn't going to tell anybody about what happened. Men don't boast about not having a pecker, or one that's no longer working. Besides, it's our word against his."

A smile spread across Theresa's brown face. "You go and get some peaches, and we will make us a peach pie."

While they were working in the kitchen, Maggie turned on the radio to listen to the news and hopefully some music. A reporter was discussing the escape of a German prisoner from the POW camp near Crestview. Authorities stated that a massive manhunt was underway. Bloodhounds had followed his trail through the woods until they had come to the road and had then lost it completely. The authorities believed that he had had an accomplice with a vehicle and the search was now widening to include a large portion of the Panhandle.

Maggie listened as a description of the missing prisoner was given and listeners were advised to keep an eye out for anyone suspicious. Then she turned the radio dial until she found a station playing Tommy Dorsey and his orchestra. Lost in her own thoughts and unaffected by the news bulletin, she swayed to the music as she and Theresa went about their chores.

Chapter Twenty

J IM GARRISON STROLLED INTO WORK AT THE SHERIFF'S OFFICE AT 8:00 o'clock sharp. His title of sheriff of Walton County carried a nice ring to it—even though the entire force consisted only of him and his deputy, Bill.

Jim lived in an apartment over a garage in town belonging to a widow named Sadie Moon. The home sat on 2 acres of manicured lawn with azaleas, camellias, and large, shady magnolia trees. Sadie Moon found the presence of a man reassuring, but also enjoyed the role of matchmaker to the local ladies.

After a few dates that she had set up, Jim sat down with her one evening over a cup of coffee and homemade pound cake and gently asked her not to make any more arrangements on his behalf. He was perfectly able to take care of his personal life without her assistance. She was hurt by his request but reluctantly complied.

Little did she know that the girls she thought appropriate for him to meet were not as they appeared. One such girl whom she had introduced at a church social liked to be blindfolded and handcuffed to her bed and have Jim ravish her. Another, a teacher in the elementary school, got turned on by the exciting risk of having sex outside where there was the possibility of being seen. Jim had fun with these women and their unusual taste, but had not found the right woman yet.

Being sheriff in a small, Southern rural county meant breaking up fights in the juke joints and hauling drunks to jail, as well as separating fighting couples so that they did not kill each other. Most of the time, he and Bill patrolled the country roads, helping farmers round up loose livestock and occasionally issuing speeding tickets. He had been in charge since the previous sheriff had been fired for taking bribes from moonshiners 2 years before.

Jim was honest but was also pragmatic. He quickly learned who was making and selling liquor and knew that these moonshiners were like everyone else in the county—poor and struggling to survive. He would drive his black-and-white police car out to their farms, and as he sipped iced tea on the front porch, would patiently but firmly let them know that he knew what they were doing.

He established a clear set of rules. First, any liquor had to be safe to drink. Too many moonshiners ran their liquor through old car radiators that contained high levels of lead, leading to blindness. Second, if liquor were being made, there could be no dead squirrels or other animals thrown into the vat to speed up the fermentation. Most importantly, only enough liquor could be made for a family's own consumption. Anyone caught making large quantities for mass distribution would be dealt with severely.

Word soon spread that the sheriff was a fair and decent man. When trouble did arise, he and Bill were given deference and respect.

He also had to deal with the Negro community. With good reason, they were suspicious of any police authority, and it took a while for him to establish a good relationship with them. He decided to meet with the black church leaders and explain that he intended to enforce the law without prejudice, a rather novel approach to them. He had the same problems with the black citizens that he had with the whites, and he dealt with them both the same way.

The sheriff marveled at how many black men could get into so much trouble with a knife. He decided that white men liked to shoot, and black men liked to cut. He had spent his entire 28 years living in south Alabama where blacks and whites lived in separate communities, and it was all he knew. Eventually, the blacks began to trust him and that helped him keep his ear to the ground for any emerging problems.

When he walked into work that morning, Bill was waiting for him with a cup of coffee.

"Have you heard the news?"

"What news is that? Has another soldier from around here been killed?"

"No, a German prisoner escaped from the camp. It happened last night sometime. The army's got the dogs and everybody out trying to catch him."

"Well, that is interesting. How did he get out?"

"From what I heard on the radio, he cut the fences and escaped. The dogs lost the scent at the road. They think someone picked him up. Some official just called here and wants you to help find him."

"Seems like a good idea to me. Hold the fort here and I'll drive over and see what we can do."

He drove the patrol car over to the POW camp and found the place to be in total bedlam. Both the army and civilian police were meeting in the exercise field near the inner fence. When Jim approached, Sam Connell, the only police officer from Crestview, saw him and walked over. Jim greeted him with a quick handshake. "Hi, Sam, what do you know?" As they frequently worked together searching for suspects or speeding drivers that might have crossed into the other's domain, they had become friends.

"A prisoner named Dieter Braun escaped in the middle of the night by cutting the two fences and crawling under them."

Pointing to a man with a clipboard, he said, "He can give you a picture of the escapee."

"Thanks, Sam. Good to see you again. Say hello to Mary Jane for me."

Jim introduced himself to the official and took a head-shot photo of Braun. The picture looked like a booking photo taken at the jail, except that there seemed to be more of a look of defiance than seen in the typical jailhouse mug shots.

Walking over to the fence, he dropped to his knee to examine where the prisoner had broken through. The cut had clearly been made by a wire cutter. *Strange, how would a prisoner gain access to such a tool? He couldn't—which means that someone from the outside helped him.* Bill had said the scent had been lost at the road. *If someone had helped him escape, this Dieter Braun must be someone important. This is too complex for just a simple escape because the prisoner was tired of being a POW.*

Jim left the camp and walked around the perimeter fence. Searching in the thicket, he found footprints in the sandy soil close to the narrow path that was used as a passage to the pasture. Although the army had been trampling through the area that morning looking for clues, they had not noticed that someone had been standing a mere 10 feet away from the path. Speaking to no one in particular, Jim said, "Yep, this guy had an accomplice. Now we have *two* people to find."

When he arrived back at the station, he brought Bill up on all he had seen. "Let's split up and check all the stores and farms between here and the camp and ask if anyone has seen any strangers today. If anyone has seen anything unusual, give me a call. I'll do the same here in town and will work my way south."

Jim took the picture of Braun and gave it to Bill. "Show this to people and see if they recognize him."

Jim made his way south of town while Bill covered the west. No one had seen or heard anything unusual. As Jim worked his way back to the office, he decided to stop in at the various stores to inquire if the owners had seen anything unusual enough to report. He was at his third stop when he hit a promising lead. The owner of the hardware store was sitting behind the counter entering some figures into a bookkeeping journal when he entered.

"Hey, Homer, how are you today?"

"Hey, Jim, doing fine, I guess. Wish we would get some rain. Things getting mighty dry. Whatcha need today?"

"Don't need to buy anything today, thanks. I don't know if you heard, but one of those German prisoners over at the camp escaped last night. I'm trying to find out if anybody has seen or heard anything out of the ordinary."

"No, can't say that I have seen anybody come by here today. Don't guess they would come in and buy anything on their way out of town, anyway," he chuckled. "We don't get a lot of strangers coming through town. I pretty much know everybody that lives within 10 miles, and most of them owe me money. If I hear anything, I'll let you know."

"Thanks, Homer. Take care and give my regards to your wife. See you in church on Sunday."

He turned to walk out the door when Homer called out, "Hey, you know, Sheriff, there was a man that came in a couple days ago. He said he worked for the road department. I never saw him before, but that wouldn't be unusual if he wasn't from around here. He bought a hand ax and a wire cutter. Said he was doing survey work or something like that and needed to cut some fences to get to some markers."

Chill bumps radiated from Jim's neck to his arms. He knew he might be on to something now. "Did he say anything else?"

"The only thing I remember is that he said that he had seen some prison workers in a field and wanted to know if there was a prison around here. I told him about the POW camp."

"What did he look like."

"He was about 30 years old. Maybe 6 feet tall, I think. Brown hair. Wore cotton work pants and a casual shirt. Just kind of normal looking, I'd say. You think he mighta had something to do with the German escape?"

"Don't know, Bill, but wire cutters were used to cut the fences around the camp, so that is a connection. Did you see what he was driving?"

"I looked out the window when he was leaving, and I think I saw him drive away in '36 or '37 Ford. Dark gray."

"Thanks. If you think of anything else, give me a call."

Jim had an intuitive feeling that anyone who escaped would head toward the coast. It seemed natural that the only way out of the country would be by water. Maybe a boat would pick him up. The idea that Braun and his accomplice would attempt to drive long distance seemed impractical. Also, where would they drive to that would be better than boarding a boat nearby? He continued south toward the sea with a vague hope that he might find some clue. It was the best idea that he could come up with at the moment.

He worked his way further south than he had earlier and crossed the bridge that passed over the bay, stopping at every gas station and store on the highway. No one had seen anything unusual and a '36 or '37 gray Ford was too common to arouse interest, much less suspicion. By now, it was getting late in the afternoon, so Jim decided it was time to return to DeFuniak Springs. He had paperwork that had piled up while he was out of the office, and he thought he might watch the local high-school baseball team play over at the ball field.

As he was driving north, he passed a pickup truck at the side of the road with a flat tire. A black man was struggling to get the tire off the rim. Jim pulled off the road ahead of the truck and walked back to see if he could be of assistance. He noticed there was a black woman, probably the man's wife, sitting in the passenger seat. As he approached, he could see fear register in both their eyes. He was aware that interaction with the police usually meant trouble for black people. For this reason, Jim felt the best way to develop better relations with the black community was to reach out more than most police officials and give a little assistance when possible.

Theresa saw the police officer approach the truck and was sure he was here to arrest her for her assistance with the caper she and Maggie had committed the day before.

"Hi, can I help you with that?" the officer said with a smile. Robert looked warily back at him. No white man—and certainly no policeman—had ever offered to help him in any way that he could recall. He was so afraid he stammered. "No suh, I got this under control. We'll be fine. I'll have this tire fixed in no time, and we'll be off, I promise."

Jim could see the man was scared to death. "Look, I didn't stop to give you a hard time. Let me help you. Then we can both be on our way."

The man seemed to relax a little, and Theresa almost fainted from relief.

After the two men had changed the tire together without speaking, Jim wiped his dirty hands on his pants and said, "I'm looking for two men driving a '36 or '37 Ford sedan. One of them is an escapee from the POW camp out near Eglin Field. Have you seen a car like that today?"

"No suh, we ain't seen anything like that. Have you, Theresa?"

"No, I ain't either." She was so happy not to be arrested she was almost giddy.

Jim remembered the other thing that he had asked people during the day. "One of them, the man that helped the prisoner escape, may have been hiding out in the area for a few days. Have you seen anyone around that you hadn't noticed before?"

Before Theresa could signal Robert not to say anything more, he replied, "The only thing we noticed is a car comin' and goin' with its lights off down the road next to our house.

Like they didn't want anyone to know they was comin' and goin'."

Theresa thought she was going to have a heart attack. *Damn you, Robert,* she said to herself. *The last thing I need is for a policeman to find out where we took John Logan.*

"That's interesting. Show me where that place is, please."

Smiling, Robert was now full of confidence and pride. A white man—a police officer, no less—had stopped and helped them and had not hassled them. On top of that, the policeman had actually given credence to something he said.

As they drove toward their home, Theresa was beside herself with worry, but could not show any indication of fear to Robert. Robert was in high spirits, however, and could not keep from rattling on about the good fortune of being treated well by the policeman. When they reached the driveway to their house, Robert pulled over and told Jim to continue on down the sand road. Jim waved goodbye and headed in that direction to check out what might be there. Theresa broke out into a cold sweat.

Chapter Twenty=One

CHRISTIAN WAS RELIEVED THE ESCAPE HAD GONE SO SMOOTHLY AND was enjoying a temporary moment of personal accomplishment. Perhaps he was better at this mission than he had expected, although he knew there was no way that he could kill innocent people like Maggie. So far, he and Dieter were on schedule for the rendezvous with the boat and were lounging on the blankets they had spread on the floor of the house. They could not leave until dark and were trying to rest before the next phase of the escape began. It would be a long night, involving both luck and physical stamina.

Christian planned to drive over to Grayton Beach before midnight, leaving the car hidden behind a vacant house, and then walk the mile or so to the raft. They had eaten the fruit he had bought the day before, but neither was very hungry. They were both nervous and edgy. Neither man spoke, though each gained a volume of knowledge of each other through silent observation. Christian had quickly determined that Dieter Braun was a dangerous ally. Braun was pleased that the führer had gone to the expense and effort to send Christian to get him out.

Instead of expressing appreciation to Christian, however, Braun's arrogance hinted an undertone of superiority. His demeanor telegraphed to Christian the unspoken message that Braun considered himself more important than Christian or any of the other soldiers back at the camp. He acted as if it were his divine right to have been rescued. It was clear to Christian that Dieter would sacrifice him without a second thought and was thankful he had not shared all of the details of the escape with him.

After only a few hours, Christian became extremely irritated and was desperate to board the submarine and create some space between himself and Braun. He had spent enough time observing Gestapo and SS agents to know that their authority created their identity. Braun was no different.

They both heard the car as it turned into the driveway. Quickly, they crawled over to a window on their hands and knees and peered over the window ledge and were extremely startled to see a police car.

"How the hell did he know we were here?" asked Dieter.

"He doesn't know," responded Christian in a clipped voice. He wasn't about to explain what had happened yesterday.

"Let's get the hell out of here before he gets out of his car."

Christian grabbed the Luger, and they quickly slipped out the door, bolted through the backyard, and into the pine thicket. The undergrowth was thick. They only had to travel 20 feet before they were hidden from view. Silently, they crouched in the palmettos and watched as the police car came to a stop. The officer climbed out and walked slowly toward the house, looking for signs of activity.

As Jim walked around the house, it didn't take long for him to see that people had, indeed, been there recently. Footprints were everywhere. Car tracks were still fresh, and the remains of the burnt outhouse still smelled smoky. A trail of dried blood led toward the drive. *Someone was hurt and bled pretty badly.* He walked up the steps to the back porch and carefully opened the door, calling out to see if anyone were inside. When he received no response, he stepped in. He walked from room to room, finding evidence of recent habitation.

Blankets were spread on the floor, and remains of fruit were piled in a corner of the main room. *Maybe just vagrants.* As he walked out the back door and started across the yard, he noticed fresh tire tracks leading to the barn. Quickly, he unlatched the barn door and as it swung back, he knew he had hit pay dirt.

A gray 1937 Ford was parked inside. Peering through the windows of the car, he saw a hand ax and wire cutters lying on the backseat. He now knew the escapee and his accomplice could not be far. Had they seen him coming and run into the woods? He was probably being watched, so he had to be very careful. He closed the barn door and casually walked back to his car as if nothing had aroused his suspicion.

Christian and Braun had to make a quick decision. They could not tell from the officer's actions if he had found what he was looking for. He seemed to be taking his time and was not acting as if he had found anything of importance that produced a sense of urgency. It would not have been a long shot to think that the officials figured that another person was involved, but certainly they could not know the type of car he was driving.

One thing for sure was that the Germans couldn't stay here any longer. Should they attempt to intervene and capture the police officer, or should they escape into the forest and make their way toward the beach on foot?

Christian knew the beach was about 5 or 6 miles away, but the route was through thick palmetto, scrub oak, and wax myrtle forests. Traveling that distance on foot would be brutal. They would barely make it in time to signal U-67. Christian had an intuitive sense that the policeman was looking for them. He could not take a chance.

As the officer was walking to his car, Christian raced from the forest and, in quick strides, slipped up behind the officer, pointing the Luger in the center of his back. Dieter Braun was left sitting on his knees in the woods, shocked by the sudden decision Christian had made. Impulsively, he jumped up and followed Christian into the yard.

Jim had heard movement behind him, but before he could do anything more than turn toward the source, a pistol was pointed directly at him.

"Hit the ground now! Spread your arms and legs out on the ground—now! Face down! Do it, or I swear I'll shoot you!"

"OK, OK, don't do anything you'll be sorry for. I'm going down," the officer said, dropping to the sand.

Dieter Braun approached Christian and in German, shouted, "Shoot him. He has seen us and can identify us."

"Shut up, Dieter. I'm not going to shoot him unless it's necessary. There is no reason to kill him if we don't have to."

Christian reached down and unbuttoned the snap on the holster attached to Jim's belt, withdrew his revolver, and stuffed it behind his back. Then he ordered Dieter to take one of Jim's shoelaces and tie his hands behind his back. When that had been completed, Christian directed Braun to help Jim to his feet.

"Let's take him inside. We can deal with him better there."

"I still think you should just shoot him."

Christian didn't respond. He had to think, and arguing with Dieter was pointless. Killing seemed to be his one solution to everything. Once inside the house, Christian led Jim to the metal bed frame and told him to lie down. He then told Braun to take the other shoelace and tie him to the bed frame so that he could not stand up. After that, he took one of Jim's socks and stuffed it into his mouth, used his knife to cut a strip from the blanket, and wrapped it around Jim's head to hold the sock in place.

Jim was remarkably calm during the ordeal. He saw that the man in charge was cool and efficient, and Jim quickly assessed that if he did not resist, he would have a better chance of survival. When he was tied securely to the bed, Christian looked down at the officer.

"I don't know how you were able to find us so fast, and it really doesn't matter. We're going to leave you here. I assume that eventually, you'll be missed and someone will come looking for you. By then, we'll be gone. Don't underestimate me, however. If I see you again, I *will* shoot you without a second thought. Do you understand me?"

Jim looked up and nodded. He had every intention of seeing the stranger again, and he was sure that he would not be as considerate.

"I'm telling you, Christian, we need to kill him. If we don't, he'll be a problem."

"I've made the decision. I've come a long damn way to pluck you out of your predicament, and I've put myself in a lot of danger in doing so. Until we're in the clear, I'll continue to direct this operation. Do you understand?" Dieter Braun did not like taking orders from anyone and turned away seething.

The three men remained in the room until the sun set. Each man was deep in his own thoughts. Jim believed as long as the one called Christian was in charge, he might survive. If the man called Braun was to take over, he was a dead man. Fortunately, Christian held both pistols. There was nothing for him to do except wait. Bill was the only person that knew where Jim had gone, and it would be much later in the evening before he would begin to worry. Also, there were miles and miles of roads between DeFuniak Springs and the coast to cover when he did become concerned.

Christian was thankful he had not shared with Dieter specific details about how they would rendezvous with the submarine. Although he would have preferred to keep both pistols, there was no reason for him to have two while Braun was unarmed. After giving this some thought, Christian told Braun that he was going out to the well for some water. When he was out of sight, he took out the Luger and removed the bullets. Christian would offer Braun his choice. If his instinct was correct, Braun would choose the German Luger over the American gun. It was a risk that

Christian had to take, but a calculated one. He still had the Luger shells in his pocket if Braun chose the other pistol.

Braun just wanted to get back to Germany. He did not care if Christian made it or not. His country needed him, and he had been sent for by Hitler himself. He would do whatever was necessary to make sure that he was on the boat back to the fatherland. It irked him that Christian would not divulge more information regarding the pickup. He also thought it was a mistake to let the policeman live. It could only lead to trouble.

At 10:00 o'clock, Christian told Braun he wanted to go to the point of rendezvous. They left Jim tied up to the bed and went out to the barn. On the way out to the car, Christian took the key from the patrol car and tossed it into the woods. He then ripped the police radio from the dashboard, severing the cord from the transmitter. "No reason to give him a vehicle or the ability to communicate if he does get free," he commented to Dieter as they climbed into their Ford and drove away.

Chapter Twenty-Two

CHRISTIAN AND BRAUN DROVE TO GRAYTON BEACH. THE TOWN was quiet and dark from the blackout. He parked the car in a sand alley behind an unoccupied house two blocks from their destination. Christian was confident the car would not be found until morning, and by then, he planned to be long gone. They walked to the house he had broken into on his first night and entered through the back door just as he had done before. Peering out a window, Christian could tell from the moving shadows behind her shades that Maggie was at home and alone. He could hear faint strains of Frank Sinatra coming from the radio in her house.

"I think we should have killed that policeman and hidden his body in the woods. No one would have found him for days."

"I don't kill people just to make life easier for me, so for the last time, shut up and get some rest. We're going to have to leave soon, so it's better if we just stay quiet until then."

The two men sat silently, each in their own thoughts. After a while, Christian rose to stretch and peer out of the small slit in the bottom of the window to see if there were any activity on the street. He was confident that he had secured the policeman tightly and unless someone had known where to look for him, he would be there for a while. He heard Braun rise behind him as he walked into the kitchen to get some water from the sink. Braun did not see the table in the middle of the kitchen because of the darkness and stumbled into it, knocking it several feet across the floor, crashing into the wall.

"Shit, I didn't see it in the dark." Both men froze. The sound was clearly loud enough to be heard outside. Christian crept to the window facing Maggie's house and watched for any indication that she had heard a noise. Her house was now completely dark, and after a few minutes of nervous anticipation, they began to relax.

Maggie was just drifting off to sleep when she heard a loud noise that startled her. She lay quietly for a few minutes as her eyes became accustomed to the darkness. Was someone in the house? Ever since John Logan, she had been uneasy, subconsciously fearing that he would come back to retaliate for what she had done to him. She reached under her bed for the pistol that she had taken from him and pulled it under the light blanket. The cold metal of the gun against her chest was so unsettling she had to force herself to breathe normally. Would she be able to actually shoot him? She thought about what he had done to Theresa and a coldness overcame her as she realized she could pull the trigger, if necessary.

Other than the usual night sounds of cicadas and frogs, it was quiet. Still, she sensed something was not right. Her heart was pounding in her chest. She had always trusted her instinct, so she rolled out of bed and crouched on the floor, her ears alert for any unusual sound. Hearing nothing, she stood and tiptoed to the front window, peering out into the street. Nothing. There were no pedestrians or vehicles moving about. A clock on the bedside table indicated it was 11:16. She walked into the kitchen and gazed out the window at the house next door. Then she realized something about the house was not quite right. Since it had been unoccupied, she had been able to see through the windows, even at night. Tonight, shades had been pulled down, and it was totally dark. Someone had been in—or was still in—that house.

Willing herself to stay calm, she sat in a kitchen chair trying to think of what to do.

There was no police force in Grayton Beach, and there was no one to call for help. She was terrified that it might be Logan. He may have returned to harm her after all. *Better to take action before he does*, she concluded.

Breathing deeply to calm her frayed nerves, she changed into shorts and a blouse and slipped into a pair of leather sandals. Picking up the .32 caliber pistol, she quietly opened the back door, careful not to let the hinges squeak, and slipped out, staying close to the house in the shadows. A thin myrtle hedge separated the two houses, but it was easy to slip between the sparse, gangly branches to reach the backyard. Working her way to the back of the house, she crawled on hands and knees until she reached the back porch.

From the light of the moon, she could see that the back door had been breached and wood had splintered on the frame. With the pistol in one hand and a fleeting sense of self-confidence, she kicked the door open and shouted, "John Logan, you low-life son of a bitch, come out of there right now before I come in and blow the rest of your manhood to hell."

It took Christian just a second to identify the voice and another several seconds to get over the shock.

"It's just me, Maggie, don't shoot."

She did not recognize the voice but was greatly relieved that it wasn't Logan. "Who's in there? Come out so I can see you."

Christian appeared out of the darkness with his hands up so she could see that he wasn't armed.

"Christian? Is that you? What in God's name are you doing here?"

Suddenly, a hand appeared from behind her covering her mouth, and she was knocked to her knees with a hard push and held there. A voice speaking in German said to Christian, "This is getting messier by the hour. What are we going to do with her?"

Christian replied in German, "Let's take her to her house. I'll figure out how best to deal with it."

Listening to the conversation, Maggie realized she had come face to face with the enemy. She was being held captive by two Germans.

Christian picked Maggie up from the floor and with his hand covering her mouth said, "Be quiet and you won't get hurt. We're going to go back to your house, and if you cooperate, you'll be fine. I really don't want to hurt you, but I will, if necessary. Now nod if you understand me."

Maggie was overcome with fear. She nodded compliantly, her eyes wide with disbelief.

"Good girl. Now walk in front of me and don't make a sound." Christian felt ashamed seeing Maggie's terror. But he had a mission to complete, and he didn't want Braun to see a weakness in him that would cause any difficulties when they returned to Germany.

Once inside Maggie's house, Christian told Braun to find some rope or cord so they could tie her to a chair. Rummaging around the house, Braun found some heavy twine in a drawer. Pulling her arms around a straight-backed kitchen chair, he secured her tightly.

Maggie looked at Christian and then at Braun and said, "I know who you are. You're the German who escaped from the POW camp, and you," she said to Christian, "helped him escape. You're waiting here for a boat to pick you up, aren't you? What are you going to do with me?"

Christian replied, "Quite frankly, I don't know what we're going to do with you. We have two options. We can take you back with us to Germany on the boat or leave you here for someone to find you. If we took you home with us, I'm sure there would be a job you could do to help in the war effort."

There was a slight twinkle in his eyes when he mentioned taking her back to Germany, and neither Braun nor Maggie could tell whether he was serious or not. The idea of being shanghaied caused her to become nauseous. She looked at Christian to see if he were serious. He smiled as he said, "But I don't think that that would work very well for any of us."

They sat for a while in silence. Christian and Maggie stared at each other. He knew she probably hated him, and he didn't want her to. He wasn't quite sure what to say. He admired her calm demeanor and quiet confidence after being kidnapped by two Germans. If she were frightened, she didn't show it.

"You've been an enigma to me ever since I first saw you. Who are you? You don't know it, but I was hiding in that old farmhouse and saw what you did to that man. I have no idea what he did to deserve that, but I'll give you credit, you have balls." Christian then realized he had given her the ultimate guy compliment and blushed. "Was he the man you thought was hiding when you came over next door?"

"Yes, I thought he was going to continue to harass me and my servant, and I was tired of it and pissed off. Guess I created a problem for all of us, huh?"

The fact that he had seen what she and Theresa had done to Logan caused her a great deal of embarrassment. It was like getting caught making love; an act too personal to be seen by others. But in this circumstance, it might actually work in her favor. Maybe he would think twice before he did anything to her. Even in this strange situation, she felt comfortable with him. She felt that whatever happened, he would not allow any harm to come to her. Unfortunately, she didn't have the same feeling with the other man who appeared wary of her and extremely hostile.

"Are you the German who escaped from the camp up near DeFuniak Springs?"

He nodded as he kept watch at the kitchen window. Turning to her, he said in broken English, "I was captured in France and sent here. I am an officer in the German army, and my services are important to my country. They sent him to help me escape. We are being taken back to France in a U-boat. There, I will continue my work to help defeat the Allies, and when the war is over, I will come back and personally see those guards at the camp are given the kind of treatment they deserve."

Maggie looked over at Christian and could see from the slight roll in his eyes that he was exasperated with the prisoner.

Looking Christian in the eye, she asked, "How did you get into this? You don't seem the type. When you helped me back from the lake after I cut my foot, I would have sworn that you were a typical American. Are you a traitor?"

"No, Maggie, I'm not. I was born in Germany but raised and educated in America. Matter of fact, right in Atlanta. I have a degree from Georgia Tech in civil engineering. I went back to Germany before the war without any intention of joining the military. Officially, I am not even in the military.

"Last month, I was told if I didn't help this man escape I would be conscripted into the army and sent to the Russian front. This is the lesser of two bad choices that I had to make. If I can get him home, they will let me go back to designing transportation logistics.

"The only time I have fired a gun is when some French Resistance fighters were shooting at me while I was trying to save some lives. I guess you could say I'm on a special operation. I'm not in the SS, nor am I a member of the Nazi Party. I'm just an unlucky guy with the right background to suit their purpose."

They sat for while without speaking. After a few minutes, Christian looked at Maggie. "You are a very unusual person. You're young and attractive and live alone. Why are you here?"

Maggie told him how she had lost her fiancé at Pearl Harbor and moved here until she could decide what she would do. She told him how John Logan had tricked her and then abused Theresa and spoke of how she eventually planned to move back to her hometown of Birmingham and resume her life as before.

Christian listened to every word, mesmerized by the soft Southern accent that he had not heard in years. There was no way he was going to allow anything to happen to her, even if it meant jeopardizing his mission. He had never known a woman like this. She was not subservient like so many young girls he knew who wanted to marry and settle down as the traditional hausfrau, nor was she aloof like the society ladies he had met at functions in Berlin. He thought of Rose then. He hadn't thought of her in years. She was the polar opposite of Maggie. Maggie was refreshingly open, defiant, and confident. He couldn't help but stare at her in admiration.

Maggie stared back, knowing he was interested in her on a primal level that he could not deny, even if he were unwilling to accept it. She felt a closeness between them, but he was a German agent in spite of how he chose to define it, and she was the All-American Girl who should not have feelings for her country's mortal enemy.

Their eye contact was abruptly halted when Christian looked away and went to the window to see if anything had changed. There was no activity on the street. The only movement was the branches of the tall pine trees swaying in the breeze.

At midnight, Christian told Braun that it was time to go. "The submarine will be at the site to pick us up. We need to walk down and inflate the raft so we'll be ready to go immediately."

Braun seemed pleased to hear this and nodded his approval as he started for the door. Christian rose and walked over to Maggie. Leaning over and looking into her eyes, he whispered, "I am leaving you here. I'm sure you will be discovered in the morning. I'm sorry we didn't have an opportunity to meet under better circumstances.

"Maggie, I hope you will not judge me harshly because I'm German. This fellow Logan was an American and that did not make him a good person. Being German does not make me a bad person. If our countries were not engaged in this stupid war, I would have liked very much to have become better acquainted. You're a very exciting and courageous woman. Good luck with your life. Someone will find you in the morning. By then, we will hopefully be gone and out of your life for good." Although he had a smile on his lips, the sadness in his eyes betrayed him.

Christian found a clean towel in a drawer and folding it into a long narrow roll, wrapped it around her head, covering her mouth but making sure she could breathe through her nose. He then turned to Braun and indicated that it was time to go. Maggie watched them as they went to the back door. She wished she had the courage to tell him that she understood. As Christian opened the door to leave, he looked back and his eyes locked onto Maggie's. Without a further word, he turned off all the lights and, leaving Maggie in total darkness, walked out the door.

Chapter Twenty-Three

THERESA AND ROBERT SAT ON THEIR FRONT PORCH, ENJOYING THE cool breeze before retiring to bed. Their small home seemed to hold the heat of the day, and their bedroom remained uncomfortably warm until well into the evening. The sandy trail in front of the house was quiet, so when Christian and Dieter drove past, the sound was as deafening as a freight train. The car had passed by slowly and without any headlights, as if the occupants wanted to avoid attention. It reminded Robert that he had not seen or heard the police car come back down the road.

"I ain't heard that policeman's car come back. I'm fixin' to drive down to the farmhouse to see if he's still there."

"That's plain crazy, Robert. What if he's settin' up a trap, and you fumble right into it? Whatever is goin' on down there, it ain't none of your business, and you is gonna get us in trouble." Theresa didn't think Robert would get into trouble but was terrified that her secret would be discovered.

"Well, I'm gonna drive down there. If I can't see nothin' from the road, I'll come right back." He bent down to give her a kiss when Theresa jumped up from her chair saying, "I'm comin' with you. I ain't sittin' here worryin' what's happened to you."

They drove the pickup slowly down the sandy trail. When they reached the farmhouse, they could just make out the silhouette of the patrol car sitting in the yard. There was no movement and no lights anywhere.

"Somethin' don't seem right. If anyone is still here, there needs to be some kind of light on. Let's drive up to the house and see if he's still there." Even Theresa was intrigued at this point.

"Let's just be careful. If anything should happen, I'll never forgive you for gettin' me in this mess."

Robert had heard that threat so many times before from her that he dismissed it without much thought. They eased the truck into the yard and parked behind the patrol car. The only sound they could hear was the chorus of cicadas and frogs. They could make out the back porch steps in the dark. As they started up, each step creaked loudly, boldly announcing their arrival. They called out as they reached the back door.

"Hello! Is anyone there?" At first there was no sound at all. Then they heard a soft muffled sound coming from one of the rooms. "Is there anyone here?" repeated Robert.

Then a very faint groan responded from within the house. With Robert leading the way and Theresa hanging on to his belt from behind, they felt their way through the rooms until they could make out the outline of a figure lying on a bed.

When they approached the dark shape, they saw it was the sheriff. There was enough moonlight coming through the window to see that he was bound to the bed, muffled.

Quickly, they unwrapped the binding from his head and removed the cloth from his mouth. Jim took a deep breath of fresh air. His first thought was that he needed to do a better job of washing his socks in the future, but his first words were, "Thank God you came. Untie me from the bed and then free my hands. The men that did this are the German escapee and his accomplice. I've got to find them before they board a submarine that's scheduled to pick them up sometime tonight."

Once the sheriff was freed, they walked outside into the dark backyard. A breeze had picked up, and the mosquitoes that had been tormenting Jim had disappeared. He opened the door to his patrol car and saw that the keys to the ignition were gone.

"Damn it, I should have known!"

"Sheriff, I think I can start the car without a key. Let me see."

Robert opened the hood and then reached under the steering column to pull some wires free. He then touched one to the starter solenoid under the hood and the other to the starter wire. The car started immediately.

"Thanks. I don't want to know how and where you learned that trick."

With a twinkle in his eyes, Robert smiled. "When you work around farm machinery all your life, you have to learn how to keep them going. Lots of times there ain't no key no way."

"I don't know where these men went, but I don't think you can help me anymore. I really appreciate you coming out here and finding me, but I want the two of you to go home and stay there." The sheriff felt his empty holster and remembered the two men had taken his service revolver. Turning to Robert he said, "They took my gun. Do you have one I can use? I'll return it as soon as possible."

"I have a .22 rifle I use for varmints, and a 12-gauge shotgun I use for bird hunting. I also have some buckshot for heavier game, if it would help."

"The shotgun would be fine. When this is over with, I'll return it and let you know what happens."

Jim followed Robert and Theresa home. Robert went inside and brought out the double barrel shotgun and a box of shells. Jim thanked them again and drove into Grayton Beach, hopeful he would find some sign the men had been there. He thought about calling Bill from a pay phone, but as it was just his luck, he had absolutely no change in his pocket. The only pay phone was at the store, and it was closed.

There was no sign of the men in Grayton Beach. They could have headed in any direction, toward Panama City or Fort Walton, or even gone inland, but his instinct told him they must have made their way to a rendezvous point on the beach to be picked up by a German boat. Long stretches of desolated beach lay in both directions. He looked for footprints, but it was fruitless. There were so many footprints in the sand that he was wasting his time.

By now, it was approaching midnight, and the entire village was in darkness. Jim was tired and dirty, but thought he might drive around the few streets to see if he noticed anything unusual. There was nothing more he could do until morning. Tomorrow, he would canvass the homeowners who were in town and people at the store to see if anyone had seen or heard anything unusual.

He drove back through the narrow, sandy and oyster-shell lanes between the few wooden houses. A few cars were parked there, but none looked like the one he sought. Then, as he was driving down a narrow, one-way drive between two large oak trees, he caught the reflection of a metal object. Slowing down and peering into the dark, he could barely make out the shape of a car bumper from behind a wax myrtle hedge behind an old storage shed. He stopped his car and walked carefully up to the vehicle.

As he approached the car, he recognized it as the Ford and moved quietly. Peering inside, he could see no one hiding. He listened intently for any noise but heard nothing except the sound of the night creatures. In the distance, he could hear the screech of an owl from the top of a pine tree.

Finding the car gave Jim a renewed sense of energy and purpose. He felt sure the Germans would go down to the beach to make their escape. He decided to go back toward the beach and then determine which direction to proceed, with the plan to intercept them before they were able to get away. He stopped the car, having no choice but to turn the engine off by reaching under the steering column and pulling the wire free that ran to the starter. The car died immediately.

The sheriff walked through the sand dunes to the wide beach. The ocean breeze was picking up, and salt spray blew into his face. The light of the moon gave the sand a gray color. Visibility was good. He looked up and down the beach to determine if he could see anybody. Finding it deserted, he took his chance and went east. Sometimes luck was all you had to go on.

Chapter Twenty=Four

LEAVING MAGGIE'S HOUSE, CHRISTIAN NOTICED THE LIGHT BREEZE had increased to a strong wind. This was not a good sign. They made their way toward the beach, keeping to the back of the houses. When they crossed the sand dunes and were on the beach, Christian realized contact with the submarine would be difficult now that the wind had whipped up the surf and each wave wore a frothy crown. If Maggie had not discovered them, they could have waited one more night for calmer weather, but that was not an option now. They had no choice but to row out to the U-boat as soon as they saw the signal.

He tried not to think of what life would be like as a captured German spy on American soil. He assumed they would line him up in front of a firing squad after they were finished torturing him. Shaking off the thought, he focused on finding the buried raft. Although the escape had been challenging, he had confidence that Kapitänleutnant Müller-Stöckheim would be waiting for them. But the kapitän had made it very clear to Christian that his rescue mission was second to his own of finding and sinking American ships. Timing was critical. Without the U-boat, he and Braun had no lifeline.

They walked along the water's edge where the sand was firmer. He estimated it was probably a half-mile to the buried raft. They had sufficient time as long as the U-boat remained there until 3:00 A.M., as Müller-Stöckheim had promised.

It only took a few minutes for them to reach the crossed driftwood. Scooping away the sand with their bare hands, they quickly uncovered the deflated raft and two short paddles. Then Christian located the hand pump. Inserting the needle into the raft, he began to inflate it. When the raft was fully inflated, Christian pulled out a flashlight that had been stored in one of the canvas pockets, stood up, and walked to the shoreline.

Braun's eyes moved in the direction of the ocean. Pointing the light straight out into the black void of the Gulf, Christian signaled with the series of predesignated flashes. He waited for 10 seconds and then repeated the flashes, and again for the third time. Nothing. He realized he had been holding his breath with nervous anticipation and forced himself to breathe deeply. *Come on, come on. Where are you?* His mind was racing. Why wasn't the U-boat there? *Shit!*

Finally, he saw a short burst of light cutting through the darkness. He turned to Braun as he grabbed one side of the raft and began dragging it toward the water, yelling over the crashing surf and wind, "Let's go! It's going to be tough in this surf!"

Braun nodded in agreement and quickly took the other side of the raft and began to drag it through the sand. As they started toward the water, out of the corner of his eye, Christian noticed a lone figure on the beach coming their way.

Luck was, indeed, with Jim tonight. He had been walking for only a few minutes when he saw what looked to be a dim light flashing in the distance. He had kept his eyes on the sand searching for footprints and had only looked up for a second when he saw the flash ahead of him. As he focused on the source, he saw it again, and then a third time. It was a signal. He knew they were a short distance in front of him. He then saw another flash coming from far out in the water. Without a doubt now, he knew he had found them.

Knowing he didn't have much time, Jim sprinted over the sand dunes and then toward the two figures silhouetted against the skyline a couple hundred yards ahead of him. When he was closer to the men and still hidden by the dunes, he carefully opened the breech of the double barrel shotgun and inserted a shell in each side. Silently, he closed the gun, being careful to minimize the sound of the click as it seated itself.

Crouching low, he continued through the soft sand and low vegetation that covered the back of the dunes. Finally, he dropped to his stomach, held the gun with both arms, crawled to the top of the dune, and peered into the darkness. The men were at the waterline preparing to board the raft and row out to sea. It was now or never because the shotgun only had a limited range. Hoping to catch them off guard, he slid down the sand dune, slipping in the soft sand and causing a squeak as the particles of the fine grains squished beneath his feet. Bringing the gun to his shoulder, he shouted at the top of his lungs, "Stop right there and raise your hands!"

Having spotted the figure earlier, Christian told Braun someone might be coming and they needed to hurry, so he was not taken by surprise by the man's sudden appearance. Christian dropped to his knees in the surf behind the raft, lifted his pistol with both hands, and fired.

At the same time, Braun reached up and fired his Luger, only to hear a dull click. Christian's shot hit Jim in the left shoulder, knocking him backward. As he fell, Jim pulled both triggers on the double barrel shotgun. Braun staggered back. Most of his face disappeared. He was dead before he hit the water. The pellets from the shotgun had grazed Christian's shoulder, cutting a searing tear through the skin but not deep into the flesh.

Jim was on the sand, desperately trying to keep calm and reload the shotgun. He was in agony from the wound to his shoulder and was bleeding heavily. Christian sprinted toward the prostrate figure. He reached for the gun, the barrel still hot, and pulled it out of Jim's hands.

Christian recognized Jim from the farmhouse and aimed his pistol directly at his chest as he cocked the lever to fire. He was pumped up with adrenaline and was in survival mode. Kill or be killed. As they made eye contact for a moment, Christian realized what he was about to do. Jim was unarmed. It would be murder—as simple as that. He would have to live with the consequences for the rest of his life. If he could get to the U-boat, this would be a senseless act.

He lowered the pistol and reached over to see the damage to Jim's shoulder. He was bleeding, but the wound did not look life threatening. Jim never broke eye contact with

Christian during the whole incident. Perhaps it was the only way to maintain his sense of dignity in a situation where he was completely powerless. If he were going to die, he would do it with dignity.

When Christian had lowered his gun, Jim briefly closed his eyes and gave a silent prayer of thanks. Then Christian spoke, and Jim was surprised by his perfect English. At the farmhouse, the two men had spoken in German.

"I think you'll be all right. I have some first aid supplies and a small vial of morphine. Lie here and don't move. I'll patch you up enough for you to get back to town."

Walking down to the shoreline, he heaved the shotgun far out into the water, eliminating the worry that Jim would be able to use it again. As he secured the raft from the surf, he noticed that the shotgun pellets had missed puncturing the raft's skin. Jim had fired high, saving the raft and his chance to row out to the submarine. He found the first aid kit in the pouch and returned to Jim, finding him attempting to rise but with no success. Christian picked up a small piece of driftwood and said, "Bite on this. I'm going to give you a shot of morphine and dress the wound. It'll hurt like hell, but you'll be better off."

Christian prepared the syrette containing morphine and jabbed Jim in the thigh, injecting the drug. He then ripped open Jim's shirt so that he could get to the wound. Tearing open a packet of gauze and tape, he applied a patch to his shoulder, stemming the blood flow. Jim bit hard on the driftwood and breathed deeply through his nose. The pain was almost more than he could bear. But soon, the morphine took effect, and he began to relax.

Christian went back to the water to see if he could find Braun, but in the darkness and surf, the body was not visible. He had no choice but to leave Braun's body to the elements. He had been sent to rescue Braun and bring him home, and he had failed in his mission. He had no idea what would happen to him when he returned to Germany, but at this point, he had no choice but to get to U-67 before it left. He knew they were waiting for him and every minute was vital.

Christian helped Jim to his feet. At this point, the morphine had rendered him helpless.

"I have to leave," Christian told him. "I'm sorry that this happened to you. The fact that I'm here was out of my control, but I'm not important. You killed the important man. I think that you will be okay if you get some medical help as soon as you can. When you get back to town, go to the fourth house on the left of the main road. Inside, you will find a woman tied up. Free her and have her take you to a hospital. Her name is Maggie."

Christian wanted Jim to tell Maggie more . . . that he was sorry that they met under these circumstances. He would have liked to know her better. But one look into Jim's eyes and Christian realized the officer would be lucky just to make it to Maggie's house.

"What's your name?" slurred Jim.

Knowing that it made no difference, Christian responded, "My name is Christian. Now I have to go."

He turned and walked into the surf, grabbing the side of the flimsy rubber raft and throwing himself into it. Then he began to paddle out into the darkness. As soon as he began to paddle, he realized the wind and surf had increased considerably since he had left Maggie's house. Every stroke caused the raft to spin. Any forward motion was slowed by the high surf and wind in his face. Salt spray clouded his vision and within a minute, he was soaked to the skin. Christian paddled as hard as he could, stopping occasionally to catch his breath. When he ceased rowing, even for a moment, he could feel the raft drifting back to shore.

At this rate, it would take him hours to row out to the boat. Still, he pressed harder, hoping that he could overcome the waves and wind. When he guessed that he had covered less than a quarter of the distance, he realized he no longer had the strength to make it. He had no choice but to let the wind carry him back to the beach. Tomorrow night he would try again. There was no way to signal the U-boat so his only hope was Kapitänleutnant Müller-Stöckheim would determine the weather was preventing him from making it and would return the following night in calmer seas.

Exhausted, he lay down in the raft and let the waves and wind carry him back to the beach. Salt water soaked into his shoulder wound, and it felt like it was on fire. A feeling of despondency overcame him. He had failed to deliver Braun, and he could not even save himself. He was exhausted and in severe pain. Weary and despondent, he rested his head on the side of the raft. His body was submerged in water inside the raft. Exhausted, he closed his eyes. He did not care what happened to him anymore.

Almost a mile away, a seaman was standing in the conning tower of U-67 scanning the darkness through binoculars for sight of the raft. All that was visible was waves and ocean spray. After half an hour, he was replaced by another sailor. Gratefully, the sailor climbed down the ladder into the warmth and dryness on the interior and found the kapitän.

"Kapitän, I cannot see any sign of them. The waves are running 2 to 3 meters, and the wind is blowing at

25 knots. It would be almost impossible to row a raft in this weather."

"I think they must have tried, but cannot make it tonight. I'll give them one more night and hope the seas are calmer tomorrow. That will be the last chance. After tomorrow night, we navigate west to New Orleans. We're beginning to get low on provisions and fuel and are down to only a few remaining torpedoes. Pass the word we'll head out toward the shipping channel and spend the day looking for enemy ships," the kapitän replied.

At the mention that they would be going home soon, a quiet hurrah spread through the vessel. Kapitänleutnant Müller-Stöckheim hoped that Christian and Braun would be able to make it out to the boat tomorrow night. If not, he would be forced to leave them. Maybe the weather would improve. It was all he could do. *Such is war,* he reflected to himself.

Chapter Twenty-Five

Jɪᴍ ᴡᴀᴛᴄʜᴇᴅ Cʜʀɪsᴛɪᴀɴ ʀᴏᴡ ᴏᴜᴛ ɪɴᴛᴏ ᴛʜᴇ ᴡᴀᴠᴇs ʙᴜᴛ ʜᴀᴅ ɴᴇɪᴛʜᴇʀ the strength nor weapons to prevent him. He could see Christian was struggling but could only assume he would make it eventually. The morphine made him drowsy and standing was an effort. Walking slowly to keep his mind and body oriented, Jim made his way back to town and following Christian's instructions, he located the house he had described.

Jim stumbled to the front door and knocked, as much a formality as anything, because he had been told that the woman was tied up and could not answer the door. When there was no response, he picked up a heavy ashtray from the porch table and used it to break the glass door panel. Carefully, he reached inside, turned the lock, and swung it open.

Maggie heard the knock and then the shatter of glass falling to the floor. Her body was alert, and her mind was racing as she began to yell as loudly as she could through her gag.

Jim could hear a muffled voice coming from the next room. Turning on a lamp in the living room, he realized the noise emanated from the kitchen. Walking in that direction, he saw Maggie tied to the chair. After locating the light switch, he turned it on, picked up a knife from the counter, and cut the cords that held her arms and ankles to the chair. Then he untied the cloth from her head, allowing her to breathe.

As Maggie's eyes adjusted to the overhead light, she saw the man was wearing a police uniform. Hungrily, she filled her lungs with deep gulps of fresh air.

"Thank you. I had no idea how long it would be before someone found me." Maggie could tell immediately the officer was in need of medical help. She jumped up and took him by the elbow, leading him to the sofa in the living room. "We need to get you to a hospital. Let me grab my keys and I'll take you."

"Thanks, I appreciate it."

"Oh, by the way, my name is Maggie."

"Jim Garrison. I'm the sheriff in DeFuniak Springs." Jim knew the morphine was having an effect on him, but he couldn't seem to stop talking. It was unlike him to reveal any information to a civilian about an active case, but his thoughts flooded his mind and flowed unchecked out of his mouth.

"I've lost a lot of blood, but I think I'll be all right. I was chasing two German spies. I shot one. The other got away on a raft. I need to let the authorities know what happened. I guess they're the ones that tied you up."

At the mention one of the Germans had been shot, Maggie felt her heart sink. She was afraid to ask which of them had been shot, but she had to know. She hoped with all her heart that it was not Christian. The thought made her ill.

"Which one did you shoot?"

"The one who escaped from the POW camp near Crestview yesterday. Apparently, the other one, whose name is Christian, was sent here to get him out. I found them in an old, dilapidated house while they were waiting for the escape vessel, but they overpowered me. I should have been more careful. They tied me up, and I overheard bits and pieces of their conversation when they spoke English. The one called Christian treated me well under the circumstances, and he's the one that patched me up on the beach after he shot me. I must have missed him with my shotgun, but I damn sure didn't miss the other one. He's shark bait by now."

A tremendous relief spread over Maggie's entire body. She barely heard the rest of what he was saying. Although she appeared calm, she was a jumble of conflicting thoughts and emotions as she struggled to make sense of all that had happened. She was supposed to hate all Germans. They were the enemy. But she liked Christian and felt she could trust him.

"There's a hospital in DeFuniak Springs. If you don't mind, take me there. I'd appreciate it. They took my keys when they left me tied up, but a colored family found me, and the husband hotwired my police car to get it started. I'll have to send for a tow truck to pick it up."

After helping Jim into the passenger seat of her car, Maggie backed out of the sandy drive and drove north toward the hospital. As they passed the road that turned toward the farmhouse, Jim mentioned to her it was the place where he had found the two Germans and where a colored couple had helped him.

"Were their names Robert and Theresa?" she asked.

"Yeah, how did you know that?"

"Because Theresa is my maid and cook. I know them both. They are good people."

"You're right about that. I helped them fix a flat tire. They suggested I take a look at the farmhouse and then came looking for me when they realized they had not seen me come back down the road. I borrowed his shotgun which I used to kill the German. How did you get involved in this?"

"The one called Christian was walking on the beach the other day and helped me when I cut my foot on a piece of broken glass. He told me he worked for the road department. Later, I ran into him just north of here, but we did not speak."

She was careful not to tell Jim the exact circumstances under which Christian had observed them when she and Theresa had taken John Logan to that same farmhouse. The less Jim knew the better.

"Then earlier tonight, I heard a noise next door and thought it might be a man who's been bothering me, so I went over there to see if it was him. They were hiding in the house and surprised me. They brought me back to my house and tied me up. The one called Braun wanted to kill me, but the other one, Christian, would not allow that to happen; in fact, he was very careful not to harm me in any way. We talked a bit, and I got a sense he was a man who seemed to be thrust into circumstances that were beyond his control."

"It's interesting that you say that because when they had me tied up at the farmhouse and after he shot me, he seemed more concerned with my well-being than I would have thought a German spy would be. I think that he was out of his element. He could have killed me easily on the beach but didn't. He even talked to me like the whole thing was an unfortunate set of circumstances. But he's a spy on American soil, and if I had been able to, I would have shot him dead in a second."

As they drove north to the hospital, Maggie realized she had reached the point of exhaustion and could not deal with the situation anymore. It was such a relief not to think about anything but getting Jim to the hospital. She would try to absorb it all later.

Jim rested his head on the seat back. The morphine and the trauma of his wound finally overpowered his ability to stay conscious. Soon he was sound asleep. When they reached the outskirts of DeFuniak Springs, Maggie gently awakened Jim to ask how to get to the hospital. Through slurred speech, he gave her instructions how to find the small country hospital.

A nurse helped Maggie get Jim out of her car and into the emergency room. Immediately afterward, the nurse called the only doctor in town. In a few minutes, he arrived and began to attend to Jim's wounds. Maggie informed the doctor Jim had been shot by a German spy and that the spy had administered morphine and put the bandage on before he escaped.

After what seemed like hours, the doctor pronounced Jim in stable condition and said he would be fine in a few days. He was lucky the shot had missed vital organs and the bleeding had been staunched, otherwise, he could have bled to death. He needed to stay in the hospital for a couple of days to rest and heal.

Visibly relieved, Maggie told the nurse she would come back and visit in a couple of days. She was dead on her feet and just wanted to go home and sleep. On the way back to her cottage, she thought about Christian sailing back to Germany. It seemed impossible he had been with her only a few hours ago, and now he was gone. Why was she even thinking about him? *He's a German spy, for God's sake.* Her world had been completely turned upside down. She silently wished him well as her car made its return trip down the dark lonely road to Grayton Beach.

Chapter Twenty-Six

THE RAFT, PROPELLED BY THE FORCE OF THE WAVES, SLID ONTO THE beach and stopped abruptly as the waves reversed and moved back out to sea. The sudden change shook Christian from his semiconscious state. His body was shutting down as a result of muscle fatigue, the trauma of his wound, and from the exhaustion of trying to stay in the raft during the roller-coaster ride in the stormy waves. Suddenly, another large wave crashed on the shore and threatened to lift the raft up and suck it back out to sea. Quickly, Christian rolled out of the raft and swallowed a mouthful of water as he splashed headfirst into the shallow surf.

Weak and light-headed, he crawled on hands and knees, coughing to clear his lungs. After a minute, he regained enough energy to stand. With strength he did not know he possessed, he pulled the raft out of the surf and dragged it across the beach and behind a sand dune.

Catching his breath for a few minutes, he finally opened the valve and slowly began to deflate the raft. It emitted a musty odor as air hissed from the narrow opening. Although Christian's optimism had taken a huge hit, his survival instinct had kicked in. Summoning all his remaining strength, he began digging a shallow hole in the dune with both hands. When the depression was deep enough, he pressed the remaining air from the raft and pushed it into the hole. He then covered it with sand and marked the spot with driftwood once again.

The sand dunes provided shelter from the strong winds. Christian lay on his back, looking at the brilliant stars overhead, trying to figure out his next move. He had already exhausted his options for hiding in Grayton Beach. He could go back to town in the hope his car would still be there, but that created the risk of being caught on the road. The car would be recognized as soon as the sheriff was able to put out a police alert.

Christian started toward town and discovered *something* had actually gone in his favor. The wind had blown the raft in a westerly direction, leaving him a long way from where the Americans would be looking for evidence of where he had departed. A small smile formed on his haggard face, and the saltwater that had dried around his mouth cracked. He turned east. In a few minutes, he walked through the sand path from the beach to the road. All was quiet and dark. As he walked toward Maggie's house, he saw her car was gone. Christian guessed Jim had made it to her house, and she had taken him to the hospital.

Suddenly, a feeling of complete calm enveloped him. He knew at that moment his fate lay in Maggie's hands. He was exhausted and in pain and had nowhere to hide. He felt exposed, vulnerable, and defeated. It was now up to Maggie to either help him or turn him in. It was a decision he would accept without regret.

He walked up to her front door and without knocking, entered her house. As he suspected, she was not there. Making his way through the dark house, he found the bathroom. Closing the door, he pulled the shade over the window and turned on the light. There was a simple medicine cabinet over the pedestal sink containing a few cosmetics and medical supplies, including a small bottle of tincture of Merthiolate antiseptic that would suffice for his wound.

Christian unbuttoned his shirt and examined his wound for the first time. The shotgun pellets had peppered the fleshy part of his upper left arm, and it was still seeping blood. He felt better knowing the shot had exited because it would help minimize infection. However, he knew the seawater contained bacteria, and he would need real medical assistance soon. He took some toilet tissue and poured some of the antiseptic solution on the tissue, then dabbed the medicine onto his shoulder, grimacing with the sting.

While he was standing at the sink, he looked in the mirror and was shocked by what he saw reflected. He had aged 10 years in 2 days, and he felt as bad as he looked. He stripped off his wet clothes, climbed into the shower, and let the warm water wash away the salt and sand. Realizing he did not have any other clothes to wear, he reluctantly rinsed out the ones he had just shed in the shower and squeezed as much of the water out of them as he could. Having to put his wet clothes back on was an extremely unpleasant prospect, and redressing in wet garments would irritate his already-white and wrinkled skin. Fortunately, with his body heat and the warm weather, however, it wouldn't take too long for them to dry.

Now, all he could do was to wait for Maggie to return. Looking down again at the wet clothes and continuing to wrestle with the idea of getting completely dressed in them, he decided to put his trousers back on, but not the cold, wet shirt, and lay on the bedroom floor to keep the mattress from getting wet.

As he lay there, he was conscious of the quiet. The only sound in the house was the repeated tick from a windup clock that sat on the bedside table. He breathed deeply and could smell the faint fragrance of Chanel No. 5 softly floating throughout the house. He could not help but smile. He had smelled that same scent on women in Berlin. *What a small world we are becoming.* Soon, he dozed but woke up with a jolt when he thought he heard a noise. When he moved, the pain in his shoulder flared up. At the sound of a car door slamming, he stood up, ran his fingers through his hair to look a little more presentable, and waited for her to enter.

Chapter Twenty-Seven

J<small>IM</small> STRUGGLED TO RELEASE HIMSELF FROM THE DRUG-INDUCED roller-coaster ride. But, floating in a world of make-believe, free from pain, was difficult to give up. He had slept through much of the day and was tempted to close his eyes again when the nurse came into the room to check on him.

As the effects of sleep and drugs subsided, he was jolted into recalling what had happened to him and why he was in the hospital. Immediately, Jim insisted the nurse call Bill. When his partner had arrived, Jim filled him in on all that had happened. Jim instructed Bill to notify the military and then to return to the crime scene to check for any evidence, either the remains of the dead German or any clues that could be helpful to the case. When he had completed that assignment, Jim asked him to arrange to have his car towed back to DeFuniak Springs for repair.

When he thought the meeting was over, Bill started toward the door of the hospital room. Before he could exit, however, Jim called him back. "One more thing. Would you please stop by Maggie Neal's cottage and thank her for taking me to the hospital last night." Bill smiled and nodded. "Oh, and tell her I'll stop by to see her when I get out of here." Jim was itching to get out of the hospital. He wished he could be in the police car with Bill instead of this damn bed.

Later that afternoon, several officials from the military base came to take his statement. He told them all he could remember. How the Negro couple had assisted him and how the German with the perfect English had told him where to find Maggie, and even the fact that she brought him to the hospital. He left nothing out that might be significant to the case. They informed him that they would drive down the next morning and talk with her. By the time they left, he was exhausted and drifted off to sleep again.

Bill found Jim's car and called to have a tow truck pick it up, then walked down the beach and found the spot where Jim had been shot. There were bloodstains on the sand and several sets of footprints and scrapes where the raft had been dragged across the beach. But there was no sign of the dead German. He guessed that the tide had washed the body out to sea.

The wind had subsided, and the waves were lapping softly on the beach. Looking out into the water, he could see the dark shadow of the shotgun lying on the seabed about 30 feet from shore. It was too far to wade out and retrieve it. It would be useless anyway after sitting overnight in saltwater. He had seen everything he needed to see, so he decided to return to town to check on Maggie.

Chapter Twenty-Eight

Maggie slid out of her car, slamming the door as she walked toward her house. During the quiet and lonely drive back to Grayton Beach, she had relived the last few hours, hoping to make some sense out of all that had happened.

The only thing that she wanted now was a long, hot shower. She would tidy up the mess that had been made in house in the morning. It was now almost 4:00 A.M., and she was completely dead on her feet.

As Maggie flipped the kitchen light switch, she sensed movement in the darkness of the bedroom. *Oh, no! Not again. Who's here now?* Before she could scream, Christian emerged from the doorway of the bedroom, holding himself against the doorjamb for support. He spoke quietly and in a calm voice. "I've been waiting for you. I didn't know where else to go. You're the only person that I can trust."

Maggie's only response was her continued stare into his haggard face, as if she couldn't believe he was actually standing in front of her.

Christian wished he could put his arms around her to reassure her and to apologize for intruding yet again into her life, but his arms stayed on the doorjamb where he knew they belonged. He was tired of playing the role of German spy and wished he could just see her smile instead of greeting him with apprehension and distrust.

Whether it was the lateness of the hour or the sight of him, or the combination of the two, it was just too much for Maggie to deal with. Without a sound, her eyes rolled back in her head and she started to faint, falling slowly to the floor. Christian quickly covered the distance between them, grabbing her before she hit the hard surface. Taking her to the bedroom, he gently laid her on the bed. Then he went into the bathroom, returning with a wet washcloth to wipe her face. When she began to stir, she stared at him but said nothing. He seemed focused on a spot between her face and the edge of the bed.

"I'm sorry I frightened you. Please forgive me for coming back here, but I had nowhere else to go." Maggie's facial features were expressionless, so Christian continued. "The policeman found us before we could get away and killed Braun. His shot also hit me in the shoulder. I had to shoot him to protect myself. He would have killed me if I hadn't, but I only tried to wound him and not kill him. I patched him up as best I could, and I gave him some morphine so he could make it to you. I knew that you would take him to the hospital. I'm sorry to get you involved again, but I knew you would take good care of him."

Maggie said nothing.

"I tried to row out to the submarine that was waiting for me, but the wind was too strong. I got about halfway and realized I simply could not make it any further. I must have passed out from exhaustion, and when I woke up, I was back on the beach. I was going to hide out in the woods until I could rendezvous with the boat, but realized my flashlight was gone and I had no way to signal the ship. I have nowhere to hide and no way to communicate with the ship, so I came here. You are my only hope."

He moved his head and locked eyes with Maggie, willing her to say something. Nothing.

"I can't do this anymore. I'm so tired. If you wish to call the authorities, you can. They will either kill me or send me to a POW camp for interrogation. The funny thing is I really don't know anything that would help the Allies. Braun was a scientist and was needed to help design some advanced missile system, but that is all I know. I am not even in the military officially, but I don't think anyone would care about that. If I'm turned over to the Allies, I suspect I will be shot as a spy. Maybe that's what I deserve.

"Right now, I only want to get some sleep. I want to lie down beside you for a while, if that is all right with you. Don't worry. I don't have the energy to make a pass, even if I wanted to. Would you let me lie next to you for the night? Don't try to make a decision tonight, tomorrow will be soon enough."

Maggie saw the fatigue in his face and heard the weariness in his voice. But she also heard a plea for help from a man who seemed to be caught in a situation not of his own making. Somehow she believed him. If he weren't telling the truth, she guessed she'd never see the morning light. She went with her gut instinct and without saying a word, nodded slightly and moved over so that he could lie down beside her.

Having a man in her bed was, on one hand, confusing, but on the other, very comforting. It had been a long time since she had shared her bed with Charles, and after they had made love, he had always left to return to his home. Spending the night together was simply not acceptable in their social class. Tonight was different, however. Having Christian next to her seemed like the most natural thing. It was strange that she wanted to be with him, regardless of the circumstances. She would worry about what she should do tomorrow.

The only thing she insisted on for the night was that he remove his wet trousers. There was no way she was going to sleep next to someone wearing wet clothes. He stood up and removed his pants and returned to the bed. They lay next to each other under the light sheet. Although he was not touching any part of her, she could feel the warmth his body radiating. They lay in the dark, not saying anything, and soon, she could tell from Christian's breathing he was sound asleep. She lay still, afraid to move so as not to awaken him. She stared at the shadows that played across the ceiling, wondering how she ever managed to get herself into such a predicament, and soon fell into a peaceful sleep.

Maggie woke first, and looking at the clock by Christian's side of the bed, saw it was almost 9:00 A.M. Fortunately, today was Sunday and Theresa had the day off. Realizing she was still wearing the same clothes from the day before, she slipped out of bed as quietly as she could and tip-toed into the bathroom, where she stripped and climbed into the hot shower, scrubbing herself from head to toe with soap and then shampooing her hair. By the time she finished, her skin was pink from all the scrubbing, and she felt refreshed, as if she had washed some of her problems down the drain.

After she dried and wrapped her hair in a towel, Maggie put on a pair of cotton shorts and a sleeveless blouse, then went into the kitchen to make a large pot of coffee. While the coffee was brewing, she sat in the wooden porch swing, her mind blank. In a few minutes, she could hear the boiling water begin to burble up into the clear glass cap of the coffee pot, then drip down into the grounds. She always enjoyed listening to the sound of the coffeemaker. The aroma soon reached her. Maggie went into the kitchen to turn off the burner, anticipating the first, delicious sip. Carrying her favorite enamel mug, she returned to the porch swing, watching the steam rise as she tried to figure out her next step.

The obvious thing would be to notify the authorities and let them take Christian away. She could explain how he had come back and taken her hostage and that she had slipped away while he was asleep. But she realized she wanted to protect him. She wanted to be with him and get to know him. It dawned on her no one knew that he had not managed to escape the night before. She had all day and tonight to think about whether she should turn him in or allow him to try to escape again.

In a few minutes, she heard sounds coming from the house. The bathroom door squeaked and the faint sound of water running brought her attention back to the present. She walked into the kitchen, found a chipped ceramic mug, and placed it next to the stove. Then she returned to the porch. Soon after, Christian appeared in the doorway, his hair wet from the shower and wearing the now-dry trousers. He stood for a minute before he spoke.

"Good morning. I hope you don't mind, but I borrowed your razor. I couldn't turn down the opportunity to shave when I don't know when I might be able to do it again. I wonder if you might take a look at my shoulder and tell me if you think it's getting infected. Maybe I could use some more of your antiseptic, if you don't mind."

Maggie rose and walked into the kitchen. She said nothing but filled his mug with coffee and handed it to him. After looking at him and then his wound, she said, "Here, drink this. Your shoulder looks fine, but I'll put a fresh bandage on it in a few minutes. Let me fix us some breakfast first. I'll make some eggs and toast, but for right now, let's just enjoy the coffee and the morning before it becomes too hot. We need to figure out what we're going to do."

Christian smiled at her, warmed by the simple gestures. Having someone offer him breakfast was a unique experience for him. So when Maggie's voice suddenly took on an angry tone, he was stunned.

"Damn it all, Christian, do you realize what a dangerous situation I'm in because of you? I can be held as an accomplice to your actions. I could be arrested and accused of helping harbor an enemy. I think they shoot people for that. How dare you put me into this situation? What do you want from me? Do you want me to tell you what you did is okay—because it isn't. You came to America to help an enemy escape, even if he did get killed, which, by the way, I'm glad to hear. He was a real son of a bitch and quite frankly, I'm glad that he's dead." Christian looked at her and then gazed into the distance.

"You're right. I'm being very selfish. The last thing I want is for you to get into trouble because of me. What is so ironic is that I'm in this situation because I happened to be on the wrong side of the ocean at the wrong time. I spent my life in both Germany and America. If I'd stayed here after my parents died, I wouldn't be in this situation. Unfortunately, that can't be altered now, and all I can say is that I'm very sorry. I'll leave now. But before I go, I want to tell you how much I care for you. You are an amazing woman, full of compassion, independence, and resilience."

Looking directly at Maggie and placing his fingers under her chin to lift her eyes to his, Christian smiled gently and said, "Your only slight character flaw is that you believe there is goodness in people when often there isn't. But I think you see some goodness in me, or I wouldn't have been able to spend the night here. I won't let anything happen to you, I promise. I'll find a place to hide and hope the submarine shows up tonight. If I'm caught before then, at least you will not be involved. It was foolish of me to come back here. I could've hidden in the woods and found a flashlight somewhere, but the truth is I wanted to spend whatever time I have left with you."

He turned and walked into the bedroom to put on his shirt and still-damp shoes and socks. Maggie followed him and wearily sat on the bed watching him dress. Her thoughts echoed Christian's, but she didn't know what to do. They were caught up in a dangerous situation. She didn't want him to go. She wanted to help him, knowing if she didn't, he might not survive—but at what cost?

A knock on the front door interrupted the intimate moment. There was no time to come up with any plan of escape. Panic hit Maggie in the gut. Christian looked at

Maggie with resignation in his eyes. Gesturing toward the bed, she whispered, "Climb under the bed and don't make a sound. I'll see who it is."

Gathering her composure, she walked to the door, holding her mug of coffee in both hands to keep them from trembling. She could see a police officer inspecting the broken glass frame where Jim had gained entry as he waited for her to answer the door. Reaching the door, she attempted to appear calm and self-assured, an act she was sure the police officer could see right through.

"Good morning, Officer. How can I help you today?"

"Good morning, Miss Neal, I am Sheriff Garrison's deputy. My name is Bill. Sheriff Garrison asked me to stop by and see you while I was over here today. He said I was to check on you to make sure you were all right. He also said to thank you for bringing him to the hospital. He'll drop by in a day or so and thank you personally."

"Well, that's very nice of you. Would you like to sit on the porch and have a glass of iced tea while you're here?"

Her heart was pounding with fear that he would accept the invitation, but she thought if she did not show a basic courtesy, it might give him some signal that something was wrong. At that moment, Maggie knew she had crossed the line. The decision had been made. She was aiding and abetting the enemy. There was no going back now.

"No ma'am, I need to get back to DeFuniak Springs. By the way, I know a person that can replace this pane if you would like me to have him come by."

"Thanks, Officer. Maybe later in the week if that'd be convenient. I need to leave for a couple of nights. By the way, what is the latest on the man that helped the POW escape? Did he get caught or did he get away?"

"Well, from what I could tell from the beach, he was able to get away. There was no sign of him when I walked down there this morning. Too bad Sheriff Garrison didn't kill them both. He knows the one who got away was wounded, but evidently, he was able to make it to the German submarine. I think the military may want to talk to you later to see if you can shed any light on what happened. Here's my card. Please give us a call if we can help you in any way."

"Thanks for stopping by, Officer. Please tell the sheriff thanks also, and I hope he recovers soon. I'll try to stop by if I get up that way in the next few days."

Maggie turned and went back into the house, barely making it to a kitchen chair before collapsing. She sat for a minute to regain her composure and for her nerves to settle. Christian stood at a distance and had the good sense not to say a word.

"I never realized what a good actress I could be. Katherine Hepburn would be proud of my performance. I just wish it were a movie and not real. I keep thinking about all our American soldiers dying for our country, and I'm not very proud of what I've just done."

"I can't do this to you, Maggie. I'm leaving now. Thanks for all you've done for me. I'll never forget you."

"Don't leave," she whispered, surprising ever herself with her statement. "I don't know what to do, but I'd prefer you to stay here with me today. I want to spend time together as long as we can. I know it's insane, but it really is what I want. Come and tell me about who you are and what you want. I need to know if I'm out of my mind for helping you."

Christian poured a fresh mug of coffee and sat across the kitchen table from Maggie. For the next hour, neither moved as he told her his life story, from his birth in Germany to his family's move to America, and the discrimination they had suffered and his decision to return to Germany with the intention of finding a sense of purpose in helping the country recover after the First World War.

He told her about his recruitment by Colonel Schmidt to help Dieter Braun escape and the reasons he was selected. He told her about his disappointment at how the leaders had brought Germany back into another war and his shock at how they were treating Jews and other minorities. He wished he had stayed in America, but he had returned to the place of his birth, and he would have to live with that decision. When he had told her all that he could think to tell her, he was exhausted but felt a huge relief. He was also ravenous.

"Any chance we might eat some breakfast? I'm starving. I'm a decent cook and would be glad to make us an omelet if you have the ingredients."

"That's OK, I'll fix us something. Thanks for sharing your life with me."

"Thanks for listening. I'd like to ask you to do the same. I would very much like to know all about you."

Maggie made a fresh pot of coffee and squeezed some orange juice. She fried some bacon, then dropped two eggs into the hot grease just long enough to cook them sunny-side up. When they were almost cooked, she toasted four pieces of bread and placed butter and homemade strawberry jam on the table. They sat and ate their meal, each in their own world, and not a word was spoken until they had finished.

After they ate the last of the toast and jam, Christian cleaned the plates from the table, poured another mug of coffee, and moved to the sofa in the small living room.

It was not possible to sit on the porch because they could be seen easily from the street. When he had settled down, he said, "Your turn."

Maggie talked as she washed the few dishes, then sat down facing Christian, her feet tucked up under her on the opposite end of the sofa. She told him about her childhood and the tragedy of Charles's death. She had already told him why she was in Grayton Beach when she had been tied up so she finished with the comment that she was unsure how long she would stay.

As the story of her life unfolded, Christian held on to every word. She left nothing out when she revealed the events leading up to Theresa's rape by John Logan. But somehow she couldn't tell him about making love to him on the beach. That embarrassment would stay with her until she went to her grave. Christian understood her omission and didn't tell her he had seen them getting dressed when he landed on the beach.

"So, he was the one that you took out to the old farm and left in the outhouse?"

"Yes, he had tricked me and raped Theresa. I could not let him get away with it. I told Theresa what happened would stay between us, but I don't think I have to worry about you spreading the word around. It was very hard on both of us."

"I don't think it was very easy for this Logan fellow either," Christian chuckled.

Maggie, taken aback by his unexpected sense of humor, glanced at him and smiled.

"No, I expect not. I don't think he will bother anyone else again. I still can't believe I did that. I guess he is out of action forever now, but he deserved that—and more."

They sat silently for a while. They had both poured out their life histories and heaviness seemed to hang over the room. They needed some time to absorb what they had learned about each other. To break the mood, Maggie said that she realized she had not even fixed her hair or put on any makeup since getting up this morning. She announced to Christian that she was going to finish getting dressed. He smiled in return, understanding that they both needed a break from the intense moments of discovery.

Chapter Twenty-Nine

JOHN LOGAN CREPT THROUGH THE THICK UNDERBRUSH BEHIND Maggie's house, swatting at the gnats and black flies that swarmed around his face. He was soaked with sweat and was in severe pain. The only thought that kept him going was paying back that bitch for what she had done to him. His pain would be mild compared to what he had in mind for her.

It had taken him over an hour to hike from where he had parked his car a couple miles away to get to where he was now. The dense palmetto brush, scrub, and pine were so impenetrable that walking became extremely difficult, especially with his penis pulsating with pain each step of the way. Fortunately, he could now finally see the back of her house. He liked the idea she was isolated by the brush he had just come through. No one would be nearby to hear her screams.

He looked down at the bulge in his pants caused by the dressing to his wound and groaned. Never again he thought would he ever have a bulge in his pants again, certainly not the kind that he would have wanted. Now it just hurt like hell.

After he escaped from the burning outhouse, he barely made it to his car before fainting. When he came to, he realized he needed medical care and drove to Panama City, locating a doctor who ran his practice out of his home. Logan wasn't sure how reputable he was, but he didn't want anything reported to the authorities nor did he want any follow-up visits.

The doctor examined him and after suturing him, administered some medicine to prevent infection. He assumed the issue was domestic violence of some sort and chose not to inquire further. He gave Logan some painkillers. Speculating on the extraordinary circumstances and willing to take advantage of the situation, he told Logan the charge was $100, a sum five times the normal rate for the procedure.

John didn't even flinch as he fished out a $100 bill from the stack of bills in his wallet. With the visit completed to the satisfaction of both men, he left to find a place to rest. There was a seedy boarding house nearby and after paying for a room for the night, he collapsed on the lumpy mattress and let the drugs work their magic.

It was late afternoon before he awoke. Making his way to the filthy communal bathroom, he splashed water onto his face in an effort to wake himself. The pain from the wound was terrible, but he was afraid to take any more medication until he could determine his next step. One thing for sure, he was leaving the area as soon as possible.

A deep despondency settled over him. He had nowhere to go. He had no friends, and all the women he knew were either bar floozies or were women that he had taken advantage of, and they would take delight in his predicament. He would never be able to make love to a woman again, and if his male friends found out, he would be the laughing stock of the entire state.

Walking carefully to reduce the discomfort caused by the bandages, he found a café down the street and ordered coffee. As he sipped the stale coffee, he began to formulate a plan for revenge. Maggie Neal was going to pay for what she did to him. Even if it was the last thing he ever did, he was going to make her suffer like she had made him suffer, and then he would kill her. When he had made the decision about what he would do, he finished his coffee, paid, and left the café.

He went into a hardware store across the street where he bought a hunting knife in a leather sheath. The 6-inch-long sharp carbon steel blade was attached to a bone handle. The light tan leather sheath had a wonderful smell, like a new baseball glove.

Logan returned to the boarding house and decided to freshen up in the dirty bathroom. When he tried to pee, the pain almost brought him to his knees. Looking down at the raw wound, he saw that he had lost a third of his manhood. He reapplied the bandage and giving up on any further bathing, swallowed two more pain pills and collapsed on the bed. The next morning he awoke.

After another excruciating visit to the bathroom, John ate breakfast in the café and drove back to Grayton Beach, where he parked his car a quarter of a mile off the main road and down a sandy trail used by hunters and loggers. Attaching the knife to his belt, he hiked through the mottled shade of the pine forest, the thick undergrowth of palmetto palms cutting every exposed inch of skin. Now, he wished he had worn a long sleeve shirt. Gnats and flies attacked his face and eyes. Sweat trickled from every pore, and he began to think he would collapse from exhaustion and pain before he made it to his destination.

When he could finally see the back of her house, he sat in a small clearing to catch his breath and rest. Soon stinging red ants began to crawl on him and the gnats and flies increased in ferocity, so he stood up, brushed the sand off his pants, and crept toward his destination. Smiling grimly, he took the knife out of the sheath and gripped it in one hand.

While Maggie was in the bathroom, Christian sat in the living room idly thumbing through an issue of *Life* magazine. It contained articles about the war effort and rationing. There were also photographs of soldiers in combat and movie stars entertaining the troops. He could see the Americans were suffering just like the Germans, except that they seemed better off and the morale was higher here than in Germany.

He couldn't concentrate on the magazine, so he put it down and stood up to stretch. Then he walked to the front door and carefully peered out to see if anyone was walking or driving by the house, but it was quiet. The dew on the grass and flowers in the yard had evaporated under the piercing sun, and the temperature inside the house was beginning to climb. Perhaps if he were to open the back door, it would create a mild breeze and make the house a little more tolerable.

As Christian walked toward the back of the house, he caught a glimpse of movement in the woods. Through the window of a small storage room adjacent to the back door, he saw a man creeping through the low scrub toward the house. The man was carrying a large knife in one hand. Christian recognized the man Maggie had left in the outhouse.

Moving silently toward the bathroom, Christian whispered, "Maggie, stay in there and lock the door. The man that you took to the farmhouse is coming to your house from around the back, and he has a knife."

Meanwhile, Logan crept up to the screen door and peeked through, scanning for Maggie. He could see no one, but he heard a noise through the bathroom door. As he opened the screen door, the spring squeaked loudly, alerting anyone inside that someone was entering. Satisfied that no one heard him, he entered and went toward the bathroom. When he reached for the bathroom doorknob, Christian grabbed him from behind. Logan was surprised, but instinct took over, and he tried to turn and twist away.

Christian almost lost his hold but was able to grab Logan around the neck as they both crashed to the floor. Logan swung his knife wildly in an attempt to cut his attacker. With his hand free, Christian grabbed Logan's wrist and brought it down hard on his knee, forcing him to drop the knife. With both men on their knees, Christian grabbed Logan by the neck and smashed his face down hard on the floor, crushing his nose and knocking him semiconscious. Logan lost his strength immediately.

Christian picked his head up again and slammed it down even harder this time. There was no movement from Logan at all now. Turning Logan's head, Christian saw only vacant eyes staring out and realized the attacker was dead. Guessing that a piece of bone from his broken nose had penetrated his brain and killed him, Christian sat back on his knees and stared in disbelief as the blood dripped from Logan's nose onto the floor.

He stood up slowly, bent over, his hands on his knees, and took several deep breaths. When his breathing was normal again, he spoke to Maggie.

"You can come out now. He won't harm you again— ever. He's dead."

Maggie unbolted the door and cautiously looked out to where Christian stood and Logan lay. "Are you all right?"

"Yeah, I'm fine, I guess. As fine as one can be after killing someone. Maggie, he was going to kill you. It all happened so fast. One minute I was looking at a magazine, and the next, I was in hand-to-hand combat. This would be ruled as self-defense, but I'm not exactly in a position to call the sheriff and plead my case. I don't think the same laws apply to German agents."

"So what are we going to do with the body?" she asked both herself and Christian.

"Well, we have to get him out of here. That's for sure. How far do the woods go behind your house?"

"Quite a ways. I don't think there's anyone living back there for a couple of miles. Just pine trees and scrub."

"OK, I'm going to try to find some place deep in the woods to bury him. It's the only solution that I can think of."

"I guess that's as good as anything. Can you carry him by yourself?"

"Yes. You stay here and clean up the blood. I'll be back as soon as I can."

Christian lifted Logan's inert body over his shoulder. The pain from his wound throbbed, and it took a few seconds for him to find his balance, but when he could walk comfortably, he headed out the back door and through the backyard into the woods. Within a minute, he was out of sight of Maggie, who continued watching from the back porch.

Maggie returned to the house, found a mop and bucket, and filled it with warm water and soap. She scrubbed the floor where the fight had occurred until all traces of blood were gone. Then she emptied the bucket in the backyard and walked out onto the front porch and collapsed in a chair. Soon, panic was replaced with a sense of resolve. Whoever Christian was, he had the effect of creating calm within her. He exuded confidence which, in turn, gave her strength. But this had to end tonight. She could not live like this for long, or it would destroy her. *This is more than I can deal with. How crazy can things get? I'm harboring a spy in my house, who, by the way, I don't want to leave, and now we have a dead body on our hands.*

With these thoughts swirling in her head, she was brought back to the present by the arrival of a military car at the front of her house. It looked as if she were about to give her second Academy Award performance. Two men wearing U.S. Army uniforms got out of the vehicle. They saw her sitting on the porch and removed their hats as they spoke through the screen.

"Good afternoon, Miss Neal, I'm Captain John Willis, and this is Lieutenant Tim Tyson. We are from Eglin Field and are in charge of the investigation of the escaped prisoner of war. We understand that he and his accomplice held you hostage before they attempted to board a submarine. We'd like to ask you a few questions, if we could."

"Come in, gentlemen." Maggie summoned every bit of strength and nerve she had left and took a deep breath. She could only hope that Christian would be able to see their vehicle or hear them talking if he returned while they were still there.

It was not hard for her to recount the sequence of events of the night before. She had already done it once for Sheriff Garrison. Because what she told them was the truth, it was easier the second time. Still, she was shaking with fear inside. They asked her some questions about what the Germans had said to her and to each other, and wanted her description of the accomplice that had escaped. She gave them a fairly accurate description of Christian. She then offered them a glass of iced tea which they declined, saying they needed to return to the base. Captain Willis gave her his card and asked that she call him if she could think of anything more that might be relevant.

When they left, Maggie sat for a while and thought about where this was all going. Christian would be leaving tonight, and she realized that she cared deeply for him. They had been through so much in such a short period of time. She had saved him, and now he had saved her. Maggie only had one desire, and she was going to take care of it.

Chapter Thirty

CHRISTIAN SLOWLY WORKED HIS WAY THROUGH THE THICK BRUSH burdened by the dead weight of Logan on his shoulders. His breathing was labored and sweat poured from every pore in the heat and humidity. The gnats, chiggers, and flies sensed his inability to protect himself and joined in on an unexpected feast. He heard the familiar sound of a rattlesnake warning him to keep his distance, and stepped carefully. The scrubby bushes were dense, and the weedy vines armored with sharp thorns tore at Christian's exposed arms and rooted themselves firmly in his clothes. After a half-hour trek deep into the pine forest, he came to a clearing containing a shallow pond of stagnant, brackish water. Tracks showed wild pigs and deer used the pond, and the soft black mud sucked at his feet.

Surveying the pond, he could see there was no trail or road approaching the body of water. He gently lowered

Logan to the ground. He knew the feral pigs and other predators would soon feast on Logan's remains but thought it a good idea to remove any identification. He opened the dead man's wallet to look for a driver's license and came across a bundle of $100 bills—approximately $4,000 in all. Christian had no interest in the money, and he clearly couldn't take it back to Germany with him. Still, it was too much money to leave for the animals to destroy, so he stuffed it into his pocket, along with Logan's identification, and turned back toward Maggie's house.

When he was halfway back, he stopped and dug a shallow depression in the sandy soil and buried the identification. The money went into his wallet. He would ask Maggie what to do with it. Maybe she could use it.

By the time he had made it back to her house, he was drenched in sweat, dirty, and scratched up. Carefully peering from behind trees in the woods behind her house, he confirmed that no one was at the house, so he slipped up to the back door and called softly. "Maggie, are you in there?"

She walked to the door, opened it, and motioned him to come in. He was filthy and smelled.

"Go take a shower and clean up. I'll wash your clothes for you, but I don't think they'll be dry before you leave. Obviously, it's too dangerous to hang them outside."

He nodded in agreement and walked toward the bathroom, shedding his shirt on the way. His back rippled with muscles that were tight from carrying the weight of a dead man. He continued to undress, passing his dirty clothes to Maggie on the other side of the bathroom door. She held them at arm's length as if to distance herself from them as much as possible. Washing Christian's clothes was the least she could do, considering what he had just done for her.

While Christian was showering, she removed the contents of the pockets without bothering to look at them, then she placed the filthy clothes in the kitchen sink, scrubbed them with a brush, and hung them in the kitchen to dry.

The shower felt wonderful to Christian. He thoroughly scrubbed his body in an attempt to wash the whole sordid incident down the drain, along with the dirt and sweat. Then he dried off and wrapped a towel around his waist wondering what he would wear while he waited for his clothes to dry. As he walked into the bedroom, it was immediately obvious.

Maggie was standing there waiting for him. Naked. He was so surprised that he didn't know what to say. He just stood silently, soaking in her loveliness. Her body was beautiful, and her breasts protruded invitingly. Her nipples were brown and swollen, aching for his touch. Her waist tapered and then flared out to soft, round hips and long, sexy legs. The dark hair between her legs was silky and formed a perfect triangle. She was tanned above her breasts and below her thighs, but the middle of her body was a delicate white from where her bathing suit had covered her, as if it had never seen the sun. She was breathtaking to him—every square inch.

Removing the band that held her hair in place, Maggie moved toward him. Christian started to speak, but she placed her fingers gently to his lips, looked directly in his eyes, and whispered, "Don't say a word. I've never seduced a man before, but I'm willing to take the risk with you because I've never wanted anyone as much as I want you right now."

Taking him by his hand, Maggie led him to her bed, removed his towel, and allowed her eyes to linger on his magnificent body. His manhood was already responding to her, and she had never been so aroused before. Lying back, she pulled Christian down beside her and started to softly kiss his face. Then she zeroed in on his lips and let her tongue slip into his mouth for just a second before retreating. Seductively, she kissed his mouth hard, emitting a quiet moan which echoed Christian's. Maggie kissed his neck and then went south, caressing his chest and running her tongue around his nipples. By now, Christian was beginning to become very erect. As if on cue, Maggie reached down and started stroking him with a gentle touch.

Christian lay on his back and enjoyed every act she performed on him. He had never experienced such passion. Soon, she threw one leg over his thigh and drew herself on top of him. She leaned forward and with her breasts and nipples caressing his chest, held his face in both hands while she kissed him deeply and let her tongue explore every corner of his mouth.

Christian reached for her breasts, fondled them, and sucked gently first on one taut nipple then the other. Aroused even more by his mouth on her breasts, Maggie reached down, grabbed his erect manhood, and slid it inside her warm and wet canal, devouring him hungrily. Closing her eyes and breathing hard, she moved up and down and side to side, trying to take in as much of him as possible.

Christian began to move his hips up and down. Beads of sweat dripped off Maggie in the warm room, and their bodies were glistening with moisture. She kept her eyes closed, and the expression on her face was almost like someone in pain.

Christian rolled Maggie over without withdrawing from her, lay on top of her, and began moving inside her at his pace. He moved deep and hard, then soft and gentle.

She wrapped her legs around his waist and pulled him tightly to her, holding him closely as if she wanted to absorb him into her entire body. Christian continued to move with the confidence of a seasoned lover, teasing and pleasing her with a skill she never knew existed. Both tried not to climax too quickly, trying to prolong the ecstasy, but it was not long before they both peaked at the same time. They moaned while soaring to a height neither had ever experienced before.

The weight of his body was so wonderful. Maggie wanted to lie there all afternoon with him on top of her so she could feel him for as long as possible. After a few minutes, though, he slid out of her and lay beside her. They did not need to speak. Instead, they lay on the bed and watched the floating dust particles illuminated by the shaft of sunlight from the bedroom window.

The room was warm and before long, they drifted off to sleep. Maggie fell asleep first and soon was snoring lightly, much to Christian's amusement. Christian was as content as he had ever been in his life. Maggie's lovemaking was a reflection of who she was. She was exciting, caring, and passionate. She listened to her heart and was willing to risk everything if she thought it was the right thing. She was the woman he had been looking for all his life. And in a few hours, he would have to leave her forever.

Maggie rose first, around 8:00 o'clock in the evening, and dressed quietly. She didn't want to shower. She wanted the reminder of their lovemaking to perfume her body. Soon, she walked into the kitchen to check on Christian's clothes. The pants and shirt were wrinkled and still damp, so she decided she would press them with an iron to help dry them. As she was unfolding the ironing board, the squeak of the metal legs made such a commotion that it woke Christian. His first thought was that it was now even closer to the time he would have to leave. Thinking of their lovemaking earlier caused him to become aroused again. Maybe a cold shower would help, but he hated washing away her scent.

Still not a word had been said since they had made love. Strangely, the silence was more comforting than talking, and they both recognized it as such.

Maggie was first to speak. "Let's just enjoy being together tonight, Christian. I'll fix us a simple supper, and we can listen to the radio like a normal couple. When it's time for you to leave, there won't be any tears or promises. There is only now for us, Christian."

He nodded. "I agree."

Each of them wanted to say so much more, but with no tomorrow promised, each carried their thoughts within, not wishing to diminish their feelings by expressing them aloud.

Maggie went into the kitchen and prepared a simple supper of ham and potato salad. She sliced a large, juicy, ripe tomato and sprinkled it with salt and pepper. Then she cut some slices from the peach pie Theresa had made and placed it all on the kitchen table with a large pitcher of iced tea.

As they ate, they talked about everything but the horrific things that had happened over the previous 2 days. When they had finished, Christian turned on the shortwave radio so that they could pick up the latest news from the BBC. The scene was so domestic that anyone observing would think they were a typical American couple having supper on a lazy summer evening.

At 11:00 o'clock, Christian looked at his watch and announced that it was time for him to leave. Maggie nodded and said nothing. As he was gathering his possessions, he remembered the money he had taken from Logan's wallet. "I found this money on Logan. There's almost $4,000. I'll leave it here for you."

"I don't want it," Maggie replied.

"Well, I hate to see this much money go to waste. Can't you think of anyone that can use it?"

She thought for a minute and then realized the best solution. "I'll give it to Theresa and Robert. They could certainly use it."

The two lovers stood and looked at each other in awkward silence. There was nothing left to say. Finally, Christian took Maggie in his arms and pulled her close. "Maggie, I know we promised not to say anything, but I may never see you again, and I need to tell you that knowing you has made me a better person. I love you, and no matter what happens to me, I want you to know that. I'm so sorry the circumstances are what they are, but neither you nor I can change it. I wish I could stay with you, but I can't."

With tears in her eyes and a smile on her lips, Maggie said, "Just go now, Christian. I can only hope that someday when you have a smile on your face, you might remember me and this beautiful afternoon we shared."

"Before I leave, I would like to know what your plans are."

"I think it's time for me to go home. I'll go back to Birmingham and try to resume my life there. I can't stay here any longer. There are too many memories that I need to put behind me." Christian kissed Maggie and hugged her tightly for the last time.

"Try to remember me in the best light that you can. In war we lose the ability to make decisions based on our morals. We become a part of the war machine. I can't excuse what I did. I didn't have an option, but I will assume responsibility for my decisions."

"I know that, Christian. Now, please, go. This is just making it harder."

Christian released Maggie from his arms and with a resigned shrug, picked up his few belongings, walked out the door, and walked toward the beach.

He uncovered the raft, inflated it behind a sand dune, and when it was time, took a flashlight he had found in a closet at Maggie's, stood on top of the dune, and signaled out to sea.

Chapter Thirty=One

U-67 WAS SITTING 2 KILOMETERS OFFSHORE WAITING FOR Kapitänleutnant Müller-Stöckheim to give the orders to surface and wait one last time for the men they were supposed to take back to Germany. Soon, they would be returning home after more than 2 months at sea. They were low on fuel and torpedoes, but the voyage had been successful with four confirmed sinkings of American or Allied merchant ships. Two days before, they had successfully torpedoed and sunk the British tanker the *Empire Mica* off Port St. Joe, to the east of where they lay tonight. Morale was high.

At midnight, the order was given to surface and watch for Christian's signal. The seas were calm, the wind light, and the stars were clear overhead as two sailors climbed out of the hatch and onto the conning tower. Each man scanned the area toward the horizon using powerful binoculars. Tension was high. It was vital to locate the passengers and get underway. U-67 would be an easy target as the waters were too shallow to submerge and the contour of the beach acted as a barrier to escape. Focusing on the beach Christian had signaled from the evening before, they almost missed seeing the short burst of light far to the left.

For just a brief instant, one of the sailors noticed the flash from the corner of his eye. He hadn't seen the signal sooner because it came from west of their previous location. The men in the conning tower were unaware Christian had been pushed ashore by the wind almost a mile west of the original site and he had been unable to get back to the original location in time. The sailor immediately relayed the position coordinates to the kapitän and then returned a short burst of light back to Christian. Müller-Stöckheim gave the order to turn and head west and in toward the beach as far as possible without running aground or being spotted by beach patrols. Batteries were used for propulsion instead of the diesel engines to eliminate engine noise.

When Christian saw the flash, he pulled the raft into the light surf, climbed aboard, and started stroking his paddle toward the boat. The conditions were easier than the previous night, and soon, he was far enough offshore to be picked up. Taking a chance he could not be seen from the shore, he signaled again and then ceased paddling. The paddling had been very strenuous, and his injured shoulder was on fire. Maggie had cleaned it before he left and placed a fresh bandage on it, but the salt spray and sweat had turned the bandage into a useless wet glob of gauze.

A half moon shone low in the clear, star-spattered sky, casting a golden line of light across the water. Christian sat in the raft and listened for the sound of the submarine. Soon, he saw a dark silhouette moving toward him and then heard the soft voices of men calling out to him. "Approach on the starboard side and we will help you up to the bridge."

With the precision of experienced and well-trained sailors, Christian was brought onboard, the raft secured, and the boat made ready to sail. The smell of diesel fuel, cooking odors, and unwashed bodies overpowered him as he climbed down the ladder and into the control room. How quickly he had forgotten the unpleasant conditions of living on board a submarine that had been at sea for months. Space, clean air, and the scent of a woman were now luxuries he no longer would enjoy.

Kapitänleutnant Müller-Stöckheim welcomed him back and inquired after Braun. Christian relayed the story of the previous evening's gunfight and how Braun had been killed by an American policeman. He showed the kapitän his wound and told him that he had hidden in a house and found some bandages but did not tell the kapitän about Maggie.

Kapitänleutnant Müller-Stöckheim was sympathetic, but clearly disappointed to learn Christian had not been successful. He did not know what would happen to Christian, but he knew failing to deliver Braun was going to be a great blow to the Reich's war effort. Failures were expendable and ended up on the Russian front.

Müller-Stöckheim ordered the medic to tend to Christian's wound and then instructed the cook to give him something to eat. Fresh vegetables and meat had been consumed long ago. Now, the men were subsisting on very basic rations, which consisted of a perpetual pot of soup containing whatever could be found to add to the mix every day, along with stale bread. After eating Maggie's home cooked food and inhaling the stench inside the submarine, Christian could not stomach the potato soup offered to him, so instead, he found an empty bunk and fell into a deep sleep. He did not awaken for 6 hours and only then because the officer coming off watch needed a place to sleep and was not willing to give up his bunk during his short period off watch.

While Christian slept, the kapitän gave orders to head out to sea and then west toward Pensacola, Mobile, and the Mississippi Pass where they would search for more ships.

Chapter Thirty-Two

Maggie wandered around the house in a stupor, trying to absorb what had happened. She had a restless energy, as if she were adrift with no clear destination. In an attempt to bring herself back to reality, she washed the dishes from her last meal with Christian and then fell into one of the cushioned chairs on the porch. For a while, she stared into the distance in a daze, asking herself the one question which had no answer: *What in God's name was I thinking?*

On one hand, there was a deep sense of relief that he was gone; but on the other, an even greater ache of loss. Maggie didn't know who she was anymore. Living on her own had created a very different woman. She had slept with two men. The first, John Logan, had been a huge mistake. He had been a scoundrel who had not only taken advantage of her, but had caused her to question her judgment. How could she have been fooled so easily, and was *she* ultimately responsible for what had happened to Theresa? Maggie didn't even want to think about the episode at the outhouse or helping to hide Christian from the law. These had not been her proudest moments, but it seemed like the only thing to do at the time.

Christian was an enigma. He was a man who was pulled into the war and to Grayton Beach through circumstances beyond his control. Maggie had seen the real Christian Wolfe, an intelligent, decent man, challenged to perform tasks that tested his character and endurance. He seemed to be at war with himself. Was he a traitor to America, but more importantly, was *she* also a traitor for helping him?

Emotional exhaustion finally overwhelmed her and she fell asleep in the chair. Awakening later with a stiff crick in her neck, Maggie shuffled into the bedroom and without undressing, fell onto the disheveled bed where they had made love only hours before. His masculine odor still permeated the sheets. Maggie breathed in deeply to soak up every vestige of Christian that she could. She did not wake until the sound of Theresa opening the screen door the next morning brought her back to reality.

Jumping out of bed, she called out to Theresa, "Hi, I'm going to hop into the shower! Make some coffee and then we need to talk." She quickly stripped the sheets off the bed and threw them in a heap on the floor. She would wash them later, but she did not want Theresa to see or smell the residue of her and Christian's lovemaking. The less Theresa knew the better for both of them. Then she took a quick shower.

When she had showered and dressed, Maggie padded barefoot into the kitchen and poured a large cup of coffee. Theresa had brought a brown paper bag filled with fresh butterbeans and four ears of corn. She had finished shucking the corn and was picking the last of the fine, yellow silk threads from between the kernels, then she was going to start shelling the beans and put them on the stove with some ham.

"Mornin', Miss Maggie. How did the glass in the front door get broke?"

"That's what I need to talk with you about, Theresa."

Maggie then tried to recount the drama of the previous night as simply as she could. It was too complicated to re-create in detail, and the less Theresa knew, the less she would have to remember if ever asked.

Theresa looked at Maggie in disbelief and could barely string a sentence together. "Lordy, Miss Maggie, you done got yo'self smack dab into the middle of the war. Are you gonna be all right?"

Maggie waved away Theresa's concern with her hand as if shooing away an errant fly. "I haven't gotten myself into the war, but too much has happened here, and I've decided it's time for me to go back home to Birmingham. I don't know what I expected to find here. I thought I'd have time to grieve and find my bearings, but instead, I found a side of myself that I never knew existed. I don't know if I should be proud of myself or ashamed. But the best part has been knowing you, Theresa."

Maggie could see that the news was a shock to Theresa and not what she wanted to hear. Theresa looked away for a few seconds and when she looked back at Maggie, her eyes were wet with tears. "You've been a friend to me, Miss Maggie, and I'm gonna miss you very much. I know you want to return to your home and maybe you can find yo'self a good man. You deserve someone to look after you. You sure do."

"Thanks, Theresa, you've been a good friend and companion, and I'll miss you terribly. We've been through a lot in a very short period of time, and we share secrets that we will take to our graves. I feel terrible that I'm responsible for what happened to you, and I want to give you something I hope will help you and Robert get a new start in life."

Maggie pulled an envelope out of a drawer and placed it on the table between them. "There's almost $4,000 here that I kind of inherited recently. For personal reasons, I don't want it, but I want you and Robert to have it."

"Damn, Miss Maggie, that's a lot of money. You sure you want to give that much money to me?" Theresa said, as she reached over and pulled the envelope closer to her, fearing that Maggie might suddenly change her mind.

With tears in her eyes, Maggie said, "There isn't a soul more deserving than you. I hope it'll help you and Robert begin a new life." Squeezing Theresa's hand and then wiping her own eyes, she asked, "What do you think you'll do when I leave?"

"This is such a surprise. I don't know what we might do now. I think it'd be best for us to move north. Colored folks like us don't get much of a break down in this part of the country. Robert has some kin that moved up north to Baltimore. They was able to get nice jobs in the factories and was able to buy a home. This money will buy us a new car, and we can go up that away, I guess. Maybe we could even buy us a house. I'll see what Robert wants to do. I'm kinda like you, though. I've had about as much of this place as I can stand. After what happened to me here, I'd like to get a fresh start and put all this behind me, like you."

"Well, I think that's a good plan, Theresa. Let's celebrate our last day together by cooking up some of that corn and butterbeans you brought. Maybe make some cornbread and fry up some chicken. You can take the leftovers home and surprise Robert with the news."

As they rose from the table, Theresa reached out and hugged Maggie tightly around the waist. "You have been the best friend I ever had, and I'll love and remember you forever. I don't blame you for what happened to me. We were both victims of that man."

"Thank you very much, Theresa. I needed to hear that. You will always be in my mind and heart. In the envelope with the money, I've written my address in Birmingham so that we can stay in touch. Now, let's get started shelling these butterbeans before we both start to cry again."

Early the next morning, Maggie loaded her car with the few possessions that she had brought with her to Grayton Beach and drove north.

Her first stop was DeFuniak Springs where she went to the hospital to check on Jim. She did not feel she could leave the area without saying good-bye and to make sure he was recovering from his wound. When she entered his room, she saw that he was up and dressed. A white cloth sling held his arm and shoulder in place. A petite and very attractive nurse in a starched white uniform and cap was instructing him on how to take care of his shoulder. When Maggie walked into the room, Jim's face lit up with pleasure.

"Maggie, I'm so glad you came to see me. I'm being discharged and ready to leave this place. The service was good, but the food was terrible," he chuckled as he looked at the nurse. "Maggie, I would like you to meet my favorite nurse, Polly. She has been taking very good care of me."

Maggie could see from the way Polly looked at Jim and vice versa that there was a lot unspoken going on between the two of them that went beyond the patient-nurse role. She couldn't help but smile.

"I'm returning to Birmingham and wanted to say good-bye and make sure you were on the mend. We had quite an experience together. It will be one that neither of us will ever forget. I hope you have a speedy recovery. It appears that you are in good hands now."

Handing Jim a piece of paper, she added, "This is my address and telephone number in Birmingham. If you or the military officials need to talk to me, you can reach me there."

Maggie kissed Jim on the cheek and told Polly to take good care of him. Polly smiled and stated that that was exactly what she intended to do. With that, Maggie turned and walked out of the room and outside to her car. Without looking back, she headed north to Birmingham.

Chapter Thirty=Three

U-67 SPENT THE NEXT FEW DAYS CRUISING WEST TOWARD THE Mississippi Pass, south of New Orleans. During this time, they located and sank the tankers, *Paul H. Harwood, Benjamin Brewster,* and *R. W. Gallagher,* and the motor ship, *Baynard.* Being at sea for months had drained much of the crew's enthusiasm, but sinking four ships within days of each other had caused morale to soar and the excitement was palpable. It had been a good mission with a total of eight ships sunk thus far.

There were other German submarines in the area and on several occasions, the crew of U-67 heard the sounds of U-boat propellers on their hydrophones. During the day, Kapitänleutnant Müller-Stöckheim ordered the boat to the bottom of the sea, where they would remain quiet but cool. It was a strategy which was effective, but the confinement made for very long days. After dark, they would surface and prowl the shipping lanes. It felt good being able to move about and talk before submerging again, only to be smothered once more, by silence and inactivity.

The routine was broken when they began to run dangerously low on provisions and fuel. Much to the delight of the crew, early one morning in the latter days of July, Kapitänleutnant Müller-Stöckheim picked up the microphone and made the announcement they had been waiting weeks to hear. "Gentlemen, we have succeeded in our mission. It is time to return home."

Whoops of joy resonated throughout the vessel. The order was given to turn the boat and aim south through the Straits of Florida and then east to France, where their loved ones would be waiting. The long-suppressed desire for fresh fruits, vegetables, meat, and wine resurfaced, and the anticipation of home gave the men a boost to their morale. Long-simmering irritations and arguments from living in close confinement together were forgotten as the crew busily prepared the boat for the long voyage across the Atlantic. They knew that under Kapitänleutnant Müller-Stöckheim's command, they had pulled off one of the most successful voyages of the war.

The trip was uneventful until they were almost home. The boat sailed above the surface unless there was danger of being spotted. The fresh air and sunshine was a tonic for the men who would lie on the deck in calm weather, soak up the sun, and breathe the clean air for as long as possible before returning to the stale environment below. All German submarines had cockroaches on board, and U-67 was no exception. The longer the voyage, the worst the problem became until eventually, the sailors just brushed the insects off their clothes and food without further thought.

Christian's wound began to heal. After regaining his sea legs, he fell into the same daily routine as the sailors. Everyone was anxious to be going home, and he was no exception—except he really did not have a home to go to.

While the boat had spent long days submerged, Christian had had plenty of time to think about the word "home." He no longer thought of it as a place but more a person with whom he wanted to be, such as a family member or close friend. He realized that Maggie was the only person he knew who could create the desire in him to settle down. He thought about her often, knowing the chances of seeing her again were infinitesimal. He had to think about his immediate future, and she, unfortunately, was not a part of it.

During the trip, he began to reconsider returning to Berlin. He would have to meet with Schmidt and give his report of Braun's escape and death. He did not know what would happen to him because he had failed, but he was not overly concerned that he would be punished, probably only reassigned. Since he had no control over his future with the Reich, his only option would be to convince them that his language and engineering skills could be better used elsewhere.

Since Christian could not solve his immediate problem, he decided to enjoy the trip back. Being at sea again was wonderful. He took pleasure in breathing in the fresh salt air and gazing upon the blue skies during their voyage. He hoped in the future that he would be able to go to sea and not worry about enemy airplanes trying to sink the ship that he was traveling on.

The voyage went without incident—until August first, when, while cruising on the surface near the Bay of Biscay, they were spotted by an Allied bomber. They dived quickly, but not before the plane had dropped several bombs and caused some minor damage. Nerves were taut again after so many days of freedom from combat alert.

On August 8, 1942, U-67 arrived back at the port of Lorient, France, after 81 days at sea. She came into her berth flying eight pennants from her conning tower and received a hero's welcome of flowers and a military band and a personal greeting from Admiral Karl Donitz, the commander of the entire German submarine service. This was the most successful cruise of U-67 and Kapitänleutnant Müller-Stöckheim's career.

Christian watched as the submarine was docked and returned below to gather his few possessions and prepare to disembark from the vessel. After saying good-bye to the crew members and to the kapitän he had come to admire, Christian crossed the boarding plank with his seabag slung over his shoulder. He was immediately approached by a soldier wearing a crisp brown uniform.

"Herr Wolfe, I am Corporal Herder. I have been assigned to drive you and Braun back to Berlin. Please follow me."

Christian was unnerved by the promptness of his escort. It was clear Colonel Schmidt was wasting no time in getting Braun back into Germany and the severity of his failure hit him. *Might as well get that into the open right now.* "Thank you, Corporal, but Herr Braun will not be joining us."

He followed Herder to a large Daimler sedan with swastika flags on the hood and stepped into the backseat. The corporal closed the door behind him, climbed behind the wheel, started the car, and pulled away from the dock. Christian turned and looked out the back window to see the men embracing their loved ones and then the car turned a corner and the voyage was now just a memory.

Christian and Corporal Herder drove through villages and along country roads toward Berlin. Bombed and burned buildings were becoming more and more common. Occasionally, they would pass the carcass of a burnt-out military vehicle by the road.

They reached Paris by nightfall and lodged in a hotel in the Sixth Arrondissement, near Luxembourg Gardens. That evening, Christian walked through the streets of the city, amazed by so much gaiety around him in spite of the war. Cafés and restaurants were open and music flowed into the streets. As he watched the French girls flirting with the German soldiers, he wondered what would happen when the war was over. Would the French accept the German occupation, and would the pain of the invasion of their homeland fade with time?

In no mood for a party, Christian sought a quiet café where he had dinner of veal shank with fresh vegetables and a cold bottle of Chardonnay. In 2 days, he would be back in Berlin with Colonel Schmidt to report about his failed mission. Christian had a feeling that Schmidt was not going to be too sympathetic, and the thought of meeting with him was unsettling.

The next morning, Corporal Herder pulled up in front of the hotel exactly at 8:00 o'clock, and the two men followed the traffic exiting the city. It would take another 2 days to reach Berlin. As they drove through the countryside, Christian alternated between watching the farms and villages go by and dozing off in the comfortable leather seats of the Daimler. They passed troops on the highway, and their car was given the right of way as they approached the slowly moving convoys. The car with its swastika flags telegraphed the importance of its occupants, and when Herder sounded the horn, the soldiers and vehicles pulled to the side of the road to let them pass.

They drove throughout the day, stopping occasionally for a break, and by late afternoon, they were approaching the German border. The surrounding countryside varied from rolling hills and farmland to sections of forest. Now, they were traveling through a section of thick forest outside the city of Metz when he heard the unmistakable sound of a gunshot. Corporal Herder suddenly slumped over the wheel, blood seeping from his head. The bullet had killed him instantly. The car swerved, and Christian lunged over the seat, pushing Herder aside, and grabbed the steering wheel in an attempt to regain control before the car swerved into a ditch that ran along the side of the road.

Christian's adrenaline was pumping at record speed as he stepped on the accelerator, leaving a trail of smoke as he sped away. After distancing himself several kilometers from the site of the ambush, he pulled the car over to the side of the road and climbed out, his legs shaking. His survival instincts took over as he sought the pistol located in his seabag. Quickly, he returned to where Herder lay and withdrew his Luger from its holster.

Now adequately armed, he grabbed his bag and ran into the forest. His actions had been intuitive, and it was not until he was deep in the forest that he stopped to catch his breath. Shortly, he found a shallow cave on a steep bank leading down to a stream and crawled as far into it as he could. If there were any animal claiming it as a den, Christian would have to deal with it, but luckily, he was the only inhabitant.

Suddenly, it struck him what he had done. *Why did I leave the car and the opportunity to return to Berlin?* Intuitively, he knew he did not want to return to Germany and Berlin. After seeing what Germany had done under Hitler's leadership, he had lost faith in his homeland. He did not trust Schmidt and realized he now had a perfect alibi if the Germans caught him as he made his way to Switzerland. He could say that Herder had been shot and he had been taken captive by a group of Resistance fighters and interrogated. His circumstance now offered him an opportunity to think through his options.

It was decision time. He could return to the car, drive to the border, and tell the guards exactly what happened, then continue on to Berlin and to an uncertain future within the Reich. Or, he could hide in France and using his American identification, attempt to make it out of the country to safety. He knew the answer and reconciled that it could possibly be a deadly choice.

For 2 days he crept through the forests and along roadside hedges, sleeping under trees in the deep woods. Late on the second day, he saw a farm located some distance from the main road. Christian hadn't eaten since Paris and was famished. Hunger was beginning to sap his strength. He knew he could not make it much further without nourishment. He thought this would be his best opportunity to find something to eat, so he hid in the forest until midnight and long after all lights had been turned off in the farmhouse.

Then, creeping silently into the barn adjacent to the farmhouse, he stole four eggs from the caged hens while praying that they didn't start a ruckus and alert the farmer. Carefully cradling his stash, he returned to his hiding place, where he cracked the raw eggs and swallowed each one in quick succession. The result was almost immediate as he felt his energy return. With a full stomach, he burrowed under a layer of leaves and fell sound asleep.

The click of a shotgun's safety being switched off and the voices of two men standing over him speaking to him in French awakened him with a start.

Chapter Thirty-Four

CHRISTIAN SLOWLY CLIMBED OUT FROM UNDER THE LEAVES, holding both arms high in the air. He could speak some French but was not fluent. The two men standing before him, each aiming a gun at his gut, were dressed in work clothes. Christian deduced they had come from the nearby farm where he had stolen the eggs.

They were rough men, used to hard labor. Both men had deeply tanned faces with several days' growth of whiskers. One was considerably older than the other, and Christian guessed they were father and son. He could see the sun had been up for a while, and he had slept much longer than he should have. The men must have followed his tracks from the barn. The younger man spoke first.

"Who are you, and what are you doing here?"

Christian knew his life depended on his response. *I'm going to have to take a chance that they are not supporters of the Vichy government. If they think I'm German, I'm as good as dead. They'll shoot me and bury me right there.* Although being discovered by a Frenchman during his escape had been in the back of his mind, he actually had not thought about what he would say if caught. *Will they believe me if I tell them the truth?* He was afraid if he lied he would trip himself up in the deception and place himself at greater risk. *I hope my French is up to the task.*

"My name is Christian Wolfe. My driver taking me back to Berlin was shot on the road a few kilometers from here. I was sent on a mission against my will to America, which I failed to carry out, and was being transported back for questioning. En route to Berlin, my driver was killed by a sniper. I took that opportunity to escape and ran into the forest. I've been on the move since then. I hope you are not working with the Germans, because if you are, you can shoot me now. If they find me, I'm a dead man."

Neither farmer said a word. Their expressions remained fixed and unreadable. Christian didn't know if they understood his broken French, or if they simply didn't believe him.

"I have some American identification in my pocket to prove that I was in America if you would like to see it." When that still resulted in no noticeable change in their demeanor, he decided to apologize for stealing the eggs.

"Sorry I took the eggs, but I was starving. I haven't eaten in days. I'll be happy to pay you for them. I would appreciate it if you would let me go. I just want to get out of the country and away from this area. I'm sure the Germans are looking for me by now."

Finally, the younger man spoke, his expression suggesting that he believed what Christian had told him.

"Yes, they are. They were here yesterday, asking if we had seen anyone. They didn't seem to be too happy about losing you. They don't seem to know what to think about your disappearance and are trying to determine whether you were kidnapped. Come with us. We'll hide you until we can determine what to do with you. My name is Pierre, and this is my father, Olivier. This is our farm."

Christian followed the men out of the woods and into a wheat field. They walked through the rows until they reached a two-storey tan stone-and-stucco house with a weathered barrel-tile roof. The barn where Christian had stolen the eggs sat across a stone courtyard and a truck with a staked bed for transporting the crops was parked in front. The windows of the house were all open to allow fresh air to flow through. Light, lacy curtains danced with the morning breeze. A middle-aged lady in a flowered dress was removing loaves of bread from the oven and placing them on the kitchen table.

Making rudimentary introductions, Olivier said, "This is my wife, Claudette."

Christian didn't know how to respond, so he smiled in an attempt to look grateful. Olivier then spoke to his wife. "This man says his name is Christian. We found him hiding in the forest. He is the one that stole the eggs. He says he escaped from the Germans and is trying to get out of the country."

Placing her hands on her hips, which Christian read as a bad sign, Claudette looked directly into Christian's face and said, "Well, mister whoever-you-are, because of you, I don't have eggs for breakfast this morning."

Her scowl reminded Christian of being a small child scolded by his mother, but to his surprise, she continued by saying, "We're all going to have to get by on bread and jam. Would you like some coffee?"

With the reprimand complete and the preliminaries of his discovery out of the way, Christian sat at the thick wooden kitchen table with a steaming cup of the best coffee he had ever tasted in his life. Claudette pushed a plate of fresh baked bread and bowls of homemade butter and jam before him. He had to restrain himself from reaching across and taking the entire meal for himself. He didn't miss the eggs, but he knew the others did. Fortunately, they were kind enough not to make him feel any worse about stealing them than he already did.

"Now that you've eaten, what are you going to do?" the younger man asked.

"Unfortunately, I don't have a plan. I just know that I'm not going back to Berlin. If I can get to Switzerland I think I'll be safe. If I can't get to Switzerland, I'll work my way to the coast and try to make it to England. Can I stay here for a few days? I have some American dollars and would be willing to pay you. I can also help with chores. In a couple of days, I'll move on."

Olivier placed his coffee cup on the table and looked at Christian. "Well, we can certainly use the help, but I wouldn't know what to do with American dollars right now. If the Germans return and find you, we will all be shot, so you need to understand the risk we are taking. If Pierre and Claudette are willing, we will hide you for a short time. You can sleep in the barn, but you can only stay for a few days, and then you must move on."

"Thanks. I'll help you with the farm where I can. I'm an engineer, so if there is anything that you need fixing, let me know and I'll take a look at it."

"Good. You can take a look at the motor that operates the well pump. It's not working properly. Maybe you can figure out what the problem is."

When Christian finished breakfast, they walked across the courtyard to the barn. He was shown the hayloft where he could sleep. Claudette brought a light blanket and pillow for him. He stated the accommodations would be fine and asked to see the motor that operated the pump for the well.

The motor had been manufactured in 1906. The quartz insulators were cracked and dirty. Gingerly, he dismantled the motor, careful not to damage the cloth-covered wire, and cleaned the fragile pieces of quartz. Reassembling the motor, he instructed Pierre to turn the power back on. The motor worked perfectly.

"Thanks. We don't have enough money to buy another motor even if we could find one."

"Glad I can help. It's been a long time since I've used a skill to personally help someone. I'm actually a civil, not an electrical, engineer."

"We have some flooding in a field near a stream. Think you can help us figure out a way to drain the water off?"

"Now that's more in line with my strengths. Let's take a look."

For the next 2 days, Christian worked with the family, eating with them and sleeping on hay in the barn. On the evening of the second day, Olivier and Pierre left after dinner and did not return until late in the evening. Christian heard them return and watched as they climbed out of their truck. Olivier was helping Pierre into the house. The younger man seemed hurt and was holding onto his father as they walked from the truck.

At breakfast, Christian noticed that Pierre was limping. Olivier seemed worried. Christian decided to take a chance. "I know this is none of my business, but what happened?"

"We had a run-in with some German soldiers last night. Pierre was seen talking with some people connected with the Resistance. When they were approached, they ran, but Pierre was shot in the leg. Fortunately, he was just grazed, but I'm afraid that some German soldiers are going to try to find him and take him away for questioning. You need to leave before they come."

Christian thought for a minute. "You've taken a big risk just by letting me stay here, and I would like to pay you back if I can. I've made the decision to help France and the Allies win the war. I'm willing to do whatever it takes to make that happen. Maybe I could use my engineering skills somehow."

Olivier said nothing for a long time, then looked at Pierre, who nodded softly at his father. Olivier turned to Christian and spoke.

"How would you feel about working for the Resistance? We could use your expertise in speaking English. You could help us communicate with Allied pilots who have been shot down and on radio broadcasts. We are a dedicated force, but we need someone with your skills. If you're willing to work with us, we'll protect you as best we can."

Taking a sip of coffee in order to give himself a few seconds to think about his answer, he responded by saying, "Where would I live?"

"We'll work with our comrades to get you and Pierre to Lyon. Most of our intelligence is there. They can figure out where to hide you and how to make the best use of your skills. Lyon is a large city where you can hide more easily than in this area. What do you say?"

"I think it's a good plan, but why would the Resistance trust me? I could be a spy as far as you know."

The older man spoke. "I'm a good judge of character, and my gut tells me that you're telling us the truth. You'll be given small assignments at first that will not endanger any mission. As our trust grows, you will be brought closer into the inner workings and allowed more freedom. If there is ever any reason to suspect your loyalty, you will probably never know it. You'd be killed when you least expect it."

"That sounds reasonable to me," Christian said, as he looked the older man in the eye.

"Then let's put you in the back of the truck under some hay and drive toward Lyon. I'll take you part of the way and then you and Pierre will be transferred to another truck or two before you make it all the way. When you arrive in Lyon, someone will meet you and take it from there. For everyone's protection, we don't know the names of the people in Lyon or elsewhere."

The next evening at dusk, Christian and Pierre crawled out of the concealed metal box installed below the floor of a carpenter's truck and onto the busy streets of Lyon. They were met by a young man in a rough brown wool suit and a traditional beret. He introduced himself only as Jules and instructed Christian to follow him. They left the main street and walked through dark, low tunnels that ran below and between the buildings, accessed by inconspicuous doors that might have been mistaken for entrances to homes or garages.

After a short journey winding through the city, they emerged on a quiet side street and went into a building with heavy doors reinforced with wide iron bars. When they entered, Christian could see that it was both a home and a meeting place, as several men and women sat around the room in straight, wooden chairs, listening to a shortwave radio sitting on a table in the middle of the room.

Everyone looked up as Christian and Jules entered. When they saw Jules, they relaxed and turned their attention back to the radio, staring at it as if they could see what was being broadcast. For a few minutes, no one moved and nothing was said. It was only when it was clear that the broadcast was finished that a man stood, stretched as if he had been sitting for a long time, and approached Christian.

"Welcome. My name is Jean Moulin. I am the local co-ordinator for the Resistance here in Lyon. Word of your defection has traveled fast. I appreciate your interest in assisting us." Moulin introduced the other men and women in the room by their first names and then led Christian to another room where he poured each of them a glass of wine.

Christian noted that Jean wore a wool scarf around his neck even in the warm room. Later, he would be told that Moulin had been imprisoned in 1940 for refusing to sign a German document falsely blaming French Army troops for some civilian murders and had attempted to commit suicide by cutting his throat with a piece of broken glass. When released, he always wore a scarf to hide the scar.

"We need you to help us coordinate the airdrops of equipment and supplies from England. Your knowledge of English will enable us to communicate accurately with our contacts there. Another role will be locating and conceal-ing the Allied pilots before the Germans can get to them. I don't think I need to tell you that if you are caught by the Germans, you will be shown no mercy and will be killed immediately. That is, if you're lucky. If they were ever to find out who you are, they would look at you as a traitor to the Reich and then you would pray for death to come quickly. Can you live with this?"

With their eyes locked on each other, Christian simply nodded to Moulin in acceptance. There was no need for words. The moment Christian had bolted from the German Daimler, he had irrevocably altered the direction of his life. He was a man without a country, and his future extended only as far as today. Although this should have alarmed him, he felt a sense of relief. Christian Wolfe was no longer on the sidelines of life.

SEPTEMBER 1943

Chapter Thirty-Five

As Olivier had predicted, at first, Christian was only given minor assignments of observing troop movements and reporting back. After a few weeks, these increased in number and difficulty. He was asked to participate in the sabotage of German military vehicles en route to a combat zone by pouring sand into the gas tanks while the soldiers slept nearby on the ground. Soon thereafter, he was sent on a mission to wire and detonate railroad tracks on bridges the German military were using to transport men and materials.

Meanwhile, he began to communicate with England regarding supply drops and assisted with hiding the Allied pilots that had been shot down. He exhibited skill and resourcefulness, and his efforts began to be noticed by senior Resistance leaders. As the weeks passed, he assumed a leadership role to organize efforts on a larger and more dangerous scale.

He met many good and loyal French citizens, almost all of whom had suffered personally from the occupation and the war. Many families had seen spouses or children killed before their eyes by order of the German Gestapo. He held brave young men in his arms as they died attempting to escape from missions to destroy railroad lines or bridges that did not go as planned. Although each assignment was completely different, Christian adapted. But he never became accustomed to dealing with the death it generated.

On one occasion, he was staying at an apartment being used as a safe house on the outskirts of the city. It was the home of a young widow who had recently lost her husband in a failed attempt to blow up a bridge. While fearing for her husband's safety, she had supported his efforts with the Resistance, but she had not been prepared for the brutality of the Germans. Apprehended in the act of passing information to another member in the Resistance, he was shot with the other conspirator just before they were to be loaded on a truck, supposedly for a prisoner of war camp. Her grief was so deep that any attempt to console her was met without response from vacant eyes that stared through Christian as if he did not exist. Although her body was there, her mind was not connected to it.

Christian did not know how to help her, so he just encouraged her to eat and let her lie in bed day and night, hoping that she might fall asleep long enough to escape the pain for a little while. Each time he checked on her, he found her staring aimlessly at the wall or up at the ceiling.

One night when Christian was lying in his bed and reading by the light of a dim oil lamp, his door opened and she entered, wearing a thin cotton nightdress. Even in the near darkness, he could easily make out the shape of her breasts and hips as she approached him. She sat on the side of the bed, reached over, and turned off the lamp, then lay down beside him.

"Please hold me. I need to feel a man next to me and to be held."

Christian put his arms around her and held her close for a few minutes. Then she turned and kissed him hard on the mouth. "Make love to me. I want to have a man hold me and make love to me," she whispered.

"I'll hold you tonight, and you'll feel better tomorrow, but I will not make love to you," whispered Christian gently. "I cannot take the place in your heart that your husband holds, and you will only feel contempt for yourself in the morning. Your grief will pass and when it does, you will recover and life will go on. You are very young, and although you will always miss your husband, you will eventually find another man to love."

Sobbing until she was exhausted, she fell into a sound sleep in his arms. Christian found he couldn't move for fear of waking her up out of the deep sleep. He drifted in and out of sleep, waking up with a stiff neck and numb arm from holding her just as dawn was breaking. Silently, he slid out of bed, kissing her gently on the forehead while she still slept. It was time for him to go.

Word spread quickly in late June that their leader, Jean Moulin, whom Christian had met over a year earlier and had frequent communication with since, had been captured and had died in prison. Details of how he died were sketchy. It was not known whether he had been tortured to death or had committed suicide, but news of his death was devastating to everyone in the Resistance. It also gave its members a stronger resolve for their mission.

A few weeks later, Christian was sitting reading a newspaper outside a café in Aix-en-Provence waiting for his contact to arrive. Usually he felt dangerously exposed sitting outside, but today was an exceptionally beautiful day and the area of the Luberon was the most beautiful country that he had ever seen. He thought when the war was over, assuming that the Allies won, he could live here happily forever.

Sipping a cup of coffee while observing the shop owners go about their daily routine, he noticed two German soldiers enter the square and approach the café. With his senses on high alert, he kept his face hidden behind the newspaper. They strolled by the stores, greeting the shopkeepers and inspecting the merchandise that they were selling. The soldiers were talking to each other.

"I'd like to buy something nice for Helga. She'd really like a pretty scarf or some perfume. This part of France is so beautiful, and the villages are so quaint. I hope that when the war is over, I can bring her here and show her Provence. Let's just hope the war will soon end and we can come here on holiday."

"I agree with you. This is so different from any place in Germany I've ever visited. After we win the war, I could be very happy living here. I've learned to really enjoy the wines and cheeses, too. So much lighter and more flavorful than the sausages and cabbages back home, don't you think?"

Christian listened as they strolled along and window-shopped. They seemed like normal men, with natural feelings of missing their homes and loved ones. The men continued to stroll at a leisurely pace until they had passed through the square, moving toward the main boulevard that led to a large house that the military had taken over as a barrack for the soldiers.

Once the soldiers left the square and Christian began to relax, he saw his contacts entering from the opposite side. He did not know the name or the identity of who was meeting him, only that it would be a young couple acting as lovers. They were bringing information on the size of a German garrison that had set up camp 25 kilometers outside the city. The young man, who couldn't have been more than 20 years old, was accompanied by an equally young, pretty girl, and they held hands as if they were lovers walking out together on a sunny day. It bothered Christian that such young people were involved in activity this dangerous. They couldn't imagine how many lives were dependent on their ability to succeed.

They approached the café and sat at a small round table next to Christian. The young man lit a cigarette while waiting for the waiter and nervously played with the ashtray on the table. Christian ignored the couple and continued to read the newspaper, occasionally taking a sip of coffee. When the waiter had taken the couple's order and returned inside the café, the man turned and spoke to Christian.

"Excuse me. Do you know where we might find a shop called Maison Normandie?"

"Yes, it's two blocks farther down the avenue. It has blue shutters."

This was the correct question and answer, so the young man slipped an envelope from his coat pocket between the pages of a newspaper that he had brought with him. The couple took their time sipping on their aperitifs and when finished, smiled at Christian and walked away, leaving the newspaper behind. Christian reached over and picked it up before anyone could take it. Rising from his seat, he called to the couple. "Monsieur, you've left your paper."

Turning back to Christian, the young man replied, "I've finished with it. You may have it if you wish." Christian smiled in thanks and returned to his seat. Carefully unfolding the newspaper, he slipped the envelope into his pocket. He sat for a while longer and pretended to read the paper and then motioned to the waiter for his bill.

Appearing unhurried and at ease, he walked along the avenue for a few minutes, occasionally stopping to look at wares displayed in the shop windows, although he was actually studying their reflection to make sure he was not being followed. It was hard not to be paranoid, he thought. Anyone could be a spy for the Germans. He had learned not to trust anyone, and living like this, he realized, had become exhausting.

He turned down an alley between two buildings and entered a side door leading to a small foyer. Finally out of view of any observer, he hurriedly climbed the stairs leading to an apartment on the third floor. Once inside, he locked the door and removed the envelope from his pocket. Opening it, he saw a series of numbers on a plain sheet of paper. Each number designated the quantity of troops, tanks, military vehicles, and armament of the German garrison.

Having memorized the numbers, he tore the sheet into small pieces and placing them in an ashtray, lit the fragments with a match, and made sure that there was nothing left but ash. His next move would be to radio the information to the Allies from a secure site at a farmhouse outside town.

That evening, Christian was walking back to the square where he had met the young couple when a shopkeeper approached him and asked Christian if he had a match. The man held his pipe in his hands while Christian struck a match against the rough stone exterior of the shop and listened as he whispered.

"We have a serious problem. The couple you met this afternoon were followed by the Germans to a house a half-kilometer from here. Fortunately, they saw the soldiers coming to the front door and were able to subdue them. The soldiers had been sent there to arrest them. If these soldiers don't return with the couple soon, the Gestapo will become suspicious. We cannot let them take this couple. The mission will be compromised. They will be tortured until they tell what they know, then killed."

"Our only chance is to get to them before the Gestapo does. Give me the address," Christian said.

He returned to the apartment, reached behind a chest, and retrieved a Luger that he had taken from a dead German soldier. Carefully, he slid it beneath his belt behind his back and walked to the address the shopkeeper had given him.

It was an old house on a side street leading from the main boulevard. He knew he didn't have very much time before the soldiers would be missed and replacements sent. Pretending to be the older brother of the girl, he knocked hard on the door and in an angry voice shouted, "Claudette, you better come out here now! I know you're in there with your lover. I'm responsible for you, and he is not worthy of you. Our parents, rest their souls, would turn in their graves if they knew you were with him. Open the door right now!"

Christian transferred the pistol from behind his back to his pocket, his finger on the trigger, ready to pull and shoot if necessary. He was hoping whoever opened the door would instantly give him a clue about what was going on inside. As he had so often in the past, he was relying on instinct. The girl opened the door and motioned him to come in. Fear radiated from her face. Christian didn't think she would be able to talk.

"We were followed here. Someone betrayed us. Fortunately, we saw them coming up to the front door, and when they banged on the door, demanding to be let in, Jacques grabbed his shotgun. I let them in, and Jacques ordered them to lie down on the floor. We've taken their weapons, but we don't know what to do now. We sent the owner of the house to tell someone. We're so afraid. Can you please help us?"

Christian followed the girl into the living room where the young man was standing over the two soldiers, who were lying facedown with their arms outstretched. As Christian examined the men, he recognized them as the two soldiers that he had seen walking earlier in the square discussing gifts for their wives. The young man whose name was Jacques was shaking as he pointed the gun at the Germans. The situation was clearly more than he was able to deal with, and when he saw Christian, a sense of relief swept over him.

Jacques, speaking nervously, related the whole story to Christian. "I asked them what they wanted, and they said they were here to arrest us and take us to a place where we would be questioned. They had been given orders to pick up a young couple at this address and take them to headquarters. That's all that they knew."

Christian realized he was going to have to take charge of the situation. Just a few hours ago, these four people appeared to be enjoying the beautiful day, unaware of how their lives were about to collide. Only two of these four would survive, and Christian knew he was the person who would have to make that decision.

He pulled the Luger from his pocket, telling Jacques he would take over, then asked him if he had a car or truck. Jacques replied that he had access to a truck that delivered meat to the markets. Christian told him to go get it and bring it to the back of the house and to take the girl with him. The couple readily jumped at the chance to leave, almost running out the door.

"How long will it take you to bring the truck here?" asked Christian.

"No more than 15 minutes."

"Good, because time really matters. Now go and do not tell anyone. Your life may depend on your silence. When you get here, back the truck as close to the rear door as possible."

Twenty minutes later, Christian heard the truck as it drove up to the back of the house through an alley. When the vehicle had been backed up within a few feet of the door, Christian ordered Jacques to open the rear doors and then to come inside. He told the girl to stay by the truck. When Jacques entered the house, he saw Christian throw the lifeless body of one of the soldiers over his shoulder and move toward the truck. It was clear that the man who had saved them had shot and killed the two German soldiers.

"Now is not the time to be squeamish. Bring the other one quickly."

Jacques saw the blood seeping from the head of the soldier on the floor and immediately bent over and vomited. Breathing deeply to regain his composure, and with tears streaming down his cheeks, he dragged the dead man by his arms across the floor to the door where Christian lifted him over his shoulder and laid him on the floor of the truck. He then went back into the house and returned with a blanket to cover the men.

"You must both leave town now and do not return, at least until the war is over. I can't tell you where to go, but you can't stay here. I will leave the truck about 10 kilometers outside the city on the road to Avignon. I never want to see either of you again."

A sense of anger and frustration at having to kill again rose in Christian, and he lost his temper, venting as much to himself as to the young couple. "I don't know what you may have done to attract suspicion, but whatever it was caused me to have to kill two men. And what is worse, the Gestapo will now take revenge on the people of this city. You are too young and inexperienced to be involved in operations at this level. Don't volunteer for any more assignments until you have more training. Understand?"

Then Christian jumped behind the wheel of the meat truck and drove off without another word. Although he had lost his temper with the young couple, he knew that they had let something slip that put them under surveillance. Their actions had resulted in the killing of two men in cold blood. Christian understood that they were the enemy. He had looked into their pleading eyes as he pulled the trigger, feeling no remorse. He thought of how much he had changed since his days in Florida when he had refused to take the sheriff's life. Certainly, he had hardened since then, and he wondered if he would have made the same decision now. Christian cursed the war and Hitler for the millionth time. *How much longer can this madness go on?*

JULY 1944

Chapter Thirty-Six

CHRISTIAN WAS TIRED. BONE TIRED. HE HAD BEEN ON THE RUN for 2 years now, moving from place to place organizing and coordinating efforts to sabotage or infiltrate military operations in and around Lyon and Aix-en-Provence. He moved constantly, living in farmhouses, barns, or wherever members of the Resistance could hide him for a few days or a few weeks at a time.

Unfortunately, someone sympathetic to the Vichy government had leaked information to the Gestapo 2 weeks earlier that the infamous "Shadow Soldier" had been seen again in Lyon, and the Gestapo jumped at the chance to send a group of experienced trackers to find him.

Christian was uncomfortable with the name "Shadow Soldier" because it made him more of a target, and he damn sure didn't want to be captured and used as an example of what happens to members of the Resistance when caught.

Fortunately, he was able to escape once again, but the challenge of capturing the "Shadow Soldier" only intensified. The game of cat and mouse continued. His next temporary home was in the cellar of a house several kilometers outside of the city in the small town of Saint-Étienne.

Christian knew, as did everyone else in the Resistance, that there was more than one enemy to deal with at the same time. The German army was easy to recognize, but there were also many citizens of France who supported the German-approved Vichy government, and it was hard to determine who could be trusted and who could not. He had been living in Saint-Étienne for a month, a record length of time in one location for him. Just as he was beginning to relax, he received word that someone had betrayed him and within minutes, he was on the move again.

After being warned that his temporary accommodation had been compromised, he quickly grabbed a few items and jumped into the back of a delivery truck. Easing around the corner, he was able to glimpse a military truck as it sped down the street from the opposite direction. The vehicle slowed in front of his apartment building, soldiers jumping off the truck even before it came to a complete stop and surrounding the building while others kicked open the front door. The intensity and efficiency of the maneuver underscored the fact that he was a *very* wanted man. The timing of his escape had been much too close for comfort.

Christian leaned back against the interior wall of the truck, his eyes gazing up at the roof as he attempted to slow the adrenalin rush the last few minutes had inflicted on his body. The Germans had not captured him, but they were doing a hell of a job wearing him down. He had to stay focused, or he would be caught. He had lost count of the places he had stayed while working for the Resistance. He really didn't remember very much about any of them. He didn't care if he was in the city or the country; each had its own set of advantages and disadvantages.

His next hideout was a farmhouse on the edge of town where he had been for 3 days and so far seemed safe. He spent his days helping Henri, and his wife, Marie, with the day-to-day running of the farm. In the evenings, he would meet with groups of Resistance fighters to plan attacks or go out to rescue Allied pilots who had been shot down.

Both days and nights were full of physical and mental challenges, leaving Christian exhausted physically and mentally. Fatigue, constant flight from one location to another, and trusting people he did not know were factors which could bring about his death at any moment. Christian realized that these demons assaulted him most when he was tired, and with those powerful thoughts overshadowing him, he would fall into a fitful sleep.

Like everyone else in France, he had a chance to bathe only once a week, and even *he* noticed that he smelled like a barnyard. Each morning he washed with cold water and attempted to shave every few days. His hair was getting long and now curled over his collar. He had lost weight, but his muscles developed from the daily manual labor. With a hardness in his eyes and weariness etched on his face, Christian looked totally different than he had 2 years before. However, he was oblivious to the physical changes taking place in him.

As Christian came in for breakfast the next morning, he noticed that Henri was in a particularly good mood. News had arrived; the Germans were losing their grip in France.

Everyone had been watching the slow but steady advance of the Allied troops as they marched inland from Normandy and Marseilles. Since the invasion on the beaches of Normandy, the French citizens listened carefully to the short-wave broadcasts coming from the BBC and followed the movements of the Allied forces as they slowly marched toward Paris.

For the first time, there was a sense of optimism and with it, a revitalized purpose for the Resistance, and especially Christian. The Resistance grew bolder and was more willing to take chances. Christian felt if he could survive for another month or so without being caught, he might live to see the end of the war.

Up to this moment, all his thoughts had centered on staying alive and fighting the Germans. But if he made it through, what would he do? It was as if he were playing a game of musical chairs. When the music stopped, he would be without a place to sit. He had no ties to any place or anyone—except for the brief time he had spent with Maggie.

For the last 2 years he had rarely allowed himself to think about her. He had known her for only 3 days, and he didn't think he would ever see her again. Yet, he felt connected to her in a way he had never been with any other woman. But now there was nothing he could do, so he reluctantly pushed her out of his mind.

That afternoon, Christian received word that the German army was in retreat on the roads not far from the farmhouse. Everyone celebrated by opening a dusty bottle of Châteauneuf-du-Pape Henri had stored away in the cellar before the war. Christian, Henri, and Marie sat around the wooden kitchen table and sipped the rich, complex wine from small glasses. They toasted a swift conclusion to the war and each made a personal toast to a friend who had given their life for France. When they finished the bottle, Marie made omelets and a simple salad of fresh lettuce with a vinegar and olive oil dressing. It was one of the best meals Christian had ever eaten.

Late that night, they heard the sound of Allied airplanes in the distance, then the sound of antiaircraft fire. They had heard these sounds many times before and knew the Allies were bombing German strongholds. Alerted by the sight of headlights from a vehicle approaching the farm, the three of them rose from the table and peered out the window. A man jumped out of a small car and ran to the front door. Marie opened it just as the man started to knock. It was a fellow member of the Resistance who owned a neighboring farm several kilometers south of Henri and Marie.

"I need you to come with me. An American flyer has crash-landed about 10 kilometers from here. We were able to get to him before the Germans, but he has a broken arm and is pretty badly bruised. We need to give him some first aid and hide him. You are far enough away from where he crashed so they won't look here. We will try to get him back to the Allies as soon as we can, but it may take a few days to work out the logistics."

Christian and Henri followed the man in the farm truck without using headlights. The moonlight guided them along the road Henri had spent his life traveling to and from the local market. The driver pulled into a rutted path leading to a farm and then into a barn. By the time Henri had stopped the truck, the farmer was returning with the American flyer, his arm around the wounded man's shoulder for support. The pilot was bleeding and limping badly. The farmer told them the Germans had already been to the farm but before they could search the barn, had been redirected to pursue a more promising lead at another location.

"He says his name is Rex. I don't understand much English and when he speaks, it sounds completely different from any English that I have ever heard. Maybe you can understand what he says. Please take him back to your farm and hide him. I'm sure they will return here again soon looking for him."

Christian helped the American into the front seat of the truck between himself and Henri, and they immediately left to return to their farm. If the pilot had been conscious, they would have preferred to return on foot through the woods because there would have been less chance of discovery, but the distance was too far for the injured pilot, and he groaned with pain as he nodded in and out of consciousness.

When they arrived back at the farm, Christian assisted him into the house and lowered him onto an old sofa that sat against the stone wall in the living room. Marie made a simple sling from a towel and wrapped it around the flyer's shoulder. She cleaned the blood from his face, revealing only some minor cuts. Although the flyer was still quite shaken and in pain, he spoke to them for the first time.

"Damn, I thought for sure I was a goner. They got a lucky shot to my fuel line. Lucky for me the plane didn't explode. I really appreciate y'all helping me out here. Where the hell am I?"

Christian couldn't have been more shocked to hear a Southern accent coming from his mouth. He smiled. "What part of the South are you from?"

"Well, I'm from Atlanta, Georgia, home of the prettiest girls and the best cookin' in the whole damn world.

My name is Rex Hollingsworth. You speak English pretty good yourself. Where are you from?"

Since the answer involved a very long story that Christian didn't care to explain at the moment, he simply said, "My name is Christian. I lived in Atlanta as a young man and graduated from Georgia Tech. I've been gone a long time though."

"You are a Tech grad? Son-of-a- ahh, sorry, ma'am, my mama wouldn't appreciate my swearin' in front of a lady. You are a long damn way from Grant Field. How the hell did you end up here in the middle of France?"

"It's a long story and a little complicated. You go to Tech?"

"No, I went to Georgia. Graduated in '42 and joined the Army Air Corps as soon as I was out of school. I've been flying since early '43. I was assigned to fly bomber escorts, mostly P-51 Mustangs, out of England, and have been doing that for the past year. I have 37 missions under my belt. I don't think that I can call this mission much of a success, however. Can you help me get back to our side? It looks like we have the Jerries on the run now, and I don't want to miss the final punch."

"We'll try to get you back as quickly as possible, but it'll take a few days. In the meantime, you need to have your arm set and recover from the crash. Now, if you're really in a big hurry, Marie, here, has set broken bones on many farm animals and would be happy to oblige you, but if you think you can wait until morning, we'll have a local doctor set your arm and check you out." Christian smiled. When Rex realized Christian was teasing him, he laughed. "I think I'll wait for the doctor. Anybody here have any whisky? I could use a drink."

Over the next few days, Christian and Rex found they enjoyed each other's company and quickly developed a warm friendship. Rex pressed Christian for more details about why he was in France, and Christian reluctantly told him about the prejudices he and his family suffered and his eventual return to Germany, but he did not disclose his trip on U-67. There was too much at risk with the American military if he were accused of being an agent for Germany on American soil. He told Rex that he had become disillusioned with Germany and Hitler, had defected, and had spent the better part of the past 2 years working with the French Resistance.

Rex was fascinated by Christian's life story. He couldn't believe he had been saved by a Georgia Tech grad in the middle of France. Over a glass of brandy one evening, Christian asked if Rex had ever met a girl in Atlanta by the name of Rose Abbot. "We dated a few times when I was at Tech."

Rex said his parents and the Abbots were members of East Lake Country Club. Although she was a few years older than he, he had met Rose and her new husband a few times at the club. "Rumor is she has a drinking problem. She married a man who's the son of the president of one of the local banks. The word around the club is that both sets of parents put a lot of pressure on them to live beyond their means. They always seem at odds when I see them at social functions."

On the eighth day of Rex's rescue, Christian learned that the American pilot would be picked up the following night and transported to a location near the Allied lines. He would be met by a liaison that could get him through the German line and back into Allied hands. That evening as they were enjoying a simple supper of soup, crusty bread, and a local red wine, Rex asked Christian what he was going to do after the war was over.

"I'm not sure at this point. I can't go back to Berlin even if I wanted to. I may stay in France. I have fallen in love with the country and the people."

"Well, I have a proposition for you. If I can stay alive for the next few months, I'll go back home to work in my family's business. We build homes and office buildings in Atlanta. There'll be a boom in Atlanta after the war when soldiers come home and start families and businesses. Why don't you come and work with me? We'll need engineers with your skills. You should give America a second chance, and I can promise you that you can make a good living. Don't forget, you'll see the prettiest damn girls in the whole world walking down Peachtree Street."

Christian felt as if he were experiencing an epiphany. Feelings that had been suppressed for 2 years suddenly surfaced. He did not give a hoot about the girls on Peachtree Street. There was only one girl that he desperately wanted to see. He had never imagined he would have an opportunity to see her again. Long-suppressed hope resurfaced. He didn't know where she was, or if she were still single, but he decided that he was going to find out.

Without hesitation, Christian responded, "Rex, that's probably the best idea I've heard in a long time. If you're serious, I'd like to take you up on that offer."

"Great. You can stay with me until you get on your feet. My family and I'll introduce you to Atlanta society and to the business community. You'll do well. Maybe you could even take up golf. I could sponsor you at my country club." With a smile, he added, "Of course, being a Georgia

Tech grad will have a negative influence with the selection committee."

Christian laughed and retorted with the well-known fact that anyone who went to the University of Georgia did so because they couldn't get into Tech. Rex rolled his eyes and joined in the laughter.

"Let's take one step at a time, Rex. First thing is for me to get to America. That may take a while. In the meantime, you get back safely and hold a place there for me."

Later that evening, Christian found a piece of stationery and a pen, and with a glass of cognac to calm his nerves, wrote a letter. The next morning, he sealed it in an envelope and handed it to Rex. He had addressed it to Maggie Neal, Birmingham, Alabama, with a space between her name and city.

"Would you do me a favor? When you return to the States, would you please see if you could find the address of this person and mail this letter to her? I've asked her to reply to you, so if you'd give her your address, I'd appreciate it. When I arrive in Atlanta, you can give me any letter she may write back."

Rex looked at the name and city on the envelope and smiled, "Damn, Christian, you're a man of the world. You can bet your ass that I'll find her address and make sure the letter is mailed as soon as I get home. Now, you make sure you make it out of here safely and get to Atlanta as soon as you can."

Rex found a piece of paper and wrote his parents' address and phone number and gave it to Christian. "When you know your arrival time in Atlanta, wire me, and I'll meet you at the train station. You'll stay with me at my parents' home until we can find a suitable place for you. I'm looking forward to working with you and introducing you to some mighty fine bourbon and some pretty 'Georgia peaches.'"

The two men shook hands and Rex, looking every inch the typical laborer in worn and dirty farm clothes, climbed into the truck and drove away with Henri toward the front lines.

Later that evening, Henri returned to say the transfer had gone smoothly and Rex was back in Allied hands. Christian knew if he, too, could survive, he might have a future worth living for. For now though, he had more sorties to plan and people to meet.

There was great momentum within the Resistance now that the Germans were on the defensive and everyone wanted to participate. The following day, he had to meet with a Resistance fighter named Jean Renoir to discuss German troop movements. Then another group that had found some explosives wanted to know how best to use them. Christian poured a large snifter of brandy and raised a toast to Rex and to the end of the war. It looked like the worst was over. Now maybe he could relax a little. That evening, Christian drifted off to sleep, allowing himself at last to think about Maggie. His life would not be complete until he knew for sure.

He should not have let his guard down . . .

Chapter Thirty-Seven

ANTOINETTE DUBOIS WAS THE BEAUTIFUL 26-YEAR-OLD DAUGHTER of François and Margot Dubois. She knew she was pretty and despite the fact her parents were poor shopkeepers, she had never suffered from the deprivation that her fellow French citizens had during the war. There were always young men willing to give her their rationed food or sweets in an effort to woo her, so she had learned to rely on her beauty to be treated well. She realized her looks could take her away from the poor life that she had been born into, but she also knew that the young Frenchmen her age could never satisfy her needs.

The only men that had the ability to provide her with the lifestyle she wanted were the German soldiers, so she was pleased when she met and decided she was in love with a handsome lieutenant, Johann Kerner. Lieutenant Kerner was strikingly handsome in his uniform, tall with short blond hair and piercing blue eyes. He exuded a sense of confidence noticed by all with whom he interacted.

Kerner had been sent to Lyon to command a group of soldiers who were assigned to support the senior officers in the local headquarters. However, Kerner's commanding officer had also given him an order to seek out the American Resistance fighter, known only by the name of Christian. Christian had become an embarrassment to the German army, and so, a reward had been offered for his capture. Kerner made sure that the local townspeople were aware of the ample reward, and he worked hard to find the elusive "Shadow Soldier."

Now, time was running out. It was becoming clear Germany was going to lose the war so if the leaders of the Resistance were going to be brought to justice, it needed to happen soon. Kerner thought it would only be a matter of time before someone desperate for money or sympathetic to the Vichy government would let him know where he could find Christian, so he bided his time and enjoyed the sights of the beautiful city. However, he was now under pressure to find Christian as a matter of honor. He and his superiors did not want to leave Lyon with the "Shadow Soldier" still on the loose.

During the evenings, Kerner was free to visit the local cafés and nightclubs. It was in one of these small cafés where he noticed Antoinette sitting at a table with some girlfriends. When she saw him approach her, her heart skipped a beat. He was a beautiful specimen of a human being, and she was instantly smitten. He asked if he could buy her a drink. His manners were so courtly that she rose from the table, instantly leaving her friends without another word. They sat alone for the rest of the evening and by the time he had walked her home, she was madly in love.

Kerner thought that she was pretty, but felt she was immature. He could tell she was looking for someone to take care of her. Because she was a local girl and had extensive family and friends in the city, he thought she might be a good source to help him find Christian, and if it meant leading her along, well, worse things could happen than to make love to a beautiful girl and have her unwittingly be a spy for him.

Within a week, they were lovers and while he was enjoying the sex, Kerner was careful not to give her a sense that it might be a lasting relationship. Antoinette, on the other hand, was completely in love, and Kerner knew this. She would do anything he asked, which was exactly what he needed. One evening as they lay next to each other naked and exhausted from lovemaking, he made his first move.

"Antoinette, there's something I need to tell you. I'm afraid I may be reassigned soon. I was sent here to find a vicious killer, and I've been unable to locate him. If I don't find him and bring him to justice soon, my superiors are going to lose confidence in me and transfer me to the front. I need you to know this before we go too far in our relationship."

"Johann, you can't leave me. I love you. I don't know what I'd do without you. Who is this killer?"

"We only know him by the name of Christian. Some people refer him as the 'Shadow Soldier.' Have you ever heard of him? He seems to be a hero to the Resistance, but he is a cold-blooded killer who has caused us immeasurable harm."

"I can't let you go. I'll see what I can find out. I know some people that might know something. Give me a few days. In the meantime, hold me and touch me again like you did before. You know where I mean."

Over the next few days, Antoinette worked hard to find out anything she could about this man named Christian. Many people had heard of him, but no one seemed to know where he might be found. It didn't take long for her to determine if anyone did know the whereabouts of Christian, they were protecting him.

Kerner realized she needed to be more discreet and told her she was only going to drive Christian deeper underground if she were too obvious. It would be better if she were to try to gain more information by letting it be known that she was interested in helping the Resistance. Perhaps then she might meet someone who might put her in contact with Christian. As it turned out, it was easier than she thought it would be.

She had heard rumors from her parents that a cousin named Jean Renoir, who lived in Lyon, was suspected of being active in the Resistance. Jean was a few years older than Antoinette, and they had never been close, but he was a good person to start with. He owned a small wine and tobacco shop not far from Antoinette's parents' home, although Antoinette had not been in the shop for several years.

Antoinette entered Jean's shop and casually perused the selection of wine as if she were searching for something special. Jean heard the tinkle of the bell over the door and came through from the storage room in the back. His eyes lit up as he saw her.

"Hello, Antoinette, it's a pleasure to see you. May I help you select some wine?"

"Hello, Jean. I'm not here for wine today. May we speak privately?"

He motioned her to follow him back to his tiny office and closed the door. Antoinette felt claustrophobic in the small space, but she gathered her nerve and spoke.

"I overheard some German soldiers talking in a café yesterday. They were discussing the fact that they were going home and another group would be coming by train next Wednesday from Paris. I would like to get that information to the right people, but I don't know anyone. I'd guess there are people who might want that kind of information. Do you know anyone? I don't know who to tell, but my parents thought you might know someone. I don't want you to get into any trouble."

"I might know someone who may be interested in information like that. Let me see what I can do. Why don't we meet at Camille's Café at 8:00 o'clock tomorrow evening?"

The next evening, Jean met Antoinette at the café and relayed to her that he was meeting with someone the next day. Over dinner, Antoinette controlled the conversation, leading Jean from subject to subject, alternating between his personal likes and dislikes to the war and when he thought it might end. After they had finished a bottle of wine and he was relaxed, she carefully broached the subject of the Resistance.

"I'm impressed with what you do, Jean. I guess you know a lot of people that you can't talk about who are doing very brave things to help us with the war. I don't know anything about Resistance activity myself, but is there some way that I can help defeat the Germans?"

"You're a beautiful, young lady, Antoinette, and I think that you could use your charms to gain access to German headquarters and pick up valuable information. It might be dangerous, however, and you need to know that."

"I understand, Jean. What should I do?"

"I'm meeting someone tomorrow who can give you more information. His name is Christian, and he coordinates most of the activity around Lyon."

At the sound of Christian's name, Antoinette had to bite her tongue to keep from smiling. This was too easy.

"Come by my shop tomorrow at noon and I will introduce you to Christian. He might have some ideas to talk with you further about."

"Thanks, Jean. Now I feel I can play a part in bringing the war to an end."

When they left the café, Antoinette was beside herself with joy. *Johann is going to be so impressed. In just one evening I have discovered this Christian. Now all I have to do is arrange for Johann to capture him, and we can be together forever.*

Early the next morning, Antoinette went to the office where Kerner worked and sent word that she wanted to see him. She was told that he had been sent to the village of Roanne and would not return for 2 days.

Now what should I do? I set up a meeting with this Christian, and I don't know what to do or say. I know, I'll use my charms to get close to him and when Johann returns, he can capture Christian and I will be a hero.

The next day, Antoinette entered Jean's shop a few minutes before noon and waited nervously while he served some customers. A few minutes later, a handsome man with a weary look on his face entered. Jean went to the door, locked it, and flipped the "Open" sign to "Closed for Lunch." He then turned and spoke to Christian.

"This is my cousin, Antoinette. She overheard some valuable information and wanted to pass it along to someone who might be interested."

Christian turned to Antoinette and while Jean spoke, he was struck by how attractive she was. He had not been in the company of a woman that radiated such beauty and poise for as long as he could remember. Just as she hoped, Antoinette could tell he was interested in more than just information. Christian spoke first.

"Thanks for helping us. What have you heard?"

"I was in a café yesterday, and some German soldiers were trying to get me to go out with them. One of them said he only had a few days left and then his company was going to be replaced with soldiers who were coming down from Paris next Wednesday by train. If I did not go out with him, I would miss an opportunity to spend an evening with a real man who could give me some real German sausage, and he didn't mean bratwurst. Then they all laughed as if they thought that was really funny. Why do men act so stupid and adolescent?"

"Well, all men don't. That is information that we might be able to use. To show you that all men are not so coarse, would you let me buy you dinner sometime?"

"I'd like that. I'm free tomorrow night. Maybe we could meet at Camille's at 8:00 o'clock."

"I would look forward to that very much. I need to go now, but thanks again for the information."

Christian left the shop feeling good. Perhaps his team could figure out a way to sabotage the train, but at least he would be able to spend an evening with an attractive lady. Life was looking up for a change.

The next evening, Christian put on his best suit for his date with Antoinette. He had been thinking about her all day and hoped that he would make a good impression on her.

He had not been on a date for such a long time he was not sure how he should act. He could only be a gentleman and hope she would be favorably impressed. It was nice to think about the art of romance for a change, instead of the art of war.

For the first time since he had arrived in France, Christian felt he was finally able to let his guard down somewhat and enjoy himself. He was confident that Germany would be defeated soon and that the people of France would be able to get on with their lives. He had a future in America. Tonight, he could relax a little and enjoy the company of a beautiful girl.

He entered Camille's a few minutes before eight and told the waiter to bring a bottle of champagne and two glasses as soon as Antoinette arrived. He would order dinner after they had enjoyed the champagne.

At 8:00 o'clock, Antoinette entered the café, but not alone. With her were three German soldiers. She simply pointed to Christian and said, "That's him sitting there."

Christian did not have time to look for a way to escape. With guns drawn, the soldiers surrounded him and roughly tied his hands behind his back. Then, lifting him off his feet, they carried him out the door and threw him into the back of a large car.

As the soldiers began to climb into the car, shots rang out. Two of the soldiers fell immediately, bleeding from wounds. The third soldier held up his arms in surrender, but it was pointless. Jean Renoir held a pistol against the soldier's head and without hesitation, pulled the trigger. The soldier fell to the ground. Jean then walked over to the other wounded soldiers lying on the ground and shot them both in the back of the head. Then he spoke to Antoinette.

"Your parents deserve better than this. Because you are a member of my family, I cannot kill you; however, I will make sure you pay for what you have done."

Turning to a comrade, he gave his instructions.

"Take her out of town, shave her head, strip her naked, and then break her nose so that she will never be able to use her beauty again. Let her find her own way back to town. The people of Lyon and France will see where her allegiance lies. Let's see how she survives then. I will tell her parents personally so they know that it came from the family. Those good people do not deserve a daughter like this."

Jean pulled Christian from the car, untied his hands, and they walked quickly down the street.

"There was something that just didn't seem right when she came to visit me. I was suspicious and decided to investigate. I found out she was dating a German officer and had been asking about you over the past few days. I put two and two together and figured that she was trying to set you up. I've been following her."

"Jean, we've been through a lot together. Thanks for looking out for me. I let my guard down too soon and of all things, over a beautiful woman. I guess if I was going to get caught, it might as well been over a woman. Better that than being shot blowing up a train, I suppose."

Jean nodded and left Christian standing alone under a streetlight. Christian knew the shots would soon bring the police, so he moved quickly through the shadows back to Henri's farmhouse. When he was safely behind locked doors, he dropped into a chair and poured a large glass of brandy, drinking it in two gulps. He poured another, this time only half full and decided to sip it more slowly. He had been extremely lucky to have Jean watching out for him.

He had let his guard down too early and had nearly paid the ultimate price.

Women. Why is it we let women have such an effect over us? They control our big heads and our little heads also. Damn, I wish that I didn't love women so much. They are just too much fuckin' trouble. Well, I was damn lucky tonight. I owe Jean a tremendous gratitude for saving my ass. Tomorrow, I'll make sure he survived OK. I don't feel sorry for Antoinette, however. For the rest of her life, she'll show the effects of her traitorous actions. Surely she will have to leave this area and go to a larger city, like Paris. And she'll probably have to live the rest of her life working in a factory or doing some thankless, menial job, especially if word of what she did follows her.

Christian, drunk from the brandy and an overdose of adrenalin, fell onto his bed and immediately went to sleep, only to awaken in the middle of the night sicker than he had ever been in his life.

Maybe alcohol is as bad as some women, he ruminated as the bed spun under him.

Chapter Thirty-Eight

CHRISTIAN REMAINED IN THE LYON AREA AND CONTINUED TO coordinate the Resistance operations. In late August, word came that Allied forces were moving north from the Mediterranean coast having successfully completed the Italian campaign. The forces including American, French, and British soldiers, invaded the beaches between Toulon and Cannes under Operation Dragoon. With minimal resistance, they marched north. Their objective was meeting with Eisenhower's troops that were working their way west toward Paris. For the first time in 2 years, Christian and his fellow Resistance fighters felt a sense of great relief that they might even survive.

In the first week of September, Allied forces arrived in Lyon and began the liberation of the city. Crowds lined the streets to welcome the soldiers, including Christian, who joined the occasion, drinking an entire bottle of wine.

When he awoke from a drunken sleep the next morning, he had a vicious hangover, but was so happy that he considered drinking another bottle. Fortunately, he was prevented from further revelry when a friend who found him nursing a growing headache and drinking black coffee in a sidewalk café told him that he had been summoned to the building the Allied forces were using as their command offices.

Christian's first reaction was fear that his mission to Florida 2 years earlier had been discovered. As soon as he arrived, he was ushered into a room where an American officer sat at a desk. The officer looked up from his paperwork and stared intently at Christian.

"Please, have a seat. I am Major General John Dahlquist, commander of the 36th Infantry Division. One of my officers brought to my attention from a conversation he had with some of the local citizens that you are an American who has been very active in the Resistance. Would you mind telling me how you ended up here and what you did?"

Christian knew his story of how he had ended up in that farmhouse over 2 years ago was known only to him. Since he had lived in so many different safe houses in France, there was no way to trace his beginnings with the Resistance, so he merely created a new history.

"I was traveling in France and sort of got stuck here. I knew I'd be shot or imprisoned if the Germans found me, so I joined the Resistance and went underground. Out of necessity, I've been moving around and helping rescue Allied flyers shot down and translating so the pilots and locals could communicate. On a couple of occasions, I slipped into cafés and restaurants where German soldiers were congregating and sat and listened to see if I could pick up anything important. I was born in Austria, but my parents were born in Germany. We moved to America when I was small. I learned German from my parents and English in the States."

"From what we've been told, you are being a bit modest about your efforts. There seems to be a certain admiration from your fellow Resistance fighters regarding your contributions to their country and to their lives. We were told you put your own personal safety aside on several occasions when you ordered your colleagues to leave a designated meeting place or mission where you suspected a trap was being set, and on one occasion, you spared a scared young fighter the responsibility of having to kill two German soldiers by doing it yourself. You are named the 'Shadow Soldier,' are you not?"

"Yeah, well, I heard something about that from time to time, but I did what I thought needed to be done. That's all. So far as my killing German soldiers instead of letting a scared young man or girl do it, I thought I could deal with the taking of someone's life better than they could. After you have taken someone's life, you are never the same again. I wanted to spare those people that life-changing event if I could."

"What are you going to do now?"

"Assuming the war will end soon, I hope to return to America. I helped save an American flyer a few months back. He asked me to come to Atlanta and work with his construction company. I'll have to earn enough money for my passage and figure out how to get there. I hope cruise liners will be going to America soon. I'll take it a day at a time, I suppose."

"I think I can help get you home. Although you are not officially in the army, I'm going to have my corporal write an order for you to join a group of wounded soldiers who are leaving in 3 days in a convoy to Marseille. You will all be shipped to England, where the wounded will either be treated in hospitals there or returned to the States on a military transport ship. Once you get to the States, you're on your own. Would that be acceptable to you?"

Christian couldn't believe this was happening. After 2 years on the run, he was going to the place where he knew in his heart would be his home forever.

Three days later, Christian arrived at the long line of trucks and military vehicles ready for the trip to the Mediterranean coast. He approached a sergeant who was ordering soldiers and medics carrying wounded men in a sea of chaos.

"Goddamn it, Soldier, get on the fucking truck before I kick your ass up there myself! Move it along. This ain't no stroll in the fuckin' park!"

Seeing several men carrying wounded soldiers on litters, he barked, "Load those men in the ambulances, and if there's no more room, find a truck and load them the best you can. Try to make them as comfortable as possible. If I'm not happy with how they're loaded when I get over there, I'm going kick your ass to Marseille myself, do you hear me, Corpsmen?"

Christian approached the sergeant with trepidation. *This guy is not in any mood to be played with.* The sergeant had seen too many of his men die terrible deaths far away from home, and Christian could tell it had taken a toll on him. Out of the corner of his eye the sergeant saw Christian approach him.

"Who the fuck are you, and what the fuck do you want, Frenchy? I ain't got time to talk to any fuckin' civilians right now."

Christian handed the sergeant the orders that Dahlquist had given him. "I'm an American citizen. I've been working for the Resistance for the past 2 years, and I have orders from Major General Dahlquist to join the convoy back to Marseille. Then to England."

"Well, shit, I've seen it all now. Find a fuckin' seat on a truck and stay out of my soldiers' way. If you can help get some of these wounded men on board, make yourself useful. They deserve all the help they can get."

The sergeant then turned and continued to yell at the troops as they walked down the line of trucks. "Soldier, if you don't get on that goddamn truck by the time I get to you, I'm going to pick you up and throw your ass up there myself. Do you hear me?"

Christian found a truck with an available seat in the back and settled in for the 2-day journey. After another 2 days in a tent camp in Marseille, he and the other men boarded a troop transport headed for England. Christian spent almost 3 weeks in England and finally arrived in New York City in late October. The Allies had broken the code for the enigma machine, and German submarine danger was no longer a serious problem. The trip across the Atlantic was uneventful.

When Christian disembarked carrying the few items he owned in a worn leather bag, he heard another sergeant shouting at the men as they walked off the ship.

"All right, men, listen up! Those soldiers going to any place west of the Mississippi River go to the building on your right and you'll get further orders there. Those soldiers going to Chicago, Detroit, or other Midwest cities, go to the building in the middle. Those soldiers going South to Atlanta or New Orleans, go to the building on the left.

You'll be processed and put on trains for home. Anyone who doesn't fall into one of those three groups, see me. Good luck and Godspeed."

Christian had thought he would spend a few days in New York City and recuperate from the trip. He still had $200 that Colonel Schmidt had given him 2½ years ago and knew that he could purchase a train ticket with it. However, the idea of a free ride to Atlanta was too good to pass up. He would need some money when he arrived in Atlanta, so he followed the soldiers traveling to the southern states. An army corporal who was too busy to question Christian's civilian clothing handed him a one-way ticket to Atlanta, Georgia. Christian had just enough time before boarding the train to send Rex a telegram, informing him that he would be arriving in Atlanta in several days.

Rex Hollingsworth had arrived home in Atlanta on the last day in September 1944. By now, he had fully recovered from his injuries and was happy to be home and ready to go to work in the family business. His parents threw a large party in his honor at the country club. He felt so grateful to be alive and with family and friends again. He had lost many good friends in the war. Even more had been wounded and would never be able to work again.

Over breakfast the morning after the party, Rex told his parents he had become good friends with a young American man called Christian who was working in the French Resistance and who had saved his life. He told them Christian was a graduate of Georgia Tech in civil engineering and he had invited him to come to Atlanta after the war to work with them in the family business. Rex's father was pleased his son was home and was focused on being involved in the business. He trusted his son's decision and approved the plan.

Soon after Rex returned home, he found an address for a Margaret Neal in Birmingham. In the hope it was the same person that Christian wanted to contact, he posted the letter with his return address. Two weeks later, the letter was returned with a stamped message stating the addressee had moved without leaving a forwarding address. Rex filed the letter in a drawer to give to Christian when he arrived.

Chapter Thirty-Nine

CHRISTIAN CHANGED TRAINS IN WASHINGTON, D.C., AND ARRIVED at Union Station in Atlanta on the "Crescent," the latest evolution of train travel, pulled by new powerful diesel engines and offering fully air-conditioned cars. The trip had taken 2 long days, and Christian was more than ready to disembark. He didn't know if Rex had received his telegram and if the offer of employment were still serious. He had decided he would wait at the station for an hour or so and then find a boarding house if Rex did not show up. As he was walking toward the exit along with a large throng of soldiers, he heard his name being called.

"Christian, over here! Man, you're a sight for sore eyes! I'm glad you made it."

Giving Christian a strong handshake, he started for the exit doors. "My car is parked out front. I couldn't believe it when I got your telegram. I've only been home for a month.

You made it out of there fast. How did you get here so quickly?"

As they drove through the streets of Atlanta, Christian told Rex how he had been summoned by Major General Dahlquist and how he was given orders to travel with the soldiers back to England and then on to America. It was surreal to be back in the city that he had left so long ago with such bad feelings.

"I've rented a house in Decatur. It's easy to get to the office in downtown Atlanta, and it's also near East Lake Country Club where I play golf. You can stay with me as long as you like. First thing tomorrow, we'll go to Rich's Department Store and get you some new clothes. Then we're having dinner with my parents at the club. They're looking forward to meeting you."

When they reached Rex's home and Christian had been shown his room, Rex handed him the letter that had been returned.

"This is the letter you asked me to mail for you. It was returned 2 weeks after I sent it, with no forwarding address. I'm sorry."

Christian's heart sank when he saw the envelope. He had hoped more than he wanted to admit that she had responded.

"You don't know how sorry I am."

The next day, Rex and Christian drove downtown to Rich's Department Store and Rex directed Christian to the men's department so he could buy the necessary clothes to begin work. Rex instructed the salesman to put the clothes on his account and told Christian he could pay him back when his paychecks began to come in.

"While you're being fitted, I'm going upstairs to get a package my mother asked me to pick up. I'll be back in a few minutes."

While Rex was waiting for the elevator, a tall, slim lady joined him. Rex had never seen her before. With her hazel eyes and cute off center nose, she was beautiful.

"Hello, do you work here?"

"Yes, I'm the president's secretary. Do you shop here often?"

"No, but from what I can see from the merchandise today, I may shop here more frequently now."

She knew the stranger was flirting unabashedly with her, but she thought he was cute, and she could tell he was successful in his profession. The elevator door opened, and they both entered. Rex pressed the button for the second floor, and the girl pressed the button for the third floor, where the executive offices were located.

The elevator arrived at the second floor all too quickly, and Rex smiled at the attractive lady as he exited, saying, "Have a nice day. I hope to see you again soon."

After he located the package for his mother and it was wrapped, he returned to the first floor, finding Christian with an armful of bags.

"Wow, I just talked to the most attractive girl I've seen in a long time. She's the secretary to the president of the store. I'll have to come back and ask her out. Are you ready to go?"

"Yeah, think so. Thanks for advancing me the cost of all of this. I'll pay you back as soon as I receive my first paycheck."

"Don't worry about it. We need to go back and freshen up now. We don't want to be late for dinner."

Chapter Forty

ON THE OTHER SIDE OF TOWN, MAGGIE AND HER BEAU, ANSLEY, were dining at the Druid Hills Country Club. They were discussing where they would spend Thanksgiving and Christmas. Ansley was from Nashville. He was looking forward to taking Maggie home with him soon to introduce her to his family. Maggie knew this would be a major step in their relationship. She thought she was finally ready. Ansley would be a perfect husband, and she had finally decided to put Christian behind her. At least she tried to.

Maggie had returned to Atlanta the previous Sunday evening from a trip to Birmingham to see her parents and was glad to be back. After leaving Grayton Beach 2½ years earlier, she returned to Birmingham with the intention of resuming her life and teaching again. However, a sense of restlessness and discontent overwhelmed her. She longed to have her own children, and although she loved her job, it was a constant reminder of what she was missing.

Grayton Beach and the war had made her a different person. Her previous comfortable life in Birmingham seemed trite now; meaningless. In the fall of 1943, she told her parents that she was moving to Atlanta for a fresh start. She then visited Charles's parents to tell them about her plans and to say good-bye. Charles's mother, Margaret, was not only supportive of Maggie's decision, but had a suggestion.

"As you know, I graduated from Agnes Scott College in Atlanta before I married Charles's father. One of my best school friends recently wrote me that she was now widowed. I could tell from the tone of her letter that she was lonely. Her husband was a very successful lawyer in Atlanta, and she lives in a beautiful home right on Peachtree Road. I'm going to call her and ask if you can stay with her until you find a place of your own."

Margaret excused herself and in a few minutes, returned with a smile on her face. "It's all settled. My friend Frances Ashwood is looking forward to having you stay with her. She is well connected in Atlanta and is excited about introducing you to her friends."

Handing Maggie a folded note with the address and telephone number, she told Maggie Frances would be expecting her sometime the following Saturday afternoon.

Because she had such a fondness and respect for Margaret, Maggie knew she would be in good hands until she could find a job and get settled. She returned to her apartment to sort through the things she would take. There was a stack of mail, including a letter from Theresa. Maggie and

Theresa had written often. They had a special affection for each other.

Theresa and Robert had moved to Baltimore, Maryland, and Robert had found work quickly. Within a year, their daughter was born, and Theresa had called Maggie to tell her the good news and to ask her blessing to name her Maggie. Maggie responded with a resounding yes and immediately ordered a new crib from Sears and Roebuck to be shipped to her little namesake.

She made a mental note to write to Theresa to let her know her new address in Atlanta and realized for the first time in a long time she felt good about her life again.

Late Saturday afternoon, Maggie drove up the driveway to Frances Ashwood's home. The two-storey brick house with white columns supporting a large, shady porch sat back from the road on 2 acres of manicured lawn surrounded by azaleas. Several large magnolia trees shaded the house from the summer sun. The drive circled in front of the house, and Maggie parked and rang the doorbell. A stocky Negro lady wearing a black dress with a crisply starched white apron opened the door and invited her into the foyer.

"Well, well, well, you must be Miss Maggie. We been expecting you. Please come in and I'll let Mrs. Ashwood know you've arrived. I'll have Lincoln, the gardener, take your bags upstairs to your room."

Maggie heard a voice coming from the large, curving staircase that led upstairs from the foyer.

"Thank you, Eula Mae. Welcome, Maggie. I'm Frances. I'm so pleased that you have agreed to spend some time here with me. Margaret has told me so much about you. I've asked Eula Mae to serve us some iced tea and pound cake.

I think that'll last us until cocktail time. Lincoln will take your things to your room."

When Maggie was shown to her large bedroom she was astonished. It had high ceilings and French windows that overlooked the lawn and an adjacent bathroom that was bigger than her bedroom in Birmingham.

"I could sure get used to this," she whispered to herself.

When she had unpacked her belongings and freshened up, Maggie went back downstairs to find Frances reading in the study.

"Maggie, I'd like you to feel free to make this your home for as long as you like. Eula Mae will make us breakfast and dinner every day, except Sunday night. That's when we will go to the country club for a light supper. I tend to be out and about during the day, so I don't ask Eula Mae to fix lunch. I hope that is acceptable to you."

"That would be perfect, Mrs. Ashwood. I'll start looking for a job on Monday, so I'll be out during the day also."

"Please call me Frances. One of my late husband's largest clients is Rich's Department Store. I took the liberty of asking and found out that the president needs an assistant. If you're interested, why don't you go talk to him on Monday? I think the salary would be better than teaching, and you would get a discount on all your purchases. The Bell Bomber airplane factory up in Marietta is also hiring, but it's a long drive up there and when the war is over, they'll replace the women workers with men."

Over the next months, Maggie settled into her new life. Her job at Rich's was intellectually challenging, and she could not have been happier with her decision. Maggie lived with Frances for 6 months and then decided it was time to find a place of her own. She found a small bungalow for rent in a pleasant neighborhood only a block from Piedmont Park, where she could walk and picnic when the weather was nice. She remained close to Frances but began to develop her own friends and enjoyed dating the young professional lawyers, bankers, and businessmen that were beginning to take a role in Atlanta's growth. She continued to join Frances for dinner on Sundays at the club. Maggie always looked forward to these evenings.

One such Sunday, Frances introduced Maggie to Ansley Dunwoody, a smart, charming, and handsome lawyer who had recently joined the club. He and Maggie seemed to have similar interests and began dating on a casual basis. Maggie was still emotionally scarred from all that had happened with John Logan and Christian and wanted to approach any new relationship with caution. She tried hard not to think about John Logan, but she still worried about Christian and hoped that he was safe.

As the year flew by, Maggie felt increasingly comfortable with her new life. She and Ansley saw a great deal more of each other and in early fall, he asked her to marry him. She happily accepted, and they set a wedding date for Easter of the following year.

Chapter Forty-One

Rex and Christian strolled into the dining room at East Lake Country Club. Rex was looking forward to introducing Christian to his parents, and Annabel and Hamilton Hollingsworth were excited to meet the man who had saved their only son from certain death. Annabel attempted to hold her emotions in check but was overcome as she embraced Christian. Hamilton shook Christian's hand, and in a show of gratitude, pulled the young man into a bear hug. Usually, Rex would have been embarrassed by such a public expression by his parents, but he knew how fortunate he was to be back in Atlanta. Many American pilots had not been so lucky. It was a moment of truth—a humbling experience reserved only for the survivors of war. The emotion of the moment passed quickly. Soon, they were talking like old friends and ordered cocktails.

Cocktails arrived, and the conversation flowed easily. Christian envied the warm family ties that Rex had. The familiar embraces had stirred a loneliness in him that he had kept locked away since his parents had died. He thought of how brave they had been to leave Germany to start a new life in America. Thinking about them was always bittersweet, but tonight, Christian invited them into his mind and enjoyed their presence. Had it not been for their decision, Christian would never have come to America as a child and certainly would never have returned on a German mission years later. Fate had positioned him to meet both Maggie and Rex.

For the first time in years Christian felt optimistic. Surrounded by Rex and his family, he felt as if he finally belonged. Life had taken him on an incredible journey.

Yesterday, he had been in the depths of war with its destruction and violence. Tomorrow, he would have a new career, friends, and perhaps a family. But there was one person who bridged the gap between his past and his future. Maggie. She was the only thing in the war that had made sense to him.

"Christian," asked Rex, "what are you having to eat?"

"I'm sorry, I was miles away."

Addressing the waiter, he ordered his meal. With laughter in his eyes, he struggled to leave his tangled thoughts and join in the celebration.

Relaxed and enjoying the conversation, he suddenly saw her enter the dining room from the corner of his eye. Instantly, his heart skipped a beat and chills ran up his spine. The lady was being escorted by a man toward a table across the room. Christian excused himself and walked over to the table where she and her dining companion were taking their seats.

Chapter Forty-Two

"HELLO, ROSE."

Rose looked up at Christian and was so startled she knocked her martini glass off the table, shattering the crystal goblet on the marble floor. All conversation in the room ceased as the diners turned to see the source of the noise.

"I'm sorry if I startled you. I just wanted to say hello," Christian said apologetically. "I've just recently returned from the war, and it's a treat to see a familiar face."

Christian was attempting to make polite conversation while Rose gathered her composure. It was abundantly clear she was embarrassed to see him. He could also tell from her expression she was drunk. In a slurring voice, she introduced her husband and suddenly the conversation died. After a few awkward seconds of silence, Christian excused himself and returned to his table. Glancing discreetly with his peripheral vision, he noticed another martini had been promptly delivered to Rose's table and within a few minutes, yet another.

He wasn't sure how he felt about meeting her again. What had happened between them seemed a lifetime ago. He was no longer the naïve young man he had been when he had asked for her hand in marriage. Christian shrugged off the negative feelings and rejoined the animated banter with Rex and his parents.

By the time Christian and his party left the dining room, Rose and her husband had already departed, fortunately relieving him of yet another uncomfortable encounter. But it did make him wonder if that same awkwardness would occur if he ever saw Maggie again. There was quite a difference between being a rejected suitor and being an agent sent on a mission from Germany who made love to a beautiful woman who also risked her own life to help him escape capture. No matter how awkward it might be, he could only hope he would get the chance to find out.

Christian began his work with the Hollingsworth family company the following week and felt immediately comfortable. Using his engineering skills energized him and made him feel like he was part of a building process instead of being involved in destruction. The days passed quickly, and Christian poured himself into his work from early morning to late in the evening. One day, Rex teased Christian that if he continued to work this hard he would soon be running the company, leaving him, the unemployed son of the former owner, unable to afford the lifestyle he was now enjoying enormously. Christian just laughed, taking pleasure in the moment.

Later in the week, Christian told Rex he needed to return to Rich's Department Store to pick up the suit that had been altered for him. Rex suggested he accompany Christian to see if he could find the attractive girl he had met there. Rex loved to flirt and was not afraid to risk rejection from a beautiful woman. He hoped she would be available to go out on a date.

They entered the store on two separate missions: Rex walked directly toward the elevator while Christian veered off toward the men's department. Rex adjusted his tie and pulled down his shirt sleeves, mentally rehearsing what he would say as the elevator ascended to the executive floor. There, he found Maggie preparing to leave for the day. Beaming with confidence, he approached her with a huge smile.

"Hello, we met briefly the other day at the elevator. Since there is no one else available to do it for me, I would like to formally introduce myself. My name is Rex Hollingsworth. I'm in the construction business and getting settled in Atlanta again after being away for over 2 years in the war. I'd like very much to ask you out for a cup of coffee or perhaps dinner, if you're free."

"Well, Mr. Hollingsworth, it's so nice of you to take the time to find me and introduce yourself," Maggie replied. "You seem a nice person and under different circumstances, I'd like to get to know you. But I don't think my fiancé would warm to the idea of me dating you during our engagement. I hope that you can understand."

Damn. Rex was truly disappointed. Well, it had been a good try but timing was everything, and this ship had already sailed. "I'm truly sorry to hear you're taken. He certainly is one lucky man. Sorry to have bothered you." Walking toward the elevators, Rex stopped and turned back to her. "By the way, I don't think I got your name."

Realizing just how difficult it must have been for him to introduce himself to her, Maggie gently smiled and responded, "My name is Maggie, Maggie Neal." He nodded in return, and his expression changed. Thinking that somehow she had given him some encouragement, she took on her most professional tone and continued, "Now, if you will excuse me," Maggie continued, "I really do need to leave."

Rex could tell he was making her uncomfortable, so he smiled and gave her a wink as he headed back to the elevator.

Maggie had turned around to gather her things and to hide the growing smile on her face when she heard the ring of the elevator doors closing, announcing his departure. Then she laughed out loud and shook her head in disbelief. He had been a charming and persistent man, and she had to admit that it had made her day a little bit more interesting.

Christian, meanwhile, was waiting on the ground floor when Rex finally emerged from the elevator.

"From the look on your face, it doesn't appear you had much luck with the lady today."

"Damn it all. No, I didn't. It seems she has a beau and was not open to my Southern charm. Well, there are a lot of attractive girls in Atlanta, and I'll find a belle of my own soon. After all, who can resist someone as handsome as me?"

Christian laughed. He had to admire Rex's tenacity when it came to the ladies. The woman who eventually married Rex would certainly have her hands full, but she would also have one of the best men that Christian had ever known. Christian turned to Rex saying, "I think we both need a drink. What do you say?"

No response was needed or expected.

After a strong bourbon on the rocks as a predinner cocktail at home, they decided to go to a restaurant for dinner. As they drove down Peachtree Road, the men discussed some of the construction jobs that they were bidding on and the problems associated with getting materials during the war. Nothing was going to be built until rationing was over, but they were planning to be ready when the time came.

They found a restaurant offering good Southern food and settled for plates of fried chicken, turnip greens, mashed potatoes, and sweet iced tea. Christian had not eaten Southern cuisine since leaving years earlier, and he realized as good as the food in Atlanta and the South was, it was no match for the food that he eaten in France. He missed the wines and cheeses and crusty breads. He was not sure if anyone in Atlanta had ever tasted good wine or the flavorful cheeses that were common on every table in French homes and cafés. In fact, he wondered if anyone here had ever eaten coq au vin instead of fried chicken.

The conversation ranged from work to sports and inevitably moved on to women. Rex knew Christian was so intent on establishing himself in the building business that he hadn't made time to seek out female companionship since arriving in Atlanta. The only time Rex had seen Christian show any interest was when he had given him the letter for the girl in Birmingham. Rex knew that the war had been a difficult time for Christian, but he felt that Christian needed to establish a personal life now. He thought that mentioning the letter might be a good place to start to see where things went from there.

"I'm sorry the letter you asked me to mail was returned. It's none of my business, of course, but was she special to you?"

"Yes, she was. We had only a short time together, but she stays constantly on my mind. I was hoping to see her again. I don't know what happened to her or where she is. Maybe someday I'll find her. You never know."

Suddenly, Rex was struck by a thought that jolted him, and he froze in disbelief. Quickly gathering his thoughts and attempting to regain his composure, Rex slowly placed his fork on his plate, then spoke.

"You're going to be glad my charms failed me this afternoon. Goddamn, Christian, is she tall with light brown hair, hazel eyes, and a nose that's not exactly straight?"

"How in the hell would you know that? And how does your charm have anything to do with it?"

"Your Maggie is here."

"What?!"

"She's the girl I tried to ask out this afternoon. I asked her what her name was and she told me it was Maggie Neal. I didn't make the connection until just this minute. She's the secretary to the president of Rich's. Unfortunately, she also told me she's engaged to be married, but a lot of women say that to fight off an unwanted suitor so it may or may not be true."

Christian's thoughts were a-jumble. He couldn't believe she was actually here in Atlanta. *Is she really engaged to be married? Would she even want to see me?* He looked at Rex, then through the plate-glass window onto Peachtree Street, then back to Rex. Christian wanted to be careful about what he revealed to Rex concerning his relationship with Maggie, so he attempted to act calmer than he felt.

"Yes, I want to see her, but if she's engaged, it might not be a good idea. We haven't been in touch in a long time, and she may not want to see me again. I don't want to just barge into her life now."

But in reality, that was *exactly* what he wanted. If she were engaged, he didn't have much time. He needed to think fast. He tried to appear casual in his response to Rex, not wishing to show his growing anxiety. "I'm not sure what I want to do, but I'll think of something."

Rex thought for a minute and then said with a smile, "Don't worry, I have an idea."

Chapter Forty-Three

MAGGIE WAS TYPING A LETTER WHEN SHE SAW REX OPEN THE DOOR to the executive offices and approach her. With a weary sigh of resignation, she stopped typing and looked up. *Why is it that some men simply cannot give up on a lost cause?* she wondered.

"Good afternoon, Mr. Hollingsworth. How can I help you today?"

"Hello, Miss Neal. You can relax. I'm not here to ask you out again."

Relieved, she leaned back in her chair and waited to hear why he had returned.

"I'm here to give you some information. When I was stationed in France toward the end of the war, I met a man named Christian Wolfe."

It was a good thing Maggie had remained seated, because she thought she might faint. Hearing his name after 2 long years came as a total and unexpected shock. How many times had she thought about him and wondered where he was, or even if he were still alive? Attempting to compose herself, she nodded for him to continue.

"Christian saved my life in France. He gave me a letter to mail as soon as I returned to America. It was a letter to a Maggie Neal in Birmingham, Alabama. The letter was returned to me with no forwarding address."

Maggie felt devastated. Christian had attempted to contact her. Rex instantly went from being a nuisance to the most important person in her life. He continued.

"When you told me your name yesterday, I didn't realize until later that you may be the very person Christian was trying to contact. Did you move here from Birmingham?"

"Yes, I am the same person. Do you still have the letter?" Her mind was racing with questions. *Why was Christian in France helping American soldiers? Did he not return to Germany?*

She thought that she might weep from joy. He had survived and had been thinking of her.

"Yes, I do. It's in my desk at home. I'll bring it early next week if that is okay with you?"

"That would be fine, and Rex, thank you for making the connection. It means a lot to me." *A week! How am I possibly going to be able to wait a whole week to read the letter?*

As he turned to leave, Rex smiled and said, "Whatever you and he had was very important to him. I'll see you next week."

As soon as Rex disappeared into the elevator, Maggie lowered her head into her hands and finally released the tears that had been threatening to erupt. It was only then she thought of all the questions she should have asked Rex. Rex hadn't said whether Christian was alive or dead.

Maggie jumped, startled by the ringing of the phone. The switchboard operator announced that Ansley was on the line. Gathering her composure, she waited for him to be put through, feeling guilty about her feelings for Christian.

"Hello, sweetheart. I hope you're having a good day. Listen, Friday night, one of the senior partners here is throwing a big bash at East Lake Country Club for some of our clients. I have to be there and am hoping that you'll join me. I think it'll be fun. There'll be a band and a lot of good food and drinks. Can I plan on picking you up about 7:00 o'clock? Also, I've been asked to play golf on Saturday with some new clients. I have the feeling that I may be on track for junior partnership soon, and I feel like partying."

Listening to Ansley's confident voice reassured Maggie. Putting the thought of Christian aside, she felt a little calmer.

"The party sounds nice, Ansley. I'm looking forward to it, and congratulations on the potential partnership. You deserve it. I'll see you at 7:00 Friday night."

As soon as she was off the phone, her thoughts strayed back to Christian. There were so many unanswered questions, but what mattered most to her was the fact Christian had thought about her enough to write her a letter. She tried to convince herself that the letter would help her reach some closure and accept that the past was over. Christian was most likely starting a new life of his own, and so was she. The war was effectively over, but what had happened between them would always be a secret shared only by two souls thrown together in a little town called Grayton Beach.

Returning to the present, Maggie decided she wanted to look especially pretty for Ansley and the party, so she went downstairs and bought a new dress and made an appointment to have her hair done at the salon.

By the time Friday evening came, Maggie had made peace with herself. When Ansley arrived to take her to the party, he whistled appreciatively. She gave him a long kiss and told him that she was looking forward to a special weekend together.

On the drive over to the country club, Ansley told Maggie who would be at the party that he knew. There would be clients of other lawyers so he would not know everyone. He would need to spend a few minutes with some of the guests, but he would not leave her alone for long.

"Just give me a drink and I'll be fine," she reassured him.

Chapter Forty-Four

Rex walked into Christian's office on Friday as Christian was reviewing some drawings concerning the water and sewer lines for a new subdivision they were hoping to start as soon as construction materials were available. Christian attempted to use his time efficiently before the construction work began and reviewing plans and anticipating problems could save valuable time later. Pulling himself away from his work, he focused his attention on his friend.

Rex took a seat with the ease of a man about to play a game of tennis. He always seemed to have a gleam in his eye and a smile that indicated he had a secret. Christian could only attribute his laid-back manner to being raised in the South. His mannerisms actually worked well for him in business. Although some unsuspecting businessmen actually equated a lower intelligence level with his affable Southern charm, this "good ol' boy" had a rapier-sharp mind capable of computing mathematical figures faster mentally than most people could using pen and paper.

Life for Rex was something to be enjoyed. Christian sometimes envied him. His affluent childhood had been one of privilege—the right schools, the right social club affiliations, the right friends, and two loving parents. He seemed to expect happiness as the natural order of things, and because of this, it seemed to happen. So far in Christian's life, because of his childhood and the perils of his war experiences, he expected things to be difficult—and they had been. He hoped that in knowing Rex, his luck would change.

"Don't forget we're going to East Lake tonight. Our law firm is throwing a big party for their clients, and God knows we have forked over enough money to warrant a nice evening. I understand that a lot of the law firms' secretaries will also be there. You never know, we might even get lucky. The law firm only hires beautiful single girls, and they are not allowed to date the lawyers there."

Christian looked up and smiled. "Well, it's been a long, long time since I have 'gotten lucky,' so let's cross our fingers and hope for the best."

"Mom and Dad won't be going, so we will be representing the company. Let's drive over to East Lake about 7:00 o'clock, perform our business duties, and then spend the remainder of the evening checking out the single ladies. I'm ready for a few drinks and a lot of laughs with the opposite sex."

"Rex, if I can have a few drinks and a good dinner that I don't have to pay for, that'll be enough for me. Meeting a girl and getting laid is beyond my expectations."

"See, Christian, there you go again. You've got to think more positively!"

Christian couldn't help being caught up in Rex's excitement and as he went back to reviewing his construction plans, his mood was lighter, and he found himself smiling at the possibility of having an enjoyable evening out.

Arriving at the clubhouse shortly after 7:00, Christian and Rex were met by a black valet who opened the car doors for each of them.

"Good evening, Mr. Hollingsworth. I'll take the car and park it for you. We are all glad that you are home from the war safe and sound."

"Good evening, Joshua. It's nice to be home. This is my friend, Christian Wolfe. He saved my life during the war and has come to Atlanta to work with me and Dad. I hope he'll be able to join East Lake one day—even if he *did* go to Georgia Tech. Do you think we should allow him to join?"

"I suppose that won't be a problem, Mr. Rex, considerin' that more'n half of the members here went there."

"Now, Joshua, don't go telling him that. He's going to think that he's as important as a Georgia man."

"Mr. Rex, I ain't gonna get in the middle of that argument. Now you have a nice evening, and I'll have your car waiting when you are ready to leave."

As they walked up the steps to the club, Christian reflected on the conversation Rex had had with Joshua. Whenever Rex introduced him, he always mentioned that he had been the man to save his life during the war. Christian was always touched that Rex added that to the conversation, but it also embarrassed him. He hoped that in time Rex would stop doing it.

The two men walked through the doors of the clubhouse and went directly to the bar, where they each ordered a drink and watched the other partygoers as they waited for their host to join them. Rex had known Alex Morgan, the family lawyer, all his life, but as the firm had grown over the years, there were a number of younger lawyers that he did not know. As they were enjoying their drinks, Rex saw Alex enter the bar and approach them.

"Welcome home, Rex. Grace and I have been worrying about you ever since you joined the air corps. I understand you had quite an adventure in France. We are so glad you're home safe and sound."

"Thanks, Alex, I am damn sure glad to be home again. I would like to introduce you to the man who saved my life when I was shot down over France. This is Christian Wolfe. It seems I had to go all the way to France to meet him, when he actually lived in Atlanta as a child and graduated from Tech a few years before I graduated from Georgia. He has come to Atlanta to work with me and Dad."

Christian stood and shook Alex's hand.

"Christian, it's a pleasure to meet you. Hamilton and Rex will do a good job of teaching you the business and introducing you to the right people in Atlanta. Speaking, of whom, I would like to introduce you both to a young associate of ours. He and his fiancée are in the dining room. Would you like to join us for a drink before dinner?"

They followed Alex out of the bar and into the dining room, where a couple was sitting at a table with their backs to them. As they approached, Alex spoke to get their attention.

Arising from their seats and turning toward them, the gentleman eased his arm around the lady's waist to include her in the introduction.

"This is my associate, Ansley Dunwoody, and his fiancée, Maggie Neal. Ansley and Maggie, this is Rex Hollingsworth, an old friend and client of mine, and his friend and associate, Christian Wolfe."

Rex would no longer need to worry about a plan to reunite Christian and Maggie. Fate had created a situation clearly identifiable as just about the worst-case scenario.

Unaware of any tension, Ansley reached out to shake hands, giving Maggie a second to recover from the shock of seeing Christian. Then, using her polished acting skills that she had last applied in Grayton Beach, Maggie smiled at the two men and mouthed the appropriate greeting. She could tell that Christian was as shocked as she was, but he appeared to be in total control, including a quick-thinking comment to save the awkwardness of the moment.

"It's nice to meet you," he said. "You look familiar to me. I think that we may have met sometime in the past. Did you ever live in Birmingham or maybe on the coast of Florida? I spent some time in Alabama and North Florida several years ago and think perhaps we may have met somewhere around there."

Rex stood and watched Christian work a true miracle. The reunion could have been a disaster, but he had handled the situation masterfully. In an attempt to eliminate any uncomfortable silence, Rex took Christian's arm and, motioning him to turn away, spoke for both of them.

"It was very nice to meet you. We look forward to spending time with you this evening, but Christian and I are meeting some ladies, and I believe I just heard them arrive. If you would excuse us, we will leave you to your drinks. I hope we can chat later."

Christian smiled at Ansley and Maggie. "It was nice meeting you, Ansley, and to see you again, Maggie." With a look that telegraphed hope, he added, "Perhaps later we might talk more to establish where we might have met."

Smiling, Maggie looked Christian directly in the eye. "Yes, I would like that very much."

After Ansley and Alex had excused themselves, they walked over to greet a group of businessmen who had just arrived. This gave Maggie the opportunity she desperately needed to process what had just happened. Trying to keep her frayed nerves under control, she sat down at her chair and began to shake uncontrollably.

Christian had always entered her life in unexpected ways. She should have known that receiving a letter from him would have been too predictable. At that thought, a smile formed and all the tension was released. He was alive, and he was here in Atlanta. And for that, Maggie was grateful.

He was the same, yet different. He had aged, or should she say, matured, probably from his experiences in Europe, whatever they had been. The war had obviously taken a toll on him, but yet, he radiated a maturity and confidence that made her think of all the reasons she had been attracted to him when they first met. He had a few more lines in his face now, and his hair was longer, but those eyes that could pierce her soul were the same. He could read her thoughts, and she knew it. Maggie took a large sip of her bourbon and accepted the fact that her life had become complicated once again.

As they entered the bar, Rex could see that Christian was lost in his thoughts.

"I'll be damned, Christian. I can't believe the two of you ended up here tonight."

"Me neither. Thanks for pulling me away. That was quick thinking. If we'd stayed much longer, it was going to be obvious that something was going on. Damn, she looks so good. The last time I saw her, she was pretty, but tonight, she's beautiful."

Rex had an idea. "I'll tell Alex that I'd like to spend a few minutes with him and Ansley later to discuss some legal issues. That'll give you some time with Maggie."

"Thanks, Rex. I really want to talk to her before she leaves tonight."

Like Maggie, Christian was trying to confront his feelings. He had been as surprised as she had but had learned to act quickly in times of crisis. This was a crisis of a different sort, certainly not a life-threatening one, but it seemed to have the same effect on him physically. He took a long drink of bourbon and thought about what he wanted to say to her. The pretty secretaries from the law firm never made the acquaintance of either Christian or Rex that evening . . .

Chapter Forty-Five

CHRISTIAN POSITIONED HIMSELF AT A TABLE ACROSS THE ROOM FROM Maggie, purposely facing away from her so she was not within view. He had always been able to focus on a task, weigh each component, and come to a logical conclusion. But now, his thought process was clouded by emotion. He needed some time to gather his thoughts and to determine his next step.

He wanted desperately to look into her eyes and discover if there were any chance she might postpone her wedding, at least for a while. They needed some time to catch up. So much had happened to him in 2 years, and he was eager to learn what direction Maggie's life had taken. It was imperative to Christian that he redeem himself in her eyes. They had been in a precarious situation when they were last together, but somehow in the midst of all of the mayhem, trust and love had blossomed. Nothing else had mattered then.

He needed to talk to her tonight, but he had no idea what to say. He would have to rely on his instinct. It had gotten him out of many sticky situations during the war, and so maybe it wouldn't fail him when he so desperately needed it now.

Tonight, he knew that at least he looked decent. He was wearing a tailored suit and tie that he had just bought that week. He was glad Maggie did not have to see him in the worn and dated French country clothes of the past 2 years. And if she had seen some of the haircuts, she would have laughed out loud. Still, he felt as nervous as a teenager on a first date.

Soon, the call for dinner was made, and the guests settled to enjoy the delicious food and wine. When the plates had been cleared, a band began to play the latest songs and people rose to dance. Christian took a furtive glance behind him and saw that Maggie and Ansley were still sitting at their table. Rex noticed Christian's movement and whispered in his ear.

"Now's as good a time as any. I'm going over and talk with Alex and Ansley. Good luck."

He stood up, moving deliberately toward Maggie's table. His senses were on high alert, and he found that his nervousness had been replaced by determination and confidence. Life would go on either with Maggie or without, but he was not willing to give up without a fight.

Rex was already across the room engaging Alex and Ansley in conversation at the table. Christian saw the two men rise from their seats and follow Rex into the bar where they could talk more easily. At that moment, Maggie turned to watch the band playing and caught sight of Christian moving toward her. The only thing she had time to do was to take a deep breath in a futile attempt to slow her racing heartbeat.

Not wanting to dominate the situation by towering over her, he slipped into the seat next to her. "Hello, Maggie. This was as much of a surprise for me as it must have been for you, although I think I may have had the advantage of knowing you were in Atlanta. I can't believe I'm sitting here with you, Maggie. You're even more beautiful than I remember, if that's possible."

"I never thought I'd see you again, Christian. You've changed. You've matured and seem to be content with yourself."

"Maggie Neal, are you telling me that I look old and weary?"

Maggie resisted a slight giggle and responded, "Men don't get older, they just mature."

"I'll take that as a compliment, thank you. I presume you were able to go back home without any problems from the authorities. I worried about you getting into trouble and me not being there to help. I've thought about you and hoped you'd been able to put everything that happened in Grayton Beach behind you. I understand that you are engaged to be married. When is the big event?"

As much as Christian wanted to tell Maggie how he still felt about her and how the thought of her had seen him through some seriously bad times, he knew that this was neither the time nor the place.

"We are supposed to be married in the spring. But I don't want to talk about my engagement. I'm so glad to see you are safe. Forgive me but I am in such a state of shock tonight that I don't know what to say. I've thought of you so often and wondered where you were. I never thought that I would see you again."

"That's perfectly all right, Maggie. I understand completely. I'd love to tell you about the life I lived for the past 2 years sometime. Considering the circumstances of what I was doing when we met, I think that you might appreciate what I did after we parted. Maybe we can talk more someday soon."

Maggie's mind was racing. She desperately wanted to know more, but she knew that she didn't have much time before Ansley would rejoin her. Her independent streak rose. She was not about to let an opportunity to learn about Christian's life for the past 2 years pass her by. And if she were really honest with herself, she *wanted* to spend time with the man she had always found intriguing.

"Ansley is playing golf tomorrow morning. Why don't you meet me at the entrance to Piedmont Park at 10:00 o'clock. We can talk then."

"I'd like that very much. I'm looking forward to seeing you tomorrow. By the way, did I tell you how pretty you look tonight?"

Stifling a laugh, she replied, "Yes, I think you did, sir. And did I tell you how mature you look tonight?"

"Yes, you did. I'll see you tomorrow morning. Good night, Maggie."

"Good night, Christian."

Christian ordered a double bourbon from the bar to calm his nerves. Being with her for just those few minutes had stirred up all the feelings that he had kept such a tight lid on since the night he had left her. *Damn it all*, he thought, *what is it about her that does this to me?*

Rex saw his friend enter and after ordering a drink for himself, inquired how it had gone.

"Fine, I guess. I don't know what it is, Rex, but that woman has a way of turning me upside down. I have to bring this to a head and get on with life."

Maggie was still recovering from her conversation with Christian when Alex and Ansley returned to the table. She was glad she had someone around to take her mind off Christian, so when Ansley asked her to dance, she jumped at the opportunity. Soon they were holding each other close, the warmth of their bodies mingling in the night air.

After a few more dances, Maggie told Ansley she was beginning to tire and would like to call it a night. As they were saying their good-byes, Maggie looked to see if Christian was still there, and when she couldn't find him, a deep sense of disappointment enveloped her.

When Ansley dropped her off at her home, she gave him a quick kiss and wished him well at his golf outing the next day. Soon, she climbed into bed and turned off the light, but after hours of tossing and turning, sleep still would not come. She hadn't seen Christian for over 2 years, and yet tonight, after only a few minutes, it was as if they had never been apart. Finally, the effects of the drinks and wine, along with the large dinner, sedated her and she drifted off to sleep, only to awaken a little after 2 A.M. Lying in bed, she could see the full moon shining through the bare branches near her window.

Damn it, if only he had not showed up in my life again. I had done such a good job of locking all thoughts of him away so that I could get on with life. Why is there still such an attraction?

She thought instead of Ansley and the future they had planned together. Safe. Secure. Predictable. She had only spent a couple of days with Christian. She didn't know enough about him to know what kind of person he really was. Although he had been in her heart for a long time, maybe it had been just the danger and excitement that excited her. *Does he like music or art or sports or politics or—for Christ's sake, does he like everyday things like asparagus?* She knew everything about Ansley, and he knew the same about her. Almost. She wanted a loving husband and a cottage with a white picket fence. Ansley was the perfect fit for her. Finally, Maggie fell asleep with a sense of resolution.

Chapter Forty-Six

THEY SAT AT THE BAR ELBOW TO ELBOW, SIPPING BOURBON AFTER THE crowd had left, but Christian and Rex couldn't have been further apart in their thoughts. Christian was in a state of disbelief, and Rex, in one of his rare, reflective moments, was examining the frivolity of his life in comparison to Christian's. He began to think he was getting tired of chasing secretaries, hoping to get lucky. Maybe it was time to settle down. He smiled and wondered whether he should blame this improbable thought on the quantity of liquor he had consumed over the course of the evening.

The bar at the club was closing, so Rex had Joshua bring the car to the front and they drove home, more than slightly inebriated. Christian undressed, tumbled into bed, and immediately fell asleep, only to wake with a pounding headache at 3 A.M. Moving slowly in an attempt to keep the pounding from increasing, he located some aspirin in the bathroom cabinet and carefully reversed his path back to his bedroom. By the time he settled himself back into his bed, he was wide-awake.

The full moon illuminated the room with a soft, pale glow. Soon, Christian found himself gliding toward the window like a sleepwalker. He was rewarded by a spectacular vision. The moon was a solitary ball, floating in an otherwise empty indigo blue sky. It seemed so close. Christian could see the dark craters creating a contrast within the marbled smoothness of the sphere. There was something mystical about humans and the moon. It gave hope to the possibility of two lovers uniting by thinking of each other while staring at the moon.

He recalled how many times he had seen the same moonlight up the French countryside and how it had either saved him or had created imminent danger, depending on whether he needed light or darkness to complete his missions. He remembered with sadness, the evening when an Allied soldier had parachuted from his burning plane, only to be shot by German soldiers who could easily see the descending parachute under a similar full moon. But he could also remember the evening he and two other members of the Resistance were able to escape capture because the night was so dark that a platoon of German soldiers walked within 10 feet of them lying in an open field without discovering them.

I'm so glad that part of my life is behind me. The people here in Atlanta have no idea how lucky they are not to have an invading force take over their country, rape, and plunder their land and people. The war never reached their shores, and they don't have to put their lives on the line every day just to survive.

Then he remembered that the people of Atlanta had been invaded by General Sherman's troops less than 100 years earlier. Smiling, he thought that maybe he wasn't being completely fair, at least to the citizens of Atlanta.

Reluctantly returning to bed, he thought about all the French people that he had known. Some were alive because of things he had done to protect or save them, and conversely, he knew that he was alive because of things they had done to protect him. He shuddered slightly and decided, once again, that he needed to put the war behind him as much as possible. It was not going to be easy, but his life and circumstances were changed now and full of promise. He thought again of Maggie and the effect she still had on him. He knew how he felt, but he needed to know how she felt about him. He would find out in a few hours. With that thought, he fell into a restless sleep.

At 10:00 o'clock the next morning, Christian walked into Piedmont Park. It was a warm fall day with a cloudless blue sky. The large oak trees that had been planted almost a hundred years earlier spread their branches majestically up toward the sky, allowing just enough sun to come through and create dappled patterns of light on the green grass. Squirrels scampered up and down the trees or paused suddenly as they moved across the open field in search of their winter stash of nuts. People were out strolling through the park and enjoying the beautiful day.

Christian was aware of the contrast between the harmony of his surroundings and his churning feeling of dread inside him. It all came down to this moment. After 2 years of longing, Maggie would now decide their fate. He had stopped at a florist's shop on his way to buy a bouquet of red roses. Adjusting his tie and smoothing his jacket, he scanned the park. Then he saw her sitting on a bench under a large oak tree. Their eyes met. With a smile on his lips and a lead weight in his chest, Christian briskly walked toward her and to his destiny.

Maggie had deliberately chosen the bench because it was off the main path but still in the open. She wanted to avoid any rumors about her seeing another man during her engagement to Ansley. She could always say she just happened to run into him in the park. But in reality, she didn't care who saw her. There was no way in hell that she was not going to see Christian again, even if it created a problem.

Maggie watched Christian approach. He had a smooth gait and the confidence of a man who knew his own worth. Years of traveling around the world and most recently in occupied France gave him a different look from American men. Then she saw the bouquet of roses, and her heart skipped a beat. *Damn! Why did he have to be so thoughtful?*

Now she began to shake slightly. Her palms started to perspire, and her stomach felt queasy. She only had a few seconds to take a deep breath to calm her nerves before he would be beside her. Standing up and wiping her hands on her dress, she smiled as he arrived and stood in front of her.

Christian greeted Maggie in the French manner with a kiss on each cheek. Maggie was taken aback by the gesture while Christian was unfazed. Both then stepped back slightly, and Christian handed Maggie the flowers.

"Thank you for meeting me. You look as beautiful as I remembered. I've thought of you so many times since we parted that you have become a permanent fixture in my mind."

"Christian, I never thought I would ever get to see you again. I was convinced that you had returned to Germany.

I can't imagine how you came to be in France helping American pilots. I want to know what happened after you left that night. I want you to tell me everything, so I can understand what you went through. And I want to know why you came to Atlanta."

"Whoa, hold on a minute. I'm still in shock from being this close to you after 2 long years. Let's at least take a seat before I start." They sat side by side as Christian told Maggie everything that had happened to him since they had seen each other. He told her about the trip home on U-67 and how he had been met by a driver who was to take him back to Germany and how the driver had been killed, allowing him the opportunity to escape into the woods and resulting in his impromptu decision not to return to Germany.

Pausing a moment to gather all his thoughts, he told her about being discovered by the French farmer and soon after joining the Resistance. He explained that his command of both English and German had been valuable to the Allied forces. In the process he had also become fluent in French. He continued on, telling her about the Allied soldiers he had met and the various places he had lived, and eventually explaining how he'd come to know Rex and found himself in Atlanta.

"Maggie, I've never been able to stop thinking about you and the time we had in Grayton Beach. It gave me strength to make it through the war."

Maggie sat silently as her mind raced forward. *What is he really saying? That he loves me? It sure sounds that way. Am I reading something into what he's saying?*

"I wrote you a letter while I was in France and asked Rex to mail it when he returned home. He did, but it was returned with no forwarding address."

"Rex told me of the letter and promised to bring it to me. Do you still have it?"

"Yes, but enough about me. I want to know what happened to *you*."

Maggie stood up from the bench and motioned him to follow her. "It's a beautiful day, and I'm tired of sitting on this hard bench. Let's walk a while."

As they strolled along the path, admiring the trees wearing their fall colors, she told him about returning to Birmingham, only to find herself restless and unhappy. She told him that she had received a letter from Jim Garrison, the policeman Christian had shot, telling her he had recovered fully. Ironically, he and the nurse who had taken care of him in the hospital had fallen in love, so in a strange way, that episode had a happy ending.

Then she told him about becoming friends with Frances Ashwood, how she started working at Rich's Department Store, and she was now settled in Atlanta. She finished by telling him how she had met and was planning to marry Ansley in the spring.

Although Rex had told him that she was engaged, when Christian heard Maggie tell him about her wedding, a heavy feeling of nausea rose up from his gut.

They walked some more and found they were back at the bench where they had started. They had been together for almost 2 hours, though both thought that it had seemed like a mere minute. Neither Maggie nor Christian wanted it to end. Then she remembered the letter that he had written her.

"When can I have the letter you wrote to me?"

"I brought it with me. You can have it now."

He retrieved the letter from his back pocket and handed it to her. "Do you want to read it now or wait?"

"I want to read it now." She sat on the bench and carefully opened the envelope, trying hard not to rip it. Extracting the folded note, she turned away from Christian so he could not see her reaction as she read. Christian rose from the bench and walked a few feet away, giving her privacy.

Dear Maggie,

I hope this letter will find you. I am in France and have been working with the French Resistance since returning from America. The story of how I ended up here is too long for this letter, but I wanted you to know that I never returned to Germany. I have thought of you and the brief time that we spent together so many times that it will forever be part of my life. My feelings for you are unchanged.

It has been 2 years, and I have no way of knowing where you are or what your circumstances are. If you are married and happy, then I am happy for you.

I helped save an American pilot from Atlanta, and I have asked him to mail this letter to you when he returns home. If you receive this letter, I would love to hear from you. He will give you a return address and will let me know if you respond. He has offered me a position with his company, and I plan to give America another chance. I will come to America and will begin working in Atlanta as soon as the war is over. If you are still free, I would like to see you.

Please respond to this if at all possible, even if you do not care to see me again.

Christian

She read the letter twice before she folded it and slipped it tenderly back into the envelope, then with a smile on her lips, she placed the letter in her purse. A moment later, she stood as if getting ready to leave. Christian wasn't ready for her to do so. He stood in front of her and looked her straight in the eye.

"Maggie, I wrote that letter more than 2 years after we were together. I realized after we parted I was in love with you. My feelings have not changed. I survived those years by relying on my gut instincts and in the belief that I was doing the right thing. I learned to trust my instincts, and those instincts tell me that you have the same feelings for me. I'm going to ask you to take the risk and give us a chance together."

"Christian, things have changed. I'm an engaged woman now."

"So become an unengaged woman and marry me."

"You always seem to come into my life and turn it upside down. Ansley is stable and secure."

"You mean terribly boring."

"Christian, do you see what you do? Ansley and I want the cute little cottage with the white picket fence and a yard for the kids to play in."

"So do I, just without Ansley in the picture."

"Why do you have to be so difficult?"

"Me? I go back to war, miss you terribly, write you a letter that unfortunately you don't receive, and *you* get engaged to a man you're not even in love with, but who happens to be stable."

They looked each other in the eye and then began to laugh. They had been together less than 2 hours after being apart for 2 years, and it was as if nothing had changed between them. "Christian, you make it all sound so easy. But

Ansley is a wonderful man, and I have made a promise to him."

Suddenly Christian's demeanor changed. His face hardened. "Answer me now, Maggie, once and for all. I won't ask you again. I love you. Our lives will continue with or without each other, but please marry me so that we can spend the rest of our lives happily together."

The moment stretched out into a long silence. Christian's heart was beating so strongly in his chest he knew she could hear it. Time seemed to stop for both of them. Maggie's mind was racing and then suddenly, a peaceful calm spread over her like a warm blanket. Reaching out, she took both of Christian's hands in hers. She brought her face close to his and simply answered him with her eyes. No words needed to be spoken. Her decision was clear.

Afterword

U-67 CONTINUED TO SAIL FROM LORIENT, FRANCE, UNDER THE command of Kapitänleutnant Günter Müller-Stöckheim. On November 27, 1942, he was awarded the Knights Cross, and on July 1, 1943, he was promoted to korvettenkapitän. On July 16, 1943, while cruising on the surface in the Sargasso Sea in the middle of the Atlantic Ocean, U-67 was spotted by a pilot flying a Grumman TBF Avenger bomber flying off the escort carrier USS *Cole*. The submarine was unable to dive in time and was destroyed by bombs from the plane. Only three of 51 crew members survived the sinking. Korvettenkapitän Müller-Stöckheim died with his men.

Jean Moulin continued his efforts to unify the various resistance organizations at the request of General Charles de Gaulle, a difficult task because each organization wished to keep its independence. On June 21, 1943, Moulin was arrested and taken to prison where he was tortured by Klaus Barbie, head of Gestapo in France. He never revealed any information to his captors. On July 8, 1943, he died. It is unclear if his death were due to the torture or a suicide attempt. Many believed that Barbie beat him to death.

Major General John Dahlquist continued his command, pushing the retreating German army through France for the remainder of the war. After the war, he continued a distinguished career, serving in Germany and Washington, D.C. He retired as a four-star general. On June 30, 1975, he died and was buried at Arlington Cemetery.

Note: There were prisoner of war camps located in Florida and throughout the Southeast U.S., including one near Eglin Field. The camp at Eglin Field was not established until later during the war. The author took a little literary license to change the date to fit within the story line.

Acknowledgments

A SPECIAL THANKS TO MARIE HARVEY FOR BEING MY GREATEST supporter and sounding board, as well as helping me see life through Maggie's eyes.

To Beverly Swerling Martin, Jennet Walton and Alanna Boutin, for their superb editing.

To Polly Willis, Mary Nic Harvey, and Brian Harvey, for being the first readers of the manuscript and providing valuable suggestions for improvement.

My appreciation to Larry Anderson, DO, for providing information and answers relating to medical issues.

In memory of Kapitänleutnant Günter Müller-Stöckheim, captain of U-67 and a true German hero.

In memory of Jean Moulin, founding member of the French Resistance, who gave his life for his country.

Finally, to Grayton Beach, Florida, the entire country of France, and Atlanta, Georgia, for being wonderful places in which to visit, live, and write about.

Photo by Jan Connell

JAMES HARVEY SPENT HIS CHILDHOOD YEARS IN SOUTH ALABAMA and the Panhandle of Florida where he became fascinated with stories of how German U-boats roamed the Gulf of Mexico during WWII. James now lives in North Georgia and the Panhandle of Florida with his wife Marie. When he isn't writing, he can be found fly fishing the local trout streams and Florida Keys.